P9-BYQ-194

For treasunds life.

♡

Christine Brae

# In This Life

## CHRISTINE BRAE

*In This Life*
Copyright © 2016 by Christine Brae

Cover Design by Lindsay Sparkes

Editing by Jim Thomas

Interior design by Angela McLaurin, Fictional Formats

All rights reserved. No part of this book may be reproduced or transmitted in any form or by any means, electronic or mechanical, including photocopying, recording, or by any information storage and retrieval system, without permission in writing.

This is a work of fiction. Names, characters, places and incidents are the product of the author's imagination or are used fictitiously, and any resemblance to any actual persons, living or dead, events, or locales is entirely coincidental.

The author acknowledges the trademarked status and trademark owners of various products referenced in this work of fiction, which have been used without permission. The publication/use of these trademarks is not authorized, associated with, or sponsored by the trademark owner.

All rights reserved.

"Brae gently reminds us that providence will have the last laugh in this sharply written tale of heart versus mind."
**Tarryn Fisher, New York Times and USA Today Bestselling Author**

"Christine Brae's lyrical writing shines in this poignant, layered story about love, sacrifice, and destiny. Her best book to date!"
**Leylah Attar, New York Times Bestselling Author**

"Emotional, beautiful, and captivating. In This Life isn't just a story. It's a journey of self discovery. It's about finding love, making sacrifices, losing faith, and overcoming tragedy with twists and turns I never saw coming. Christine Brae's writing is poetic and so moving that at times I wasn't just reading the words on the page. I was living them."
**Pamela Sparkman, Author of the Stolen Breaths series**

*Through all the joys I've had*
*And all the tears I've shed*
*I wish that you could see*
*You never left me.*

# Table of Contents

# In This Life

# PART I:

## Best Laid Plans
## April 2005 (Anna)

"But, Mousie, thou art no thy lane,
In proving foresight may be vain;
The best-laid schemes o' mice an' men
Gang aft agley,
An' lea'e us nought but grief an' pain,
For promis'd joy!"

—Robert Burns

# ONE
## The Mission

"ONE FOR ME, please, Miss." The smiling boy reached out his bony arms before me. I resisted the urge to squeeze liquid sanitizer into his hands before dipping the ladle into the steaming cauldron and filling his filthy cup. It had been a long day, doling out watered down chicken noodle soup in the makeshift shelter supported by flimsy poles set into the sand. One of three white tents for food, medicine and emergency medical care.

"They need their daily dose of grace," I muttered, convinced of my purpose for being there.

It was a typical day in Thailand, five days since I arrived on this medical mission—a choice I made rather impulsively. I traveled here from New York with a group of idealistic twenty-somethings, ready to help the less fortunate. There were seven of us, mostly

1

med students from different parts of the world.

Ban Nam Khem, a serene fishing village located on the coast of the Andaman Sea, featured beautiful sandy beaches, crystal clear water, and a host of natural rock formations. We were there to serve at the orphanage for children affected by the tidal wave last year.

Mud and remnant debris were still evident in some places, but if you walked down the stretch of sand far enough, you were met by unexpected bursts of paradise. The stench of sweaty bodies, some close to death, pressed together in the hot, humid air, filled my nostrils despite the endless backdrop of sea and shore. This paradise, this place of beauty, was also filled with sadness and need. Everyone here was in need of something—food, shelter, hope.

For me, hope was a cold drink and a long bath, although I would have settled for a cool breeze—something to dry the sweat trickling onto the sides of my face, and to unglue my hair from the back of my neck. Or anything to drown out the taste of salt from the soppy surgical mask stuck to my skin. My movements were restricted by a thick layer of sunblock, greased fingertips and mud-caked sneakers.

As if in a fog with no chances of ever lifting, I watched people move around sluggishly. No one seemed to be in any hurry, and I was sure that the weather had much to do with the slow pace of life. Maybe it was the fear of expending too much energy. Or maybe it was the acceptance of a situation so dire, you did what you did in the course of a day knowing full well that change was unlikely.

The smiling faces that greeted me each day were nothing short of amazing. The fact that they could live in squalor and still consider themselves blessed was a gift and an inspiration, making the days go quicker and the tasks `easier to carry out.

It was early evening by the time I made my way along the winding gravel path that led to our dwelling. The house was one of the few made of stone, a sprawling white bungalow with arched windows and a raised terracotta roof. It stood out a bit like an eyesore, a solid concrete structure surrounded by bamboo huts.

Our host for the mission was a businessman who built this home in the middle of nowhere. It must have been a good investment then—who would imagine that this happy little corner of the world would one day become swallowed up by the sea? The aftermath of that disaster captured global attention and exposed this small town to an outpouring of goodness from the Western world.

I entered the house before the others got back. The smell of bacon wafted through the hall as I made my way past the sparsely decorated living room. The afternoon sun shone dimly through the tall windows, reflecting rust-colored tiles against the yellow walls.

"Hey, Spark. A bunch of us are hanging out by the beach tonight. Are you coming?" My friend and partner-in-crime, Dante Leola, called out from the kitchen. He began calling me Spark years ago, because I was always on fire. *Would you rather I call you Ants in Your Pants Anna, or Spark?* Dante said that I did everything with fearless passion. Somehow I managed to convince him to travel here with me on a whim. I packed up and left, and he came running right behind. *We need this break before we turn into adults, I told him. When else will we get to take three weeks off once you're in business school and I'm in med school?*

Dante walked towards the sink with a frying pan in his hand.

There were neatly arranged strips of bacon on a square plate by the stove. He picked up a few pieces and shoved them hungrily into his mouth. "You could've eaten straight from the pan," I said with a laugh.

"Yeah, I could have." Typical answer from someone who took no shortcuts.

"Who's going?" I asked, while proceeding directly to the refrigerator and grabbing a bottle of water. I had yet to interact with the rest of the group, having spoken briefly to them when we arrived at the airport.

"The usual. That French dude, the English guy, and those two Russian chicks." The rush of the water drowned out the sound of his voice. I watched while he rinsed the pan and laid it face down on a kitchen towel that was spread out across the marble counter. The space embodied a contemporary feel, with grey and white stone structures contrasted by wooden cabinets and solid oak barstools. It was the most updated area of the house. "Ah. The ones you hooked up with the other night," I teased.

He winked at me while drying his hands before strutting to his bedroom. He was a beautiful man, with dark brown hair cut close to his head, deep-set green eyes that smiled wider than his mouth. They were framed by dense eyelashes and lighter brows that wiggled when he stressed a point. His nose was perfect for his face, a little crooked but angled just right. His thin, pouty lips were in perfect harmony with that sexy five o'clock shadow. He carried himself with so much confidence: pushy, organized and methodical. But he had such a joie de vivre and did everything with vigor. Dante loved to work out, and it showed. His arms, his chest, his abs—everything about him was sculpted to perfection. Just like the way he lived his life.

In the middle of the house was a patio filled with colorful orchids and tropical plants. As I cut across the indoor garden, winding my way through the U-shaped corridor towards my room, I called to him. "How much time do I have? I was hoping to at least wash up and catch a quick nap."

He stuck his head out of the door as I walked past it. "Few minutes, Spark. Get on it."

I pushed his finger away from my face. "Chill! I'll be right there."

He huffed impatiently as he followed right behind, gently directing me towards my bedroom with both hands firm on my shoulders. "This from the girl who showed up an hour late to her own graduation party?"

I dug my heels in to protest his attempts to push me along. "You'll never let me live that down, will you?" I turned towards the dresser and struggled to pull open the top drawer, which had been jammed to the hilt with clothing.

And then it hit me. My life was perfect then. Those were the easy days, before my life spiraled out of control. Dante noticed the sudden twitch of my head and quietly reached for my hand as I began nervously ruffling through my things.

"Spark, are you okay? Did I say something?"

"Of course not," I responded shakily. *I'm here to forget. Don't let me lose sight of that.*

"Have you spoken to her since we arrived?" he asked quietly.

"Nope." I answered, my voice breaking.

"You know you're going to have to do it eventually, right?"

"I texted. That's enough for now." I yanked out a t-shirt and a

5

pair of shorts and threw them on the bed. "Give me fifteen minutes and I promise I won't be late."

# TWO
## The Dude

WE SAT ON the powdery sand as the sun was setting, lulled by the sound of crackling wood from a bonfire by the shore. I reached out to take a joint from Delmar Davignon, the guy from France. His weed was strong. I felt lightheaded and frisky. Sexy. Ready to forget.

"Do you like it, Anna?" he asked. His accent alone was an aphrodisiac. Long and drawn out, with a focus on his vowels and an exaggerated take on consonants.

"Good stuff," I said, putting it to my lips for a third time.

"*Zut alors*, sexy girl, I am wishing my dick was that joint right now."

"I bet you say that to all the girls." I laughed, unfazed. I had never been one to shy away from overt advances.

7

Out of the blue, Dante muttered under his breath, "Oh, I'm sure he doesn't."

I scooted my body over, away from Delmar and closer to Dante in attempt to conduct this upcoming argument in private. "What?" I asked, without masking my irritation. "He doesn't what?"

"Say that to all the girls," he answered through lips pressed tight. "Come on, Spark. Don't be naïve." *Yes, I remember. You've told me that countless times. The dangerous red hair and blue green eyes. Contrasted with the pale angelic skin, it was beguiling to some.* This was just a routine exchange between two old friends. Everything about this was normal, even the way his eyes lingered on my face long enough for me to feel his tacit affection.

"Don't worry, once he finds out how crazy I am, he'll be running in the other direction," I laughed.

"You're a walking contradiction. For some reason, dudes are into that kind of thing," he teased. He was just looking out for me, so I decided to let it go. I tapped my hand over his before pulling away and moving back towards Delmar. I was lost in the sound of the crashing waves. Every time they rolled in towards the shore, I felt the ground shift underneath my feet.

Nothing about this place was recognizable. The warm air, the tall palm trees and discarded coconut husks, and the silvery crabs slithering in and out with the tide reminded me that I was far away from home. I began to imagine the different scenarios that would have brought these people to the mission—who they were and what they had left behind. Paulina, one of the Russian twins, was tracing the outline of the King Kong tattoo on Dante's arm. He chuckled as she whispered something funny in his ear. Kingston Preston, that guy from England, was in deep conversation with the other Russian girl, Milena. I tried to listen as they rattled on about nothing. Shallow conversation—I was bored to tears.

"American girl. Would you like a beer?" Kingston said as he stood up to walk towards the cooler. He was tall and lanky, his dishwater blond hair swept neatly over his sunburned face. His teeth weren't bad. Next to the cooler was a bag filled with sports equipment—a volleyball, badminton rackets, Frisbees and a soccer ball. It didn't seem like anyone wanted to get physically active that night. At least not in that sense.

I grinned at Dante just as he caught my eye, and he flashed me a smile back. "The lady doesn't drink beer," he said with authority. "It's a good thing I brought her my stash for the trip." He pulled out a bottle of red wine from his backpack and offered it to me.

The wine was full-bodied and dry, just the way I liked it. With an empty stomach, and some strong pot, I was feeling quite content.

Delmar leaned in, brushed his lips behind my ear, and continued to tell me what he thought we should be doing instead of sitting around the fire. I let out a whoop of laugher. This guy was pretty cute. Though not my type with the blond hair and blue eyes, the fitted jeans and pretty Hermés belt.

Dante moved away from Paulina to listen in on our conversation. His eyes darted back and forth as he observed our ongoing flirtation.

"Anna!" he finally interrupted.

"What?" I asked, offering him a swig of the wine, which he completely ignored.

"Can I talk to you for a minute?"

He stood up and tipped his head towards the shore, signaling for me to follow him. I struggled to gain my balance, leaving the group by the bonfire. The farther we walked, the darker it got. Teeny tiny sparks of light shot up from the burning wood onto the open sky. *The birth of the stars.*

"What's up?" I asked, swaying and trying desperately to focus on his face. We stood in the shadowy darkness, the rumble of the waves more distinct as they washed up along the shore.

"I think you've had enough," he scolded, both hands on his waist.

"Enough what? Jesus, Tey, it's a weekend. I'm just trying to relax a little bit. You know how difficult that past month has been."

He smiled in resignation. "Spark, you're here to take a break from that shitstorm we left back home. That's why we came all the way here. Don't complicate it by doing things out of spite that you might regret. Remember, we're leaving in a couple of weeks and going back to life at home."

"Okay, boss," I said with a tinge of sarcasm.

"You also survived four years of college without a single hangover. Don't start now," he cautioned, eyes still tight and squinted.

"Dude! Relax. I'm just having fun. I wo—"

The buzzing sound rudely interrupted my oncoming tirade. I slipped the phone out of my jeans pocket and glanced at the screen "I have to take this. It's my dad," I said, walking away from him in the opposite direction.

"Spark." He took a step towards me, hesitated and then slowly turned around.

I took a deep breath. "Hi, Dad."

"Annie, I tried to call you earlier." I could hardly hear      him

10

over the waves.

"Oh, I must have still been outside with the kids. Dad, why is your voice so muffled? Are you all right?"

"Anna. Your mom collapsed at work yesterday from a severe headache. Aneurysms, they said. Close to bursting. She's going in to surgery and has been calling, asking for you, frantically trying to reach you. You need to call her, please. Come home and make it right with her."

I felt ill all of a sudden, my heart plummeting down to my feet, but maintained my composure, closing my eyes and willing my mouth to stay shut while a barrage of thoughts flooded my mind. *Think, Anna, think. There haven't been any previous diagnoses. She's been healthy until now. If found early, they could relieve the pressure and prevent any kind of rupture. Right. Yes, they can certainly nip it in the bud.*

I couldn't give in to worry. Giving in would defeat the purpose of being here. I'd be home in two weeks, and then we could get this all sorted out.

"Annie? Are you there?"

I opened my eyes and looked far out into the water. "I'm here. I'm sorry to hear that, Dad."

"I think you have to cut your trip short and fly back. We need to figure things out, as a family. Whatever your feelings are about her, about what happened—let's work it out together."

"No." I choked out that one lousy syllable. Yes to my studies. Yes to my future. Yes to my priorities. Today was a good day to say "no."

"No? Annie, she's your mother. She doesn't deserve such hatred."

"I don't believe her, Dad. She's a liar and a drama queen. She's done this to us—to you, numerous times. Played on our emotions to justify her actions. How do you know she's not just doing this to get you back?"

"She's sick. I've spoken to the doctors. She's in the hospital, and I don't know when she'll be getting out."

"People with aneurysms live a long time. She should get better." She was heartless and cold when she left us. I am her daughter after all.

"Annie. Listen to me."

I paced back and forth, stepping in and out of the water, preoccupied by the way my feet sank into the ground like it was quicksand.

"No, Dad! You listen to me!" I shouted. "She walked out on us two months ago! She has no right to expect anything from me, from us! Why does she think she can pull this crap and have us running back to her with forgiveness?" I was irate about having to repeat myself again.

"She spent twenty-four years of her life taking care of us! She's your mother." He raised his voice and spoke with authority. "You need to come home."

"She should have thought about that before she screwed around and fucked up our home. I'm here because of her. I'm not coming back. Tell her I'll pray for her, and maybe, if I'm not as angry as I am now, I'll visit her when I get there. And if I were you, I wouldn't give in to her guilt trips. Have some respect for yourself." I shook uncontrollably, reminded of the betrayal by the one I loved the most. She was my hero, the kind of woman I wanted to become. We did everything together, shared every moment of our lives until two months ago. I never imagined that she had another life. *Secrets ruin lives. And lies are born simply to protect them.*

"She has her boy toy to take care of her now. Goodbye, Dad. I'll see you in two weeks."

I slammed my phone shut and flung it far out into the darkness, into the ocean. *Let it drown beneath the waves. A symbol of an old life gone forever. Do you know what else needs to be shredded by the force of that water? This heartache.*

With my face in my hands, I leaned back until I was lying flat on the sand, ocean water lapping around my ears, my shoulders, my body. I tried to convince myself that I was filled with hatred for her, when in fact, I was hit with a longing that made me cry out. I closed my eyes, remembering the day I saw her at a restaurant on Broadway when she was supposed to be away on business. I approached her excitedly from behind, certain that this was her new editor, surely the one who called at all hours of the day with wonderful ideas about her latest article. I watched in horror as he took her hand and kissed it, and she smiled back at him, her lips parted and inviting. I clung to the chair in front of me, gasping for breath, trying to keep myself from fainting. And yet, I couldn't train my eyes off them. I'd never seen her look so happy, so young and carefree. He slid himself into the booth to sit next to her, his paws all over her like a dog in heat. I stepped forward directly into her field of vision and waited for the look of recognition on her face. Suddenly she placed her hands on his chest and pushed him out of the way.

*"Annie!" she screamed as she frantically ran out of the restaurant to chase after me. "Please, Annie! Let me explain!"*

*I stormed down the street, ignoring her pleas as she raced behind me. Her empty words meant nothing to me. When she caught up and tried to grab my shoulder, I smacked her arm so hard that her watch fell off. "Leave me alone, Mother. There's nothing to talk about."*

*"Anna, please. I haven't been happy for so long. Please. Let's go somewhere and talk. I want to be able to explain what happened."*

*I glared at her while holding my hands up to stop her from coming any closer. "Whatever your reasons are, save them. You lied to me and Dad. How could you? Michael is only thirteen!"*

*"Please!" she cried. "This has nothing to do with the love I have for you and your brother."*

*"I said I don't want to talk about this right now. I'm giving you one week to tell Dad about this, and if you don't, I will."*

*She told him that very night, begged for our forgiveness, packed her bags and never looked back.*

I left her with those words. I left the country with that anger.

A sudden movement caused the water to slosh around my face. I looked straight up at a pair of legs that were connected to a shirtless body. The clouds parted and the moon broke free. But the baseball cap on his head shielded his face away from its light.

I saw his lips move, but couldn't hear a word. My ears were submerged in the water. It was too dark to make out his face, but a shooting star skated across the sky and allowed me a glimpse of his dark brown eyes.

He knelt down next to me and scooped my head out of the water. "Hello?" he said. "Are you okay?" His voice was low and deep.

I sat up on my knees, embarrassed and overwhelmed, my hair

14

dripping wet like the rest of me.

"I'm fine. I was just chilling for a little bit."

He tried his best to suppress a smile. I could see the outline of his face, the tip of his nose, his full lips. "Oh, is that what that was?" he asked.

"It's very relaxing. You should try it sometime," I snapped back.

"Okay," he said as he began to lie down in the water. The black baseball cap bobbed up and down next to his head.

"No! Not now!" I squeaked, laughing as I lifted his head up. I still couldn't make out his face, but his hair was thick, jet black, and somewhat unruly. Loose curls were entangled between my fingers.

He let out a throaty laugh. "There was nothing relaxing about that." And although I only saw him in parts—that mouth, those lips, the perfectly aligned teeth—he put me at ease. But it was his presence, the sound of his voice, the touch of his hand on my hair that pulled me out and brought me back. "Whatever it is, it's never as bad as you think," he said.

Slowly, I straightened myself and got to my feet. "With that thought, I think I'm going to leave. I'm tired. Thanks for the laugh." I paused to collect myself. "Goodbye, stranger."

I turned toward the long stretch of sand away from the shore, into the grove of palm trees, my feet zigzagging unsteadily in front of me. As I stopped to catch my balance, I looked back to see him still seated on the sand, his legs stretched out into the water. The moon and the stars were nowhere to be found. *Were they even there to begin with?*

"Dude. My name is Dude," he called out.

I lifted my hand and signaled a wave without missing a beat.

By the time I reached the bonfire, there was nothing left but embers surrounded by beer bottles and burnt wood. The fading light of a few stars guided me on the path to my silent home. I couldn't stand to be alone with my thoughts. So I barged into Dante's room.

"I threw my—"

Milena was sitting on top of him, her head thrown back as he pushed himself against her.

"Spark, what the—" Dante grabbed Milena's hips and flung her off the bed. "Oh, shit!" He fumbled for the light switch by the night table only to find out that it didn't work. "What's wrong?" he asked.

Glaring at me, Milena scrambled to her feet, stumbling to pick up her bra and t-shirt.

"Er... Milena, I'm sorry," I slurred. I should have known better. When your best friend was a hot piece of meat like Dante, you never found him alone. And Milena had been all over him at the beach. Wait a minute, hadn't it been her twin, Paulina, that had been making the moves on him earlier? Not that it mattered, their faces were identical.

I just shook my head and gazed down at the ground. Still, it never occurred to me to leave. For all the partners we'd had, we each came first for the other, through breakups and make-ups and one night stands, our friendship was a constant. Whenever friends questioned why we weren't together, we'd laugh and say that we knew too much about each other.

Milena left the room in a huff, and Tey finally got to the light switch on the wall. I kept my focus on a ball of dust rolling around the wood floor as he searched under the covers for his underwear.

16

"Ah. Found them." He slipped them on quickly and sauntered over to me.

"I threw my phone into the ocean."

The slow blinking of his eyelids, the slight curve of his lips. Signs that he was about to say something witty. He caught himself as soon as he saw the tears pooling in the corners of my eyes. "That can be replaced," he said instead.

I gave in to my sense of helplessness and crumpled in his arms, breaking into a sob.

"My dad said she could die!" I cried. "Oh, Tey, I'm still so mad at her!"

"Do you think you should go home? We could try to get tickets tomorrow," he offered.

"No, no." I shook my head. "I'm not ready to see her."

Slowly he led me towards the bed, allowing me to collapse on the mattress. The room started to spin and I could barely get the words out between my labored breaths. Dante crawled in next to me and held me in his arms.

"I prayed for God to punish her, and now look what's happened." It was guilt that I felt, not sympathy nor compassion. Guilt for bad wishes and vengeful prayers.

"Shh. It's going to be okay. I'm here. You're wasted and you need to sleep it off. We can talk tomorrow."

I nodded my head and faced away from him as he pulled the covers around us. "Can I stay here tonight? I promise I'll leave first thing in the morning."

He held me close without uttering a sound. *Tomorrow I'm going to tell him just how much he means to me,* I thought. *I don't ever want to take him for granted.* I closed my eyes to drift off, but not before hearing him whisper, "I've got you, Spark. I'm here."

# THREE
## *Wolf Whistle*

I JUST COULDN'T get it out of my head. Memories of my mother had invaded my brain and were fixed in my thoughts. Last night, I feared divine retribution. Today, it felt possible that God and my mother had teamed up to force me into forgiveness. Nevertheless, statistics show that the odds of a ruptured brain aneurysm are one out of a hundred. *But once it bursts, that's where the fifty percent survival rate kicks in.*

Nothing about the night before made any sense. Despite the thousands of miles that separated us, the pain in my father's voice was palpable. Yet all my anger and longing seemed to dissipate once the stranger in the baseball cap appeared. Who was he and how did he pull it off?

But back to the job at hand. This schoolhouse looked just like the one in that old television show, *Little House on the Prairie*, with white stucco walls and a set of wooden stairs leading up to its entrance. Inside, an open classroom was lined with wooden desks connected together with metal arms and legs. The chalkboard extended from wall to wall, the letters of the alphabet scrawled in cursive across the top. Everything about this place brought you back to the days before computers and overhead projectors.

I sat quietly at the desk shuffling through my list of notes for today's catechism lesson while channeling my inner Laura Ingalls. My hair was braided in pigtails and tied together to keep the humidity from frizzing it out. But I was hardly dressed like a school marm, and I felt self-conscious, worried I was showing too much in my white hip-hugging shorts and fitted t-shirt. How would I have known I'd be asked to teach a religion class? Maybe no one would notice if I stayed behind my desk to conduct my lesson. I was still a bit miffed about being assigned to do this only two days after my arrival. Because I was the only practicing Catholic in the group, my arguments were futile.

She'd begun her process of entrapment simply. "You're a practicing Catholic, are you not?"

"How do you know that?"

"You filled out the application form under 'Religion.'"

"Oh. Yes, but define practicing..."

"Do you go to church?"

"Yes, but only during religious holidays."

"Good enough."

Sold. They needed a substitute and she promised it would be a fulfilling experience. So for two consecutive nights I read the lesson plan and studied its concepts. It didn't seem too difficult—

I was memorizing a textbook and would be spitting its contents back out, word for word.

"You will have someone there with you," she'd assured me. "You just have to make sure that you stick to the lesson plan. Oh, and remember, many of these children are suffering from psychiatric disorders due to the trauma of the disaster. This is why we need someone with some medical training. Go easy on them. It'll be a breeze."

My fifth grade students began filing into the room. These twice weekly classes for the children of the village were subsidized by a nearby church. I surveyed the interesting mix of students; some looked like children of expats while others were likely residents of the tiny fishing village. There was a stark contrast between the rich and the poor in this place—the well-dressed children with their nannies or bodyguards who stood right outside the door blending in with the dark-skinned local boys and girls clad in t-shirts and shorts. There was whispering and laughing and the screeching of moving chairs.

"Good morning. How are you guys?" I said, standing up nervously to walk in front of the teacher's desk, tugging at the hem of my shorts to cover more skin and crossing my arms against my chest. Darn it! I stood up. That wasn't the plan.

"Ms. Matthews is on a two-week vacation to see her family in America. My name is Anna, and I'm your substitute teacher. There are badges on your desk. Please write your name down so I can get to know you."

"Ms. Matthews is old. You're young and beautiful," a tiny dark-haired girl piped up as she affixed a name tag to her chest.

"Thank you. I know you're missing her because she's a

21

wonderful teacher."

I turned around to grab a pile of papers to hand out to the class.

"We're not missing her," a voice called from the back of the room. There was laughter, and then a wolf whistle which prompted some giggling that led to another wolf whistle. I walked around the room, papers in hand, willing myself to maintain my composure. It didn't help that I had a horrible headache from last night's fiasco.

"What's going on here?" a deep voice called from the doorway.

I never thought I would ever see someone more beautiful than Dante. And yet, there he was, standing right in front of me. He was just as surprised as I was, his deep brown eyes crinkling at the corners when he realized it was me.

It was him. The guy on the beach from last night. I would recognize that voice anywhere. It was the voice of a crooner, melodious and soothing. It had lifted me up out of the past and brought me back to the present.

And now here we stood, face to face.

Right then, I had the undeniable feeling that he was created solely for my eyes. He was Adonis personified—piercing dark eyes outlined with a kaleidoscope of colors and swirling with secrets, nose perfectly sloped and proportioned, defined cheekbones over an angular jaw lined with glorious stubble, impeccably groomed and shaped. His hair fell in slightly untamed curls above his ears. And those lips. Full, plump, luscious. They could swallow me whole.

I snapped back to attention when I tried to suppress a giggle. What was his name again? Dude?

"Mr. Grayson!" Another little girl came running up to him. He swept her in his arms, but not before two or three little girls followed suit.

"Hi! How are you, Brittany? And you, Mariela?" he said, smiling at each of them. Two of the girls had their arms wrapped around his legs. "Hey, Malee." He gingerly led each one of them back to their seats.

"Tony whistled at the new teacher," another little boy said.

Dude shook his head at the boy who I surmised was Tony before turning back towards me with a fixed gaze, his eyes trailing from my face down to my legs. He stepped towards me. "Don't mind me," he said in a hushed tone. "I'm Caroline Matthews' assistant. I help her out whenever she needs me and lead the doctrinal discussions." He brought his lips close to my ear and whispered, "They're a rowdy bunch. Caroline had a difficult time controlling them."

I smiled to myself. Control was my middle name. These kids didn't fluster me, he did. I'd excel at staying the course, just as long as he didn't look at me with those dark, mysterious eyes.

"Okay, kids. Let's get started," I said, going about my business as if he wasn't there.

He moved to the side of the room and leaned against the windowsill, observing me with a silent grin. The way he crossed his arms against his chest accentuated how fit and slim he was, and for the first time ever, I found cargo pants and sneakers extremely attractive.

"In the next two weeks, we are going to learn about the Holy Sacraments of the Church. Who knows what they are?" I asked.

A hand shot up into the air. "Marriage, baptism, holy Communion," a pretty little girl volunteered.

"Okay, marriage. What is the sacrament of marriage?"

23

More hands in the air. The room had calmed down significantly since Dude had started watching. I decided that it must be him. He had such a peaceful presence.

"It's when two people promise to be together forever."

"Very good," I said, smiling. "Now, before we start to talk about each one, can someone name the other sacraments?"

"Anointing of the sick."

"Reconciliation."

"Confirmation."

These kids knew their stuff.

"Okay, one more. Who can give me the last one?" I asked.

Silence. No one said a word.

"The sacrament of holy orders," I offered. "Who knows what that is?"

A young girl raised her hand, snickering. "When a person promises never to have sex." The class broke out in laughter.

Dude smiled and broke in. "No, Ashi, that's not quite what this sacrament is," he said. "This is the sacrament of priesthood. Celibacy is one of the requirements of this vocation, but its main purpose is to serve God through ministry just like his apostles."

The children nodded their heads in unison.

"But they still can't have sex," Tony piped in. The same Tony. The wolf whistler and apparently mature fifth grader.

This time I weighed in. "As Mr. Grayson said, celibacy is just one of the many requirements of priesthood. We will be talking about all of the sacraments in more detail in the next few weeks. Let's move back to our earlier discussion. Marriage. This is our sacrament for the day." I was suddenly surprised by my reaction to that word. Marriage. Until a few months ago, I thought my parents were the perfect examples of married life. I hardly saw them fight, never heard them argue. When Mikey was born, I watched my mother immerse herself in the joys of motherhood. Somewhere along the way, there must have been signs that should have warned me otherwise.

Another hand shot straight up in the air.

"Yes?" I said as I turned my head to find a blue-eyed boy staring right at me while holding up his nametag.

"My parents are divorced. Does that mean they're sinners?" he asked boldly.

I glanced at Dude, who patiently waited for me to respond.

"Okay, Jason. No, they're not sinners. They're just as imperfect as all of God's children. Sometimes, we think we can be with someone forever but that's not always the case. What your mom and dad decided to do has nothing to do with you, nor does it have anything to do with going against the church." I hesitated to say more because the church did frown upon divorce.

Dude finally jumped in. "Jason, we will learn more about marriage in the next few minutes, so hold on to your question and let's proceed. Everyone turn to page thirty-seven of your workbooks. Who wants to read the first paragraph?"

# FOUR
## Noodles

After an hour, we dismissed the children for the day. The subject of marriage was more interesting to them than I'd expected. By the end of the class, we'd successfully made it clear to Jason that the church had many options for remarriage, and that all was not lost just because his parents were divorced.

I moved about the classroom, collecting the worksheets that the students had left on their desks and taking a seat to jot down some notes. Dude stayed by the doorway, speaking to two young boys about the blowfish that they found on the beach. I tried not to watch, but I couldn't help noticing how at ease he was with them.

I started packing up to leave, once again lost in my musings over the conversation I had with my dad the night before. I made a mental note to get a ride to the main town to see if I could purchase a temporary phone.

"Spark, you ready?" Dante's voice startled me and knocked me out of my thoughts. He stopped to align a desk that had been pushed out of its place before strutting on towards me. Mr. OCD.

"Oh, hi. Yes, we can go."

Dude hurriedly brushed off the young boys as he darted towards the front of the room. And from where I sat, I immediately detected a difference in their demeanor. While Dude's personality was peaceful, soothing and safe, Dante had a presence that always made him the center of attention. They stood side by side, towering above me, Dante about two inches taller and a little heavier in build.

"Hey," he said to Dante, bobbing his head up and down in the macho way a man greeted another man. They both looked each other over then turned their attention back to me.

I remained seated at the desk while holding my palm up towards Dante. "This is my friend, Dante. Tey, this is…"

"Jude Grayson," he greeted with an outstretched arm. They shook hands as I stood up and walked over to Dante, who proceeded to swing his arm around me immediately. Well, well. The joke's on me. His name wasn't Dude. But I didn't know if it was any worse than Jude.

"You two know each other?" Dante asked, squinting.

"Yes," said Jude.

"No," I said.

Jude let out a chuckle. "We met last night."

"I see." Dante smirked. "Spark, we'd better get going. I'm starving—thought we'd try that place right outside of here that serves those great noodles."

"Okay, I'm ready." I gathered my books in my arms.

He took my books and turned to leave just as Jude pressed on. "I'm kind of hungry myself. Are their noodles that good?"

Dante piped up immediately. "There's another place down the road that has even better noodles. You should try that place."

"See you next week," I said before Dante led me away. I never imagined how difficult it would be to walk away from Jude Grayson.

We quietly snaked our way past buses and motorcycles toward the little shack of noodles.

"You met him last night?" he asked, breaking the silence between us.

"Yeah. He kind of walked in on me just as I was having an episode at the beach."

"What kind of episode?"

"Nothing too embarrassing. I was just drowning myself in two inches of water." I laughed, feeling a bit mortified at myself.

"You were what?" He stopped in his tracks and gently nudged my arm. Two dogs and a chicken took the opportunity to dart past us.

"Yup! While you were making your moves on your Russian."

"She was hot."

"And I have to admit, he's hot," I jibed back. "And I thought his name was Dude."

"Well, it's better than Jude."

"Which is better than Dante."

He dropped my books on the street and ensnared me in a body lock. A large yellow sign with bold Thai lettering that read "Pork-

Beef, Meatballs & Chicken" stood a few feet away. "Take that back or I'm going to…" He squashed me with his arms and began to tickle me. Ambulances and cars zipped dangerously by us. It was a wonder how these food stalls could remain standing in the middle of such a busy road.

"No! Stop! Please!" I squealed with uncontrollable laughter. "You're going to get us killed!" I kicked and screamed until I broke his grip by biting his arm.

"Ouch!" He laughed and set me back on the ground.

"Ouch? You? I just broke a tooth biting into that rock," I teased, punching his arm at the same time.

We stood together for a few seconds until his look turned serious. "Spark, are you okay? Do you want to talk about it?"

My mother, the man I just met… there were so many things in my head. "Not right now. But," I said as I reached over to touch his face, "I do want to thank you for staying with me last night. I'm just so lucky to have you in my life."

"No worries," he answered lightly. "I'm always happy to interrupt my sex life for you."

"That wasn't the first time, I know. You have way too much sex." I giggled, offering him my hand at the same time.

"Let's not talk about way too much sex, Miss Liberated Woman."

It was time to change the subject. "Let's go order our food. I really need something to help get me out of this bubble."

# FIVE
## The Hut

WE SPENT A couple of hours with the group, slurping Thai noodles and drinking warm tea in one of the boat noodle shops, along the streets of Ban Nam Khem. Thoughts of my mother still lingered in my head, anger and disappointment now somehow replaced with the desire to have her back in my life. I told myself that I would figure it out by the time I returned to see her.

I glanced around more than once, hoping to catch a glimpse of Jude. These were uncharted waters for me, the thrill of something new and spontaneous—a far cry from the discipline that ruled my life for the past four years. There had been no time for relationships, and friendships were cast aside in favor of my studies. The struggle to keep up with the demands of a frenetic schedule was part and parcel of my life. Still, I looked forward to seven more years of school, determined to change people's lives, close the gap between human disparities, and discover a cure for the ailments of the world.

Dante was busy picking pieces of chicken from my plate. The sweeping motion of the chopsticks between his fingers was hypnotizing. Plate, dipping sauce, Dante's mouth. Plate, Dante's mouth. Tap, swoosh, crunch. There I was, thinking about him again. I'd never seen dark eyes surrounded by so much color. Last night at the beach, they shone like they were blue. Today at the school, they were outlined in grey. *Sectoral heterochromia. Different colors of the iris, hereditary.*

"Spark, Delmar just asked you a question." Dante brushed his hand against mine to bring me back to earth. "And did you hear what I said about Maggie?" My beautiful friend, second in my small inner circle of two.

"Huh? What? Sorry," I said while spooning noodles into my mouth. I was just comparing him to Jonathan Rhys Meyers in my head. Or Ian Somerhalder. No, it was that model. The Spanish one. He looked just like that dark-haired Spanish guy. Why couldn't I think of his name?

"Maggie," Dante stressed. "She left me a message, asking what happened to your phone. She's been trying to call to check in from Rome. Something about her fifth date with some guy named Donato and that she'll see you in a few weeks."

"Oh."

"And me, I asked whether you were coming to the beach with us tonight," the determined French guy interjected. Aha. There it was. My welcome diversion for the rest of the evening.

"Oh, yeah, sure," I answered.

The sun had gone to sleep by the time we were once again scattered around the sand, listening to loud hip-hop music, drinking, smoking a joint, and dancing around the fire. There was no place on earth more beautiful than this. The yellow sand glowed under the deep dark sky, and the sound of the waves crashing subdued us all into indifference. What we'd seen and witnessed in the past few days taught us so much about life, and bonded us together. The frailty of the human body, the resilience of the spirit. The abundance of hope or the lack of it, the ugliness of destruction and the randomness of circumstance. Just as expected, we began to couple up, Dante and Paulina, the English guy and Milena, and me and Delmar. This was the perfect set-up—a two-week trip, a two-week guy, no strings attached. I was ready to just go with the flow.

"*Mon dieu*! You are so beautiful, American girl," Delmar whispered into my neck as he pulled me closer. The art of seduction with this guy was just that. An art. He was smooth, his voice decadent like strawberries dipped in Debauve chocolate. His eyes never left yours, they seduced you into thinking you were the most beautiful creature he had ever laid eyes upon. And his hands—oh, his hands—they emitted some sort of heat that left you wanting more. Never mind the fact that his fingers were short and thick.

"Let's go," he ordered as he pulled me to my feet to lead me away from the group.

We stumbled through the sand to a secluded area away from the others, behind a large palm tree surrounded by beach grass. We kissed and grappled until my dress was down to my waist and his head was between my breasts.

32

"Are you ready for me, American girl?" He slid upwards while unbuttoning his jeans so that his lips rested on mine. My eyes remained closed—I was high and drunk and certain that I was in love with the cloudy dusk emanating from his eyes. "*Je vais te baiser*," he whispered. That sounded so much sexier than "I'm going to fuck you," didn't it? There is no lewdness in French; everything sounds so fluid and chaste.

The weight of his body as he started to push inside woke me up, and I was roused by a beautiful pair of eyes looking right into mine.

Only they were baby blues and not dusky browns.

"*Arrete! S'il vous plait!*" I pushed him off me with all my might. "I'm sorry. I can't do this!" I sprang to my feet, straightening my clothes and tying my dress back behind my neck. He was too dazed to make a move. "I'm so sorry, Delmar, please forgive me. This is crazy." I stumbled along the sand, trying to get as far away from everyone as quickly as I could. Wow, that was unsettling. I was officially losing it. I needed some time alone to summon back my sanity.

"Spark!" Dante called from behind me. "Are you okay?"

"I just need to take a walk," I yelled back. "Don't worry, I'll only be a few minutes." I shuffled briskly, embarrassed about getting carried away with sordid thoughts of some guy I just met in middle of the night.

The light along the beach slowly dissipated as I moved further away from the group, my path illuminated only by the glow of the sea foam that rolled along the shore. I could see little of what lay ahead, except for a small light that shone right above the water like a beacon in the middle of nowhere. My curiosity was piqued. I let the light lead me, half drunk and questioning myself for moving this far away from the group. I made a mental note to turn back soon. Dante was going to be worried and I was sure he would blame me for once again interrupting his sex time.

I stopped when I chanced upon a wooden structure held up by solid pillars rising high above the water, moving closer until I stood at the foot of the steep steps resembling a ladder built straight up against the landing. A Baan Rim Nam, meaning house on the water. Since the weather in Southern Thailand was prone to many typhoons and monsoon rains, these stilt houses were often built on cement posts to protect them from floating away.

The raft house looked damaged or incomplete, only partially enclosed with bundles of bamboo. Its floor was uneven and rough, made with floorboards that hurt your feet. In the middle of the open space was a battery operated lantern, the source of the light that had guided me here. A neatly made up futon lay on the floor by the window, surrounded by a blanket, some clothes, and empty beer bottles. Above the bed a large wooden crucifix was nestled between the slats of wood, held together by unrefined rope.

The front of the house was exposed to the clear, blue water. The view was unobstructed, surrounded only by dried out coconut palms held up by poles to shelter the home. It was evident that a storm had blown out part of it, leaving the toilet and sink area as the only section covered by a provisional wall. I stiffened impulsively as the floor behind me sagged with the weight of someone else.

Even before I saw him, I knew.

I felt my heart calming down, my stupor beginning to leave me. Slowly, I turned around to face him.

"You found it." Jude smiled at me. His eyes weren't dark that night. They were hazel and luminous and light. There was no formal greeting, no, "What are you doing here?" It was as if he'd been waiting for me to find him.

"I did."

"What took you so long?" he asked, his grin spreading from ear to ear.

"I've never walked this far out before," I said.

His eyes called to me, beckoning me to come closer, but his body language said otherwise. He seemed nervous. He kept his hands at his sides and rocked back and forth on his heels.

I moved closer, one tiny step at a time, until we were only an arm's length apart. Every step towards him was unintended, every emotion unexplained. I stopped when I was near enough to feel his breath on me, and as I gazed up, he looked down so that our noses were almost touching. The air around us was fraught with tension, the kind that manifested itself through the reactions of the flesh. The heat of his stare seared me, knocked the wind out of me. The compassion in his eyes grabbed hold of me in the middle of my storm and set me safely on solid ground. Just like last night, when he pulled my head out of the water.

And there it was again, that band of light that seemed to radiate just above his head. Slivery, silvery shining light.

I noticed the rise and fall of our chests in unison, and a rapid surge of energy. And as I turned to step away, he grabbed my shoulder with his right hand and spun me around before pressing me tightly against his body. I was in the arms of a stranger, but in the embrace of someone I had known for a hundred years. I couldn't explain what had just happened. We spoke in the silence, lost in the uncertainty of it all. It was both disturbing and exhilarating and I forgot where I was in the world at this very instant. All that mattered was that he was here and that he'd touched me.

"What is this? What's happening here?" I gasped. He held me up with his long, strong arms. I was dizzy, weak, and confused.

"I don't know," he whispered, cradling my head close to his chest, his other arm wrapped around my waist while mine were entwined around his neck. "We always seem to find each other."

I don't know how long we remained this way. I finally took a step back and covered my mouth to stifle a giggle, embarrassed by the giddiness of it all.

"Oh, God, I'm so drunk," I said. My cheeks and ears began to burn.

"I know." Gently, he reached out to tuck a strand of hair behind my ear before brushing his thumbs across my cheeks.

I walked towards the futon on the floor but he stayed rooted in place, watching as I moved away. "I'm going to sleep this off," I said, dropping to my knees and rolling onto the mattress. "Can we talk tomorrow?" I went about this as if it were my home, my bed, my blanket. Everything here was so comfortable, familiar and safe.

"Yes. Tomorrow."

# SIX
## *Blue*

IT WASN'T THE first time that I woke up to find a man watching me sleep. Ordinarily, I would be cringing at the creepiness, but this time it was different. The comfort of his presence, the light in his eyes, and the smile on his face were a welcome relief. It didn't hurt to open my eyes to the bright light of the sun shining across an endless body of pure, blue water. Jude was sitting next to me with two paper cups of coffee on top of a corrugated cardboard tray right by his feet.

"Hi," I said.

I sat up and steadied myself before walking towards the bathroom. A tiny wooden ledge held a razorblade and a tube of toothpaste, and a tub of water sat right underneath the sink. Above it, a shard of glass was held up on the wall by two tiny paperclips, allowing one to see only one eye through it. I guess there was no need for a mirror. All you had to do was look down upon the clear blue water to see a reflection of yourself. I spread a drop of toothpaste on my teeth and rinsed it off with a handful of water. My unkempt hair sat on the top of my head like a bird's nest. I deftly pulled it back and used some wayward strands to wrap it neatly into a bun.

I walked back towards the futon and took a seat right next to him.

"I didn't do anything stupid last night, did I?" I laughed nervously, hugging my knees to my chest.

He handed me the cup of coffee but didn't let go until he felt my fingers close around the cup to touch his. "Well, I don't know what you did before you got here, but no, nothing crazy with me," he said.

"Whew! Okay," I said, visibly relieved. "Whose place is this?"

"I found it three weeks ago. I asked around the village, and they told me that it was owned by a family of four before the typhoon."

"Where are they now? What happened to them?" I asked.

He shrugged his shoulders. "No one knows. They say that the mother and child were lost at sea and the father and son have left the village."

A broken family. Just like mine. My mood turned quickly. *Was today the day of the surgery? Why hadn't I heard from my father? Did he relay my message to her?*

"Oh. I would be afraid to stay in a house marked by tragedy," I said sadly.

He placed his paper cup on the floor and leaned back against the wall. I worried that the floor was too uneven to hold the cup upright for very long and so I kept my eye on it while he spoke.

"On the contrary, I feel their peace in this house. I can't explain it, but I sense many happy times here."

"Don't you live in the same house that I do?" I asked.

Jude swatted his hand at the mosquitoes encircling the top of our heads. "I do. I go over there to take a shower and eat sometimes. But I like to stay here after a day in the village. It helps me to decompress. I like to revel in the quiet, remind myself of the beauty of the world despite all this ugliness."

"I know what you mean. Three days ago, we had to help try to resuscitate a baby who had just stopped breathing. He was so thin, I was afraid he would break into little pieces when I held him." I paused. The memory of that little boy would forever be in my mind.

He nodded his head in understanding. And then he caught me by surprise.

"Do you do that every night? Get high like that?"

"No." I set my sights on the blueness in front of me. Sea and sky. Different shades, unequal depths. If I looked far enough, I could see the clouds bobbing up and down like balloons floating in the water.

"It's been two nights in a row." He wasn't going to give it up.

"Issues," I snapped back. I didn't feel defensive, just irritated; if he wanted to get to the bottom of it, we would. "I was mad at my mom for something. Really angry and confused. And then I found out that she's sick, which in a screwed up way pisses me off even more. I thought I could use the time here to get away from it all and do some good at the same time. You know, focus my energies on something else."

39

"Interesting. You leave your problems behind at home only to come to a place with bigger problems." The glint in his eyes remained full of kindness. He wasn't judging, he was making me think things through in my head.

"I can make a difference here. There's nothing I can do about the problems at home."

"But the people who love you, who you love, need you there. You're pouring out your efforts on strangers. Charity starts at home, they say."

I didn't bother to come up with a response. In another time, I would have lashed out, but his honesty was refreshing. He was a complete stranger to me, and already he had successfully started to chip away at the barrier.

"Who are you?" I asked, my tone quiet and almost somber. I fidgeted with the paper cup, trying my best to avoid looking at him.

"Sorry, I don't mean to be so off-putting. I don't know why but I just have this feeling that I can tell you anything and you'll take it all in stride," he answered sheepishly, his hand instinctively brushing over his thick black hair.

"Then talk to me. Who are you? And is your name really Jude? Do you have another name?" I lightened my tone and nudged him with my elbow.

"Ah." He laughed. "Jude Patrick."

"Hmm. Okay, let's see." I scrunched up my nose. "Patrick isn't any better, I'm afraid. I think I'm just going to call you by your last name."

"Okay, Blue."

I did a double take to make sure I heard him correctly. "In case you didn't notice, I have red hair, not blue."

"That's what they call redheads in Australia. They call them Blueys. That was what popped into my head the day I saw you at the house."

"And you know this term because?" I asked sarcastically.

"I lived there for a year."

"Oh." I began to twist the tip of my hair between my fingers. "Well, this hair does tend to stand out in a crowd." I consciously smoothed it down, feeling very unattractive all of a sudden. I accidentally brushed over the bun, causing my hair to cascade down over my shoulders.

He had this uncanny way of reading my mind, of providing me with assurances just by looking at me in silence. He reached his arm out and brushed his fingers against my face. "You're everything I imagined you would be. Fiery, strong. Sexy. The ultimate temptation." There was a shift in his mood. It had turned from thoughtful to playful.

I laughed sarcastically to mask my embarrassment. "All this in the ten seconds that you've spent with me?"

"I've been watching you for a while. It took you a few days to find me, but I knew you would eventually," he said with smiling eyes.

All right then, here we go. It was time to walk away from this awkward situation. I was uncomfortable, not because of what he was saying, but because if I didn't leave, this guy was going to make me want to do things I should never do in broad daylight, and in half a house that was exposed to the sky and sea. Whether in the dark or in the sunshine, his lips were still the only things that I could see.

"Hey, what time is it?" I sat on my knees in an effort to rise up and leave. "I was planning to make it to 9:30 mass." I wanted to find some quiet time to think about my mother. The past two days had given me some space to work things out in my head. Was it something he said to me? Somehow I was ready to revisit my feelings about her. I was willing to begin the process of healing. *Charity starts at home.*

"It's only eight o'clock," Jude said with a heavy sigh and tightly pressed lips before glancing at his phone and placing it back down behind him on the floor.

"Perfect! I can run home and jump in the shower before then. Hey," I addressed him with genuine gratitude on my face, "thank you for allowing me to stay here last night. Maybe I'll see you around again soon. At least in Monday's class."

"Anna—"

"I'll see you around." I stood up and walked across the hard, prickly floor towards the exit.

# SEVEN
## *Going Mid-Life*

I FORCED MY eyes open and reached for the watch on the night table. After a long nap filled with forgettable dreams, it was nearly ten o'clock in the evening and I was wide awake. How was I ever going to adjust to this jetlag? I figured I might as well join the others. Sometimes they were obnoxious, but it was still better than being alone with my thoughts. I pulled my shorts on to go out to the beach and find the rest of the gang.

The house was eerily quiet. The light in the kitchen was on, but the rest of the house was dark. I passed on another night on the beach and opted to take a quick rest instead. I quickly wandered down the hall towards the front door.

"Did you have a good nap?"

I stopped dead in my tracks at the sound of Jude's voice.

"Sorry, I didn't mean to spook you," he said.

"You have to stop popping up out of nowhere." I laughed as I turned around to face him.

He smiled timidly, hands in his pockets and shoulders touching his ears. His eyes shone in the dark like smoldering coal. "Sorry."

"What are you still doing here?" I asked, feeling shy all of a sudden.

"I had to do some reading so I decided to stay in. Where are you heading?" And when I didn't answer: "Do you mind if I tag along?"

"I'm going to find Dante. You're welcome to come with me," I said, starting to walk towards the door.

He followed right behind and then ended up by my side. No one was at the beach by the time we arrived. We walked further in silence until the stilt house came into view.

"Hey, I've got a few beers in there, do you want to hang out for a while?" His voice cracked. Once again, his movements seemed restrained.

"Sure. I'm not drinking tonight, though."

He took my hand, helping me climb the rickety steps, and led me towards the open area of the hut. He let go just as I bent down to sit right at the edge of the floor, my feet dangling and almost touching the water.

"This is so beautiful." I looked up to admire the large speckled moon, hovering close enough for me to touch. Not every situation with him should be this intense. "Look! We can see everything underneath the water," I said, trying to make light of the moment.

I wasn't sure if he'd heard me. He was at the other end of the house with his hands in the cooler. "Water okay with you?"

he asked.

"Yes, thank you," I answered, taking the water from him. In his other hand was a bottle of local brew. He took a seat next to me and sank his feet in between the swirling fish. We sat quietly, our eyes fixed on the view before us.

He broke the silence after downing a big gulp of his beer. "Don't freak out, but I think there's a spider on the side of your thigh."

"Where?" I jerked my feet out of the water.

He pointed at the pink mark, careful to avoid contact with my skin.

"Oh!" I laughed. "That's a birthmark."

"Oh, God. I'm so sorry," he said, flustered. He forced out a cough and cleared his throat as we allowed a moment of silence to pass between us. "So, have you and Leola ever... you know, gotten together?"

"What? No! Me and him? No! He's my best friend, we're not involved." This wasn't the first time someone had asked about us, and this wasn't the first time I reacted this way—incredulous.

"Seriously, he's the best friend anyone could ever have. He's great," I added.

Jude remained silent and nodded his head, although I could tell his mind was elsewhere.

I was curious about him, too. "Enough about me, what about you?" I asked. Technically speaking, I had spent the night with this guy and hardly knew anything about him.

He placed the bottle of beer on the uneven floor and leaned back on his hands while skimming his feet across the surface of the water. "My family is from New York, Westchester County specifically, and I'm the oldest of seven children."

"Wow, that's a lot! How many boys and how many girls?"

"Two boys and four girls," he answered. "My sister, Katie, is married with one baby. Mary is nineteen, Peg and Joe are fifteen, Erin is eleven, and Max is eight. My parents have been married for twenty-seven years. We're a pretty normal family."

"I've always wanted to have another sister. Mikey is great, but the age difference between us is just too wide."

"Yeah, they're all right," he said. "They give me heartburn sometimes, especially Katie. She's so outspoken that it drives me crazy. But we take care of each other."

"I thought we were a normal family too," I said, "until my mom decided to go mid-life on us."

"What does going mid-life mean?" he looked confused. A breeze rushed by and whipped my hair across my face. He watched as I battled with the breeze to keep it from flapping back and forth.

"Well, one day she woke up and decided to cheat on my dad," I muttered.

"There must have been something going on in her life or in her marriage. Sometimes it's a cry for help. A need for change." He said this so matter-of-factly that it actually sounded convincing.

"Where'd you go to school?" I asked.

"NYU. Philo major. And you?"

"Oh my gosh, me too! I went to NYU! Bio." I tried to cover up my squeak.

"I heard that you were the hotshot that got into med school," he teased. "I mean, John Hopkins med school, not just any other school."

"I think I got lucky," I said humbly. There was a price to pay for that. It was called loneliness. The vicious cycle of becoming so focused on your goals that you don't have time for anything else, and not having anyone else so you end up focused on your goals.

"I've always been amazed at how doctors can remember every single part of the body, how they can remember all those medical terms," he said. "Does it come naturally to you? Memorizing stuff? Taking tests?"

"I guess. So how about you, what's in your future?"

"I'm going for a Masters in Theology in the fall."

"Hmm. Interesting. Is it the humanities side of this that interests you?"

He nodded his head. "I've always been fascinated by the human psyche and the role that religion plays versus the influences of society. I assume we practice the same religion since we met at a catechism class, so how religious are you?" he asked.

"Unfortunately, baptism is the extent of my experience with Catholicism. My mom is a staunch churchgoer but she never really required us to follow in her footsteps." I paused to entertain an afterthought. "But I'm not a murderer nor am I an adulterer, and I want to devote my medical skills to helping the less fortunate. So I guess some of the altruism instilled by her faith has rubbed off on me."

He sat closer to me, our elbows rubbing. "It's our faith, not just hers," he emphasized. "I think it's all quite relative. I've always believed that there are limitless choices we can make to live a life of service. There is no better way or worse way of finding purpose in our lives."

"Okay, now you're getting too deep for me." I laughed. "I'm

here to unwind. No soul searching or anything like that on this trip."

"You're absolutely right! Sorry! Let's talk about lighter things. Like, are you sure you and Leola don't have anything going on?"

"Why are we going there again?" I said, laughing.

"I don't know," he responded. "Maybe because whoever it is that has your heart is a very lucky man?"

I wasn't sure if he was flirting with me. There was a breathless energy around us, a frisson brought about by heightened senses and beaming faces.

"I haven't given my heart away yet. Who's got time to deal with all that?" I lifted myself off the floor and began to roam around the house. A tattered brown leather case next to a crate of clothes immediately caught my eye. "Wait… is this a—" I exclaimed, lifting the case up and unlocking the rusty latch that held it closed. "Yes! A backgammon set! Get ready, I'm challenging you to one game before I leave."

# EIGHT
## 26 Going on 40

"HOW'D YOUR DAY go?" Jude asked as we sat on a small sandy hill a few feet away from the beach.

"It was fine. I think I'm getting used to the heat because I don't feel as exhausted anymore."

The backgammon challenge the night before had ended up being seven games instead of one. By the time Jude walked me back to the house, it was past two o'clock in the morning.

I spent part of my day at the free medical clinic in the neighboring town. A baby girl suffering from malnutrition was brought in, and the hopelessness in her parents' eyes still bothered me hours later. I imagined the same wretchedness in my father's eyes when my mother announced she was leaving. Nothing to fight for, as if he had seen it coming. Some pictures embed themselves in your head for as long as you live. Those images stayed with me.

I couldn't wait to see Jude again. What was this now? Our third date? Already I had opened up to him more than I would have done in ordinary circumstances. Anything to get my mind off the turbulence that was going on at home.

"Where are your friends tonight?"

"Not sure. I stopped by the house to change and came right here to meet you." I twisted my foot to shake off a hermit crab that had crawled its way between my toes.

I watched as he played with a piece of wood, tracing its edge in the sand. The sea was calm. It called to me, invited me to seek release, wash away my confusion. It was difficult to fathom the great loss of human life here only one year ago. What kind of rage could emerge so suddenly, damage everything in its path, when all I've seen of this sea is its serenity, its tranquility? What happened to make it so angry at the world?

I stood up and started running towards the shore.

"Where are you going?" he shouted.

"Out for a swim!" I said as I pulled my shirt over my head. I had no qualms about undressing. I felt no shame about my looks, my body, or myself. I never thought I was beautiful, but I always embraced who I was. I didn't have a workout routine. I was a runner and the benefits that running afforded me—tight calves, firm backside, toned arms—were a result and not the goal. The truth was that I had never done anything like that before either. Being with Jude just made me feel that much more uninhibited.

And heck! I'd made out with a French guy, slept in a stranger's hut, walked in on Dante having sex. Why not add skinny dipping to this trip's most memorable moments?

"Wait! Blue! What are you doing?" he yelled, following behind me.

I didn't look back as I peeled off my bra and hopped around the sand to slip my shorts off my legs. I was in nothing but my underwear as I ran into the warm ocean, the soft, compact sand under my feet. I submerged under the water then flipped over on my back to float peacefully across its surface. I closed my eyes and thought of my family. I pictured my father, lost and alone, my mother's newfound identity, and my baby brother's future. I was reminded of how they all depended on me to hold them together. My heart raced, and the stress of what was waiting for me at home began to overwhelm me. But a few seconds later, there he was, reaching out to grab me by my waist, holding me steadfast against the current. His eyes were fixed on my breasts, their tops exposed above the line of the water.

Shirtless and bare, his thick black hair slicked back, I fought the urge to touch his beautiful face. I was chest deep in the water while he was unveiled and revealed for my eyes only. We stood directly in front of each other with the force of the waves lapping against us, trying to push us together. He took one step towards me while gently taking my face in his hands. I closed my eyes to feel his touch against my skin.

"What am I going to do with you, Anna?" he asked in a hushed tone, his nose almost touching mine.

The roar of an approaching wave wasn't loud enough to distract us from this moment. Before we knew it, we were separated, tumbling and pushed roughly against the sand on the shore. I sat up after I hit the ground. I had already taken in a large amount of seawater. I hacked and choked, trying to get some air.

"Blue! Are you all right?" he asked, frantically scooping me up and carrying me away from the water.

"I'm okay, I'm okay," I said, coughing as he gently set me down on the sand. My choking fit ended in an unexpected barrage of tears.

"Come here," he said as he pulled my head close to his chest. He used his shirt to wipe my face.

I reached for my shirt and slipped it back over my head. "I'm sorry," I said. "I don't know what came over me."

"You just had a scare, that's all. It's okay, Blue. I'm here, and you're safe." He adjusted his position so that I was leaning against his solid body as I sat between his legs.

"I don't want to go home, Jude. There's just so much there waiting for me. I don't know how I can face it all," I said, still crying. I couldn't even bring myself to call home after everything I had said to my father.

"I know, I know," he whispered, his mouth against the back of my head. "I'm here doing the same thing. But what we both have to realize is that those problems, they don't go away. No matter how many times we brush them under the carpet, they'll eventually surface again, worse than they were before."

"Are you twenty-six going on forty or something?" I sniffed. "What about you? What are you running away from?" I tilted my head, allowing his lips to brush against my ears.

He hesitated. "I'm not running away. Like you, my life's path is pretty much planned out for me. It's what's going on around me that's making me confused."

"Like what?"

"Meeting someone like you, for one."

"Oh," I said, disappointed. I leaned forward until nothing about us was touching.

He quickly changed the subject. "Hey, what do you say we start walking back to the hut?" he asked as he stood up, offering me his hand. I took it. "Will Dante be looking for you? Should I text him?"

"He knows I'm with you. No need," I said as I dusted the sand off my legs and followed him back to his place.

"DID YOU WANT to change your, um, thing since you got it wet in the water? I can lend you a brand new pair of boxers," Jude offered shyly. I was in his bathroom washing my hands and cleaning up the salt water from my face and hair.

"Do you really have an extra pair? Yes, if you don't mind."

He walked over to where I was and handed me a box of Gap boxer shorts.

"You packed them like this?" I laughed, lifting my hand in the air and making a twirling motion with my fingers. He turned away as I removed my wet underwear and changed into his boxers. They were loose but comfortable, starchy new.

"Yeah. Why not? Here's a t-shirt too." He reached his arm back, making sure to keep his head facing in the opposite direction.

"Thanks." I turned around and swiped a drop of toothpaste across my teeth. "I'm so tired. I think I'm going to lie down."

I was woken up in the night by the sound of voices coming from the balcony. The floor creaked at first, light footsteps following after that, and then I heard a woman's voice. I laid on the mattress and strained with all my might to hear what was being said in hushed voices.

"What's the matter?" said the woman. "Don't you want this? Don't you want me?"

"Paulina, you've had too much to drink. Let me walk you back to the house," Jude said.

"No, no. I don't want to go back. I want to be here with you. I have wanted you from the first day I saw you."

"Please, let me walk you back home." I heard the floor creak once again. I assumed that he was trying to lead her outside. The sound of footsteps moved in my direction.

"What is she doing here?" Paulina cried, her bikini top hanging from her neck. She was slurring and swinging, and the uneven bamboo floor wasn't helping her keep her balance. He slid swiftly towards her, afraid of what she might do next. "Is she with you? Why is she with you?"

I sat up abruptly, ready to protect myself in case she decided to move any closer.

"Paulina, please. She's not with me. She was very tired and fell asleep," he said, trying to reason with her.

"What is it about her?" she yelled. "What is it about her that all of you are crazy about? First Dante, and then Delmar. Now you!"

She stomped out with Jude following right behind her. He was gone for a while, and I wondered, but I refused to let my feelings get the better of me. I walked over to the edge of the house to sit in his favorite spot. The stars were out in full force, both up in the sky and down on the water, like diamonds resting on top of a dark velvet shawl. Its fringes touched the ends of the earth and broke out into tiny little islands. I laughed when I looked down at myself to see a pair of skinny thighs sticking out of oversized boxer shorts.

It wasn't long after that when I felt him kneel down and wrap his arms around me from behind.

"Hi," he said as he leaned his cheek against mine.

"Hi." I held on to his arms and tightened them around me.

We stayed that way for a minute until he let go and sat down next to me.

"I'm sorry about all that," he said, tucking his hands under his legs again. This time his posture turned stiff. There was no dangling of the legs, no leaning back on his elbows.

"Did she have a right to get angry like that? Were you two hooking up or something?" I asked out of curiosity more than anything else.

"What? No! I just met her last night at the house!" he sounded irritated. "She's drunk and upset and homesick." There he was again, making amends for everyone else's shortcomings. He let out a deep sigh and continued. "Anna, about what I said earlier—"

I had to beat him to it. He was about to voice the truth. "Absolutely correct. We're not together," I muttered.

"It's not that simple. I'm committed to making things work back home."

I took a deep breath. "Gray, we're just having some fun," I assured him.

"You have to understand," he explained. "I wasn't expecting to meet someone like you."

*Someone like what?* "There's nothing to explain, nothing to understand. It's late and I'm going back to the house," I said instead.

55

"Please don't. We were just getting to know each other," he said, holding my arm in place.

I gently pushed his hand away. There was a lump in my throat and a heavy brewing in my gut. "All good. Crazy day tomorrow. I should go," I said with an artificial air of composure.

"Don't you ever just want to forget who you're supposed to be and just be who you really are?" he whispered.

"This is who I am, Jude. I have no idea what you're getting at," I declared, determined to have the last say. He stepped aside, allowing me to continue on. "I'm so tired, let's just call it a night. Thanks for having me over."

# NINE
## Rusty Nail

EACH DAY AT the clinic was both stressful and exhilarating. I reveled in the fast pace of emergency situations, eager to assist the patients, most of them locals who couldn't afford medical care.

"Chiayo. That's your name, right?" I said to the eight-year-old as I gently helped him lie down on the operating table. His foot had swollen three shoe sizes from stepping on a rusty nail and his skin was flushed with a very high fever. Dante usually helped out by manning the lines and preparing the paperwork, but today I needed an assistant.

Chiayo nervously nodded yes. "Okay, sweetie, my friend Dante here will hold your hands while I give you an injection, and then we're going to clean out that foot."

"We?" Dante flinched. "Who said I was going to help you?"

I rolled my eyes at him. "Tey. Look around you. There's no one else." He twisted his head all around to verify my claim.

The boy's body stiffened as I pressed the needle into his foot. "It's okay, little dude," Dante said soothingly. "She's going to make you better."

He then turned his attention to me. "So, what was with loverboy today?" Dante had seen Jude rush out of class as soon as he walked into the door. "I noticed you didn't sleep over at his place last night."

"Crazy Paulina showed up. He got all freaked out when she thought we were together," I explained.

"And? What are you upset about?"

"Nothing. He has a girlfriend."

"Did he say that?" he challenged.

"Not in so many words," I mumbled. I continued to drain the abscess from Chiayo's wound. "Almost finished," I said, concentrating on relieving this boy's pain.

"Well, unless you want a long-term thing, I don't see what the problem is. I've changed my opinion. This guy seems to be taking your mind off things at home. It might be a good break for you."

"You're just telling me this because you want to spend time with your Russian. I don't need you to hang out with me, if that's what you're worried about," I assured him, turning my attention back to my patient.

"Okay, I'm done, Chiayo. Let me grab some bandages, and I'll wrap your foot."

Chiayo bent his head down to look at his stitches and rewarded me with a great big smile. Dante held the boy's foot as I bandaged it.

"Jesus, you're grumpy. It's not that." I heard him but didn't respond, focusing instead on the antibiotic injection going into Chiayo's arm. When it was over, Dante turned to address the boy.

"You see, I told you it would be okay. You have the best doctor in the world taking care of you. You'll be playing basketball in no time."

He was being so genial. It was the gentle side of him that seemed to only show itself with me, and I loved him so much for it. When his father passed away while we were still in school, he was forced to grow up prematurely. Dante and I were two very driven people, and our friendship was based on a common understanding of that.

"Chiayo, keep your foot wrapped for a few days, okay? And here… these should help." I reached under the table and pulled out the shortest pair of crutches. "Use these so you don't put any weight on your leg."

"Okay," he said quietly before lifting himself up and hopping with one foot on the floor. Dante held him steady while slipping the crutches under his arms. "Thank you, Dr. Dillon," Chiayo said in stilted English as he limped away. He came to a stop as he recognized his friend. "Mr. Grayson!" he squeaked excitedly.

"Got that taken care of, huh? Great job, Chiayo!" Jude paused momentarily to ruffle his hair and give him a side hug. "Say hi to your mom for me."

Dante stepped back to allow Jude to come closer, hovering close by as I dropped the instruments into a sterilizing bowl. "Hi," he said.

"Hey," I answered.

"Is your shift almost done? I thought I'd stop by and walk you home." His smile exuded warmth and sincerity, and it took a great effort for me to feign disinterest.

"I still have an hour to go."

"Oh. Can I come back to get you later?" he asked.

Another patient needed attention. The front desk had called my name. I shot a look at Dante, who nodded his head with a smirk on his face. I exhaled loudly in response. He was right. What was there to lose at that point?

"Listen," I said in a hushed tone, "I'll stop by the hut after work."

I yanked Dante's arm and rushed towards the reception area.

# TEN
## *Magic*

"HELLO?" I YELLED as I reached the top of the steps. "Anybody home?"

I made it to the hut two hours after Jude had stopped by the clinic. Nothing lit up the water tonight. The moon and the stars were swallowed by the expansive sky. Mosquitoes were out in full force, circling endlessly around the puddles of water left behind on the shore by the sweeping tide.

"Over here," Jude answered, his voice leading me towards the bedroom. I could barely make him out through the green netting that enclosed the bed and a tiny area around it. I lifted it up and crawled inside to find him sitting on the floor surrounded by little clay pots filled with citronella candles to keep the mosquitos away.

"So? What was so important?" I asked.

"Nothing, really. I just had to see you. Explain what I said last night."

I couldn't hide the confused expression on my face. Transparency was sometimes a gift and oftentimes a curse. I sat next to him, our gazes fixed on the flickering candles.

"I want us to spend the rest of your stay here together. As friends. I don't want anything to change because of what I said to Paulina last night."

"Jude, get over yourself. I don't want to sleep with you."

"I didn't say you did," he countered defensively. "I just—"

"Last night, you made sure I knew where we stood."

"Yes." He looked at me sadly. "I have to."

He leaned the weight of his body on his arms and stretched out his legs. The bottom of his jeans were perfectly frayed and torn. His feet looked so fine, his toes long and slender.

"So how do you know Chiayo?" I asked, once again impressed by the many friends he had in the village.

"I stayed with their family when—" He caught himself. "Nothing."

"What?" I insisted. "Tell me."

His tone turned softer as he avoided my eyes. "Chiayo is Lao's cousin. Lao's mom was really sick. I sat with them throughout her final nights. I also helped to build their new house by the river."

"Is that why you're here? To help people? Are you here to help people or to find yourself?" I asked, trying not to sound too emphatic about what I thought he was going to say.

"Both, I guess. Anna, the world is neither black nor white. I find myself when I help people as much as I do when I hurt the people I love. I'm trying to learn about what's important and to give as much of myself as I can. But sometimes, I can't help but wonder what's really out there for me." His eyes bore into mine, and for the first time since I'd met him, I was sure that I was falling for him. He was selfless and giving. He wanted to make a difference in the world like I did.

Jude spoke with certainty, never failing to make me see things from both points of view. His words made me realize that my mother had to hurt us to find herself. And there was nothing really wrong about wanting what she deserved. There was nothing really wrong about wanting to be happy. The problem was that sometimes our happiness was at someone else's detriment. We were burglars in the night, stealing someone else's laughter for our own and replacing it with tears.

"Listen, Blue, can we be friends, hang out together, and just go back to normal?"

"Believe it or not, I really can't afford any more complications in my life right now. So, of course we can be friends. I wouldn't have it any other way." I smiled with genuine affinity. My affection for him was rising to the surface.

"Good," he said. "Thank you."

I turned my head in the direction of the wooden chest. It was ornate but worn, with ivory carvings running down its sides.

"What's in here?" I asked. I got on my knees and slowly lifted its lid. Inside were bits and pieces of the life of the family that lived here—broken toys, a rusty makeup mirror, damaged pictures, tiny baby clothes. I fished in between the clothes and pulled out a funny looking contraption. "What is this?" I asked, holding it up for him to see. "Oh, a cassette player! Of course! We had one of these when I was growing up."

The beauty of this place had to do with the way time seemed to stand still. Old memories mixed with new ones, the love of a family lost and found in the companionship of two strangers.

"Yeah. It even has a tape inside of it," he said. "I've played it a few times, actually. I just changed the batteries the other day."

I placed it in the middle of the floor. He slid himself behind me and pulled me close against his chest.

"Let's hear it," I said, taking his hand and pushing it down on the PLAY button. Music started to fill the room. We swung our heads and swayed to the music, waiting for the chorus, and then belted out at the top of our lungs:

*You've got to believe in magic*
*Something stronger than the moon above*
*'Cause it's magic when two people fall in love*

"You know this song?" he asked, his eyes wide with surprise. "Were you even born yet?"

"*Zapped!* Scott Baio! My older cousins used to watch it over and over again when I was a kid!" I laughed. "And listen to you, Mr. Two Years Older than Me."

"Well then," he whispered as he stood up and offered me his hand.

I took his lead as he pulled me into his arms, and slowly, so slowly, we moved together to the words of the song. My head was buried in his shoulder while the palm of his hand lay flat on the small of my back. I could feel every breath he took, every beat of his heart. At that very moment, there was no one in the world but us, in a rundown house with a ratty old bed and millions of mosquitoes. There was no one but us, and the music and the magic.

The music drifted out, idly, languidly, until we were left dancing in complete silence. The PLAY button on the recorder popped up.

"Gray?" I muttered into his chest. We stood together in the middle of the floor, motionless but holding on tightly to each other.

"Hmm?" he answered.

"The music stopped."

"Play it again," he ordered, without any intention of releasing me.

"I can't."

"Why not?" His lips brushed against the back of my ear.

"Because I'm kind of trapped here right now."

He snapped his head up and started to laugh, sweet and joyous. We needed this, he and I. No matter what our secrets were, what life was like before we met, there was no need to know, no need to worry.

The ringing of his laughter was drowned out by a clap of thunder and then a fierce downpour of rain. Instead of running for shelter, I threw my arms up in the air and started to dance.

"Go Blue!" Jude exclaimed, as he ran back into the bedroom and retrieved his phone. He scrolled through it and picked out a hip hop song by will.i.am. Despite the weight of the rain, we jumped and twirled, his hands on my waist, my head thrown back.

We swerved left and right, moving in unison. We bounced up and down, our bodies touching, his hands on me, my hands in my hair. Not once did he remove his eyes from mine as we mouthed the words to the song.

*Look up in the mirror*
*The mirror look at me*
*The mirror be like baby you the shit*
*God dammit you the shit*

Drenched, we danced away our worries and fears. There was no need for reasons, no need for confessions.

They say that love is found in the darkest of moments, when you're lost and alone, in desperate search of answers. But that night, we found love in merriment and joy. We danced until the clouds had passed and our clothes were dry, we played backgammon into the wee hours of the morning, and slept side by side on the floor. There was no need to define who we were to each other. We were young and alive, and the future looked bright.

# ELEVEN
## *For Life*

"BLUE, DO YOU believe in fate?" Jude asked as we floated along the water in two old tires that we'd picked up from the Sunday market. They were tied securely to the bamboo posts that supported the hut to ensure that we didn't get carried away by the current. Earlier, we had talked about how we should be spending our last week at the mission. "Do you think we were meant to meet, to spend time together, despite the fact that in the end, we have to go our separate ways?"

The moon was so bright and the water was as clear as glass. I could see the little fish swimming underneath my toes. Yellow spotted boxfish and blue tangs blended in with the orange anemones, flitting harmlessly in and out of the corals on the ocean floor. Jude held a flashlight in his hands and shone it on the surface, allowing us to watch the fish go back and forth as he teased them with the light. We were in shallow water, merely chest deep, and so we felt safe and secure in our own private corner of the sea.

Separate ways. It made me sad to hear these words from him. Soon, the inevitable day would arrive and he would be nothing more than the friend I met in Thailand.

"Oh, I don't know," I answered. "If God has a plan for everyone, then what good is prayer? Wouldn't prayer be useless? I mean, assuming people did pray." Bedtime prayers were a huge deal with my mother when I was younger. Not anymore.

He laughed as he reached out for my tire and linked it firmly with his. We faced each other, our feet dangling in opposite directions.

"You tend to over think things," he said. "Fate has nothing to do with prayer, Blue. Prayer keeps you in check and gives you the blessings that you need to live out your fate."

"Okay, but if you prayed for God to change things, they wouldn't change anyway." I tried to push away from him, but he held on to the rope that drooped in the water.

"But He can give you strength, acceptance, peace."

"And so what happens to choice if everything in life is your fate?" I spun around in a circle until he reluctantly let go of me.

"Fate leads to choice and choice leads to your fate," he clarified. There was no compromise with this guy. "Think multiple choice. There's only one answer, and if you continue to choose the wrong one, you'll keep trying until you get the right one."

"What? You just confirmed that prayers don't work," I said as

I pushed away from him and drifted as I far as I could go. I continued to state my case. "There was this time in fourth grade when I was being bullied for my red hair. One day, I knew that the girls in this group were looking for me. They heard that my dad had brought me these really cool wooden pens from his trip to China, and they wanted me to hand them over. I hid in the bathroom and prayed with all my might that they wouldn't find me, but they did. And they took my pens, roughed me up, and made fun of my hair. My mom pulled me out of the school the very next day and placed me in a new one."

"Now why," he began, "why in the world would they tease you about your hair? It's the most striking feature about you. Okay, along with your eyes and your nose and your mouth," he said gently, while trying unsuccessfully to reach out for me. The light sweep of the current was too quick for him.

"Smooth talking will get you everywhere," I joked, allowing myself to drift.

"Do you think that what happened has played a part in the reason why you're so strong and so driven?" He placed the flashlight between his legs and used his hands to paddle closer to me. I thought it was adorable, the way we drifted together and came apart.

"I guess," I said. "So what you're saying is that I had to be bullied in order to get transferred to my new school? Because that new school was where I spent the happiest days of my life. I met Maggie there."

"You met her in grade school?" he asked.

"Yup. Dodgeball. Some idiot hit me on the head with the ball and took me down. The ball bounced off my big head and smacked Maggie on the same spot as she stood on the sidelines flirting with a boy. We ended up in the nurse's clinic, side by side on two stretchers." I smiled with fond remembrance.

"What happened to the idiot?"

"He became my best friend."

"No kidding?!" He laughed. "You see? I really think things happen for a reason," he said, pulling me to him so that we held hands. In fact, I clasped my fingers around his because I didn't want to float away. There was nowhere else in the world I wanted to be.

He tugged on the rope as we glided closer to the hut. "For example, do you ever wonder how come you run into so many people day in and day out and only a handful of them remain permanently in your life?"

"No," I joked. "I don't sit there and do a play-by-play of everyone I meet." *Which is why this is so unlike me, Jude.*

"So," he asked, with sincere interest, "Dante was a childhood friend? He seems so cavalier to have been friends with you for so long."

"No. He never really paid attention to me until our freshman year of college. We were in Spanish class together. We made fun of the same people, liked the same movies, worked in a group together. We love the same style of clothes, shop at the same stores... and he's been the most patient, loyal friend I could ever have since then."

"Did you guys ever, you know, hook up?"

"What? No!" I objected. "I've told you before, we're best

friends. Besides, we're too alike. But enough about me. What about you? Who's your best friend?"

"A guy named Peter. We're *not* exactly the same, though. He's a ladies man. And very laid back. Sooo… boyfriends. What about your boyfriends?" he asked.

"If you're doing this so that I ask about your girlfriend, no deal, Gray. I don't want to know about her." I kicked his tire away from me and giggled as he blanched from the sting of the saltwater in his eyes.

"Why do you keep pushing me away? I asked you a question, Blue." He grabbed my foot and used it to pull himself close to me again.

"Fine. No boyfriends, none. Lots of flings, but nothing serious. I was too busy in school."

Suddenly, he slid me towards him until we were face to face, our tires rubbing against each other like bumper cars in an amusement park. He tipped himself forward and jumped into the water between my legs. I slipped my legs inside the tire and held my arms up so that he could lift it off me.

"Blue," he sighed, "I wish things were different." The luster in his eyes was gone.

I rested my head on his chest as he clasped his hands together behind my back. There was nothing else for me to say. I too wished that everything was different, and yet I hoped that things would stay the same. I needed my mother at that very moment. I wanted to tell her that I understood. I wanted to ask her about these feelings. I wanted her to confirm whether this was love.

I lifted my head up to catch his lips slightly parted. "I have to call my mom," I said.

He acknowledged the loss of the moment. "Sure. Let's get back inside and you can use my phone," he replied, continuing to hold me close while smoothing his hands over my hair.

"Gray?"

"Hmm?" he answered dreamily.

"I'm a little freaked out. There's something rubbing against my leg."

He lifted me up gently, turning the flashlight back on and handing it over to me. I settled my feet lightly in the sand, afraid to step on something I couldn't see. He guided my hand and held the light a few inches above the water.

"Look," he said excitedly. "They're seahorses." He reached his hands down just below the surface, enclosing them in the palms of his hands.

"Cool! Why are they tangled up with each other like that?"

"It's their defense mechanism. Do you see how the male with the pouch is hanging on to her tail? He's protecting her."

I brought my face closer to the water.

"Hey, do you know what they say about seahorses?" Jude asked.

"No, but I know you're about to tell me," I teased.

"That they mate for life. One mate. One partner. For life." He emphasized this fact.

"That's just a myth. Nothing, no one, mates for life."

# TWELVE
## *I'll Call*

"WHERE'VE YOU BEEN, slowpoke? We were supposed to meet thirty minutes ago! I already found ten things for us to take home and was just waiting to see what you thought!" I greeted Dante with a kiss on the cheek. We'd arranged to meet at the open market to find some last minute souvenirs for our family back home.

He placed a firm hand on my shoulder. "Spark. Let's get out of this crowd for a while and talk." There was a tremor in his voice.

"What? What's wrong? Did you have a fight with Milena? Or Paulina?" I teased.

He shook his head sadly. "You need to call your dad," he said as he handed me his phone. "Now."

The moment I snatched the phone from him, it vibrated in my hand. I guess he couldn't wait for me to call back.

"Dad?" I answered after one ring. She was foremost on my mind. "Are you going to be seeing Mom today? Tell her I found the perfect complement to the large rock in the garden."

Dante took charge and pulled me out of the crowd into a secluded area behind one of the larger stalls.

"Annie," my dad's voice cracked. "I'm so sorry, she's gone."

I dug the phone into my ear to make sure that I heard him clearly. "Gone? What do you mean? Where'd she go, Dad? Did she leave the hospital? For where?"

"She never came out of surgery," he cried. "She's gone. Gone!" He exhaled loudly to compose himself. "Come home, Annie. Please come home."

The phone slipped from my hand on the muddy ground, stealing the world from underneath my feet, leaving me with nothing but tears. By the time Dante wiped off his phone, I was dashing through the crowd, going against traffic, unsure about my destination but certain that I had to get away.

"Spark!" Dante shoved everyone in his way to get to me.

I could only think about the previous night's phone call to my mother. Things didn't work out the way I had planned. When my call was met by a male voice on the line, I was taken aback. Her lover was a living, breathing being, with a heart, a soul, and a voice. I hung up the phone and gave it back to Jude.

I tried to push Dante back. "I have to go. Please!"

"Anna, no. I'm here. Let me stay with you," he pleaded. The comforting crush of his body managed to soothe my pain.

"No, I'll be okay," I said, shaking my head. "Will you help me get my tickets, please?"

He nodded his head and watched me walk away.

I had to find Jude. I needed to inhale the fresh air he brought into my life before I suffocated to death.

Death.

An irony, wasn't it? I'd been surrounded by it every day I'd been here, and now it had touched me from afar. All the way from the other side of the world, when I should have been buried deep in it here, holding it in my arms, begging it for forgiveness. I ran aimlessly through the village, past wooden huts and stone houses, past the squalor I had managed to overlook for two weeks.

I couldn't find him. The one who could comfort me. Jude was gone. And in a few hours, I'd be gone.

For the past few nights, we'd been inseparable. While our days were spent in service to others, we selfishly guarded the privacy of our evenings in the hut that was our temporary home. We talked endlessly about our lives, our goals, our hopes and dreams. We shared the fears we had about what was waiting for us back home. We eased the burden of our inevitable departure by living in the moment, and we sought relief in the fact that forever was nowhere in the picture. That tomorrow was something that didn't need to be discussed.

I never asked him any specifics about his future. I figured it was too late. Goals without plans are just wishes. All we had were wishes. Our goals and our plans would never intersect.

There was no way that I could leave without saying goodbye.

And so I kept searching, pacing along the shore, sinking deep into my sadness. My legs felt like lead. With every step an effort, I decided to give in. Maybe if I allowed this sinkhole to swallow me, I wouldn't have to face anything. I dropped to my knees, my face in my hands, and the sound that emerged from my throat was unknown. I keened, I wailed, I let it all out. I'd lost my mother, and my future would be filled with regret.

"Oh my God. Blue?" Jude dashed up behind me and covered me with his body. "What happened?" I could see that he'd been out running. His hair and shirt were soaked with sweat and his breathlessness told me that he had finished his run with a sprint.

"She's gone! She left me! I was going to tell her that there was nothing for me to forgive! That I loved her no matter what!" I wasn't sure whether he truly understood what I was saying. I heard my thoughts but not my words. They were buried against his chest, and his heart absorbed all my sadness. "It's too late. I'm being punished for my selfishness. I should've called her sooner, I should've gone home. I'm never going to see her again."

"Shh. No, no. It's not like that," he whispered gently as he stroked my hair and held my face. "She was sick, Blue. And now she has her peace." His voice, although soft, was marked by certainty. "Come on, let's take you home."

"I have to leave in the morning," I said, gazing up at him. His eyes were filled with consolation.

"I know. It's okay." He lightly brushed his thumbs across my cheeks to wipe away my tears before settling my head in the crook of his neck. The silence of the night was louder than it had ever been, and I could hear the thunder in the background; the impending storm had finally arrived.

He stood up slowly and bent down to scoop me in his arms, lifting me up to carry me. "I'll take you home. You need to rest. You're going on a long trip tomorrow."

"No, please. I want to stay with you. Can you please let Dante know? Let him know I'm with you so he won't worry." My voice vibrated through his skin, and I inhaled the sweet, intoxicating smell of sweat and saltwater. I couldn't bear to think that after tomorrow, my life would go on without him in it.

He nodded and used one hand to punch in a text message on his phone, the other arm still holding me up with ease, refusing to let me go. He took a few slow steps towards our make believe palace, the wooden hut at the end of the world, high above the water, almost touching the clouds. The sound of his flip-flops dredging through the sand ended at the bottom of the ladder. We'd been here many times before, but that night was different. We knew that nothing between us would ever be the same again. I kept my head buried in his neck and I heard a loud, resolute breath before he climbed the stairs with me held tight in his arms.

"Hi," he whispered as we stood right at the top of the landing, overlooking our made up kingdom.

"Hi," I answered, lifting my head up and wrapping my arms around his neck at the same time.

"Blue, there's so much I want to tell you. I don't know where to begin. I need you to know—"

"Shhh." I traced my finger along the outline of his lips. "Words don't matter now. It's too late for words."

He nodded his head with a sad smile, while lowering me and resting my head carefully on the floor.

"Jude," I breathed. "I need to feel… Please, make me feel loved."

He moved his body next to mine, trailing his fingers down from my face to my neck and slowly slipping his hand underneath my shirt. I took in a deep breath before closing my eyes and enjoying the feeling of his skin against mine. Never had I ever felt so connected to anyone in my life. He kissed me, softly at first, allowing all that pent up energy between us to possess his hands as they roamed all over my body. He began to worship my lips, reverently tracing every inch of it with his tongue. And then he stopped, searching my face for approval. We were crossing the line and there was no turning back. I nodded my head and raised my arms above my head.

He responded by lifting up my shirt, exposing me completely, and then by covering every part of me with his mouth. His touch vibrated through my skin, it scorched my pain away. It was soothing, arousing, assuring. Like a powerful ray of light that erased all the blemishes in my life.

"My God, Blue, you are so beautiful." He traced his lips downward from my breasts to my stomach and down to the red birthmark on the inside of my thigh. "I've wanted you since the first time I saw you."

In that instance I was sure that I had realized my fate: it was to lose myself to someone who I would never see again.

"Jude!" I cried out as he buried himself inside me. How on earth did I survive so long without this? He stretched me, he pervaded me, but most importantly, he filled my heart.

"Tell me. Tell me this is different. Tell me this is special," he ordered.

"It is," I said with a moan as he pushed faster and faster. "Never, never like this."

"You feel like home, Anna," he groaned, resting his arms directly above my shoulders and holding my head in place. He continued forcefully, rhythmically, and we moved together, our bodies molding perfectly in a choreographed performance. We were made for each other and the many movements in this symphony were all part of a plan. The tempo, the rhythm, the alternating touches and kisses—they all came together in a perfect composition. Beads of sweat formed on his brow; his eyes were darker than they had ever been. He tried to stop, tried to pull back, tried to slow down.

"Oh God, Blue, I can't—" he said, gasping and thrusting in deeply one last time.

I closed my eyes and imagined for once that my life was perfect. That he was the one who would save me from my sorrow.

We lay face to face in the middle of the floor, on the little mattress that had been witness to our days and nights together. In the intimacy of that moment I became panic-stricken at the thought of a future without him. I never really thought about what our lives would be like after these two weeks in paradise. Somehow, I thought that we would have more time.

*That we would talk. And plan. Or at least say goodbye.*

Once again, he read my thoughts. He enclosed me in his arms and entwined his legs around mine, saying, "I'll call Dante right when I get back to the States."

"Will you?" I asked. I never replaced my phone. I didn't need to. All this time, we'd communicated through Dante.

"Of course I will. I feel so bad that I can't be there for you. But they need me here for another month, and then I have to complete my stint in Australia for another four months."

"Five months is a long time."

"It will be over before we know it," he assured me.

I remained quiet.

"We have something, you know." There he was again, looking

at me with so much honesty. Every single truth in this world made its home in his eyes.

I turned around and faced the other way, afraid to reveal my tears, but he pulled me even closer, desperate to convince the both of us that this was more than a stop on the road to leading separate lives.

"This was meant to be. Know that, my beautiful Bluey," he repeated.

"Hmm," I muttered sleepily, safe in his arms and content with accepting who and what we were to each other.

I drifted off and was in and out of one dream after another.

"Blue? Blue, wake up. You're having a dream. Wake up, baby. You're safe here with me." He shook me lightly until I opened up my eyes to look into his face.

And suddenly it became clear to me. I saw my mother in a different light. "She died happy, Gray. My mother died knowing real love. The night that I saw her with him. She never looked at my father that way."

"Not very many people can say that they found that in their lifetime," he said, lightly tracing the outline of my face with his thumbs.

"You're still awake?" I asked in a croaky voice heavy with sleep.

"I don't want to end the night without letting you know how much I'm going to miss you."

"I'll miss you too," I whispered.

He cradled my face in his hands and kissed me.

I would always remember that kiss. It sealed my fate to him forever. With that kiss I released my heart and soul into his hands, and I knew that my life would never be the same. It was a promise kiss, a goodbye kiss, a kiss that signified the end but also the beginning.

When you lose your soul to a kiss... it's irretrievable.

"Anna," he said with his eyes closed, pressing himself to me so that there was not a bit of space between us. I felt his desire against me and it pleased me to know that he wanted me just as much. "Anna Dillon. My gift, my heart. I want you again, and again, and again."

And that was when I broke my own heart.

"What happened between us can never be replicated," I whispered. "That moment we just had. That's what I want you to remember. If you forget anything else about our time together, don't forget this." He smiled weakly at me. His face was masked in disappointment but his eyes, they showed me relief. We had sealed our connection in the physical sense. There was no need to reaffirm anything else. "And Gray?"

"Yes, Blue," he answered.

"What you said about fate. I really believe that we have the power to change it."

I yielded to my exhaustion, wondering how I could recover from the events of that night. I lost my mother and I gave away my heart. And I was left with nothing to take home with me. Not one single thing.

I woke the next morning to find a wooden strand of beads wrapped around my hand, a beautiful rosary made by the children of the mission. Despite the crashing of the waves and the piercing screams of the hungry seagulls, that day was marked by the blaring silence all around me. My mother was dead, my heart was gone, and I was left all alone.

# PART II:
## Songs of Love
## Five Years Later
## October 2005 (Anna)

"The streets of town were paved with stars;
It was such a romantic affair.
And as we kissed and said "goodnight",
A nightingale sang in Berkeley Square."

*A Nightingale Sang in Berkeley Square*
*Manhattan Transfer*

# THIRTEEN
## How Time Flies

"WELCOME BACK, BABY," Dante gushed, sticking his head in the window of the driver's seat as I unstrapped myself from the car. He greeted me excitedly with a kiss. Mikey was settled in the passenger seat, eyes closed, earphones in place, iPhone in hand.

"Hi." I kissed him back, tired as heck but happy to be able to spend two days with him at our apartment in midtown Manhattan before having to head back to work at the hospital.

We'd just arrived from the long drive from New York City to Tully Hill, a trip that we made at least once every other month. The three hour drive to the rehab facility where my father stayed was an easy one, lovely and scenic during the early fall when the bold red and golden colors of the leaves blanketed the ground, and the cool crisp air was a welcome respite from the hot days of summer.

But the hours that followed were difficult and discouraging. Michael needed to see him more than I did, and I was determined to be there for my little brother despite the toll that seeing my father took on me. Life had bombarded me with lessons, and I'd learned most of all that promises were made to be broken. I never heard from Jude again. By the time Dante arrived from Thailand one week after I left, the callback on the number that was saved to Dante's phone had been shut off. I counted the months to the day he was supposed to be done with his trip to Australia. I waited for him to call, gave him the benefit of my trust, detached myself from the world around me, and stayed suspended in anticipation. I would have tried to find him, but I didn't know where to look. Sure, I knew that he was from Westchester and all, but then I began to doubt the stories that he had told me. And then the months became years, and the years ran away with the hope I had held in my heart.

"How was your visit?" Dante asked as he pulled the handle on the car door. The parking garage looked empty. Not that it mattered because Dante held two prime spots right in front of the elevator.

"Same. Apologies, tears, Mikey having a hard time saying goodbye."

He smiled weakly before walking towards the trunk of the car.

It had been five years since my mother had passed away. I arrived back in New York in time for her funeral. It was a quiet event attended by family and friends.

And her lover, of course. He reminded me of Delmar—blond with blue eyes, a slim build, very well put together. He looked much older than his years, aged since the last time I saw him at the restaurant. The man she claimed to have loved stood steadfast among the many faces of disgust and resentment, unwavering and committed. He watched as we cried and mourned, watched as we committed her to the dust, and then he disappeared forever.

Two years later, we lost everything. The house, the cars, the money that she made and set aside for Michael's college education. My father sank into the depths of despair, found comfort in bottles of whiskey and gambled away the life we once lived. Our beautiful house in upstate New York, our cars, our things, all repossessed by banks and credit companies. I worked nights and weekends tending bar while putting myself through medical school and helping Michael survive high school. By then, Dante was well on his way to obtaining his post-graduate degree, set with a promising job as an investment banker in the city. Michael and I lived in a small apartment on campus, surviving on enough money to pay for school, buy books, and eat three sensible meals a day.

Dante was my lifeline. When I graduated from medical school, we celebrated by moving all four boxes that were left to my name into his grand apartment in Manhattan. Although I had loved him for ten years, I finally allowed myself to fall in love with him when I accepted the fact that Jude was never coming back.

In these five years, I had experienced two deaths. The death of my mother was clean cut, more defined. No matter what, there was no hope of ever seeing her again. The death of my feelings for Jude were more difficult and just as painful. Because through the agony of never gazing into those eyes again, there was hope and longing, and denial that it was really over. There was no hard stop or forced acceptance of loss like with my mother. My grief for Jude lingered and played with my head every day until I convinced myself that by now, he was probably living somewhere as a married man with a family of his own.

As a thriving second year surgical resident at the John Hopkins Medical Center, I'd been privileged enough to join the team at the Harriet Lane Pediatrics program. I wanted to play a part in a child's future, but most of all, I wanted to honor the memory of my mother. She lived her life with passion. And I found passion of my own, for the ultimate genius of the human body and the way it worked.

For four years, while I mourned the loss of Jude, Dante dated many others and I reactivated my sex life. But in the end, what Dante and I had was time tested and real and I buried myself in his love. I suffocated myself in it, and I dared not come up for air, for when I did, I feared that the air I breathed would have nothing to do with the love that he gave me. That I'd find myself breathing, consuming the love of someone else. Someone I couldn't have. Someone who didn't love me. Best to invest in the one who loves you back.

A week before I sat for the final phase of my Medical Licensing Exam, swept up in the whirlwind of love and the prospect of our exciting future, Dante and I were married. In a simple ceremony in Los Cabos, in a century-old church in front of a century-old priest. We made it official when we returned to New York. I didn't change my name professionally, nor did I share in the fruits of his financial success. All in the name of survival. Of proving to myself that I could manage through the pain. Secrets ruin lives and lies protect those secrets. I was the luckiest girl alive; I had everything I could ever want. Fate had replenished my empty cup, made up for my losses in the form of Dante. I could circle the globe a million times in search of true love, but I knew that I would always end up with him. I finally accepted my fate, and I married my best friend.

"Mikey, we're home," I said, gently nudging the arm that rested limply on the console. "Let's gather up our stuff and go inside."

Michael opened his eyes lazily and nodded as he began to collect his things. Empty candy wrappers and two bottles of Coke lay underneath his feet. Dante had already cleared the overnight bag from the trunk of the car. We followed him to the parking elevator and rode up in silence. The door swung open as he held the electronic nob to the keypad. My brother dropped his bag on the ground and ran in towards the kitchen.

Dante took my hand in his and led me down the long winding hallway of the apartment to the living room. The walls were lined with contemporary art from many of New York's top galleries. Dante was a new art collector, partial to abstract works. His particular favorite was the landscape collection by Jean Metzinger. A beautiful burst of color depicted in contrasting shapes and sizes.

"One painting a year," is what he would always plan for. So far, we'd accumulated four from that collection and about ten from other art dealers around the world.

I turned my head to address my brother, who was following right behind us. He looked so grown up, so tall and lanky, with bushy uncut hair and oversized basketball shorts. "Are you okay with being home alone tonight while Tey and I go on that double date we planned three weeks ago?"

He rolled his eyes at me. "Of course, Annie. You guys go ahead and have fun. I'm dying to get back online and do some gaming."

I shook my head, smiled at Dante, and snaked my arm around his. "I guess we're still on. We have a few hours to chill before we have to get ready for dinner."

"THAT WAS SO good, Sparky," Dante whispered in my ear as I sat enclosed between his legs in the large Jacuzzi in the middle of the bathroom suite. Above us, dusk had settled, slowly dimming the natural glow that came in through the skylight. The scent of lilacs and lilies filled the air, emanating from the many candles all around us.

The soapy water had formed clusters of bubbles which gently touched our skin. *Like the sea foam that gathered on the beaches of Thailand.* I closed my eyes but only for a brief second. For the past five years, lingering in my thoughts proved to be a bad idea for me. Too many memories. Too many tears. Too many unanswered questions and unspoken words.

"Hmm." I leaned back into him so that my head rested on his chest. My hair was spread out upon his shoulders, bobbing up and down like seaweed in the water. He gently gathered it up in his hands and tilted my head sideways so that his lips could skim my face. "Glad to be of service, Mr. Leola."

His voice grew soft. "Whatever happened to the transplant candidate you've been taking care of? The twelve-year-old?"

"Oh, Bryan?" I let out a deep sigh. "Not good. His body rejected the donated liver. He's back on the waiting list."

He wound his arms around me. "I'm sorry, baby. I hate it when you have days like that."

"I know. It really makes you wonder where God is in all of this. How could children be allowed to suffer like that? And the parents! To see their pain, their helplessness, it's just so heartbreaking." In leaving me with that rosary, Jude had brought me back to God. Ironically, having Him in my life had helped me with all my losses.

I heard a soft rustling sound coming from his throat. Dante had fallen asleep.

"Tey?" I stroked his arm softly. "Tey? Are you okay?"

"Oh. Sorry." He twitched in surprise. "This medicine is just making me so drowsy."

"What medicine? What's wrong?" I sat up and turned to face him.

"Nothing, just the new headache meds I have. The pain was unbearable last night so I took one this morning," he explained. "I'm going to sleep it off before we leave for our hot date tonight."

"I'm worried about you. Those headaches. We should probably see Afihsa sometime this week." She was a close friend from medical school who was specializing in neurology. "I spoke to her about them a few weeks ago and she suggested that we take some tests."

"They're just stress headaches, I'm sure of that. Where have you been for the last ten years? I always have headaches," he said in jest.

"It's that job of yours. You need to slow down a bit." I placed my fingers on his temples and started to rub them lightly. "Look at you. You've also lost quite a bit of weight."

"No, no. I'm fine. I'm not going to work this weekend so we can just relax and take it easy." He restlessly drummed his fingers on the edge of the tub.

"Not good enough, Leola. Promise me you're going to meet me this week at the hospital. We're going to get those tests done, okay?"

"Spark, I need to see an optometrist, not a neurosurgeon," he countered, now tapping his fingers on the exquisite checkered Italian tile.

"Yes, but—"

"Baby, it's not like what your mom had. I'm fine. I'm not going anywhere."

"You never know! One minute you're here, and the next—" I whined, clutching his restless fingers in mine.

"Never. You'll never lose me," he quickly interrupted.

"Promise?" I placed my arms on his and pulled them tighter around me.

He slid down against the tub and allowed me to place my weight on his chest. "I swear," he answered, cupping his right hand over my stomach and stroking it.

"Oh, Tey," I sighed. It broke my heart to see him want something so much. I could sense the yearning in his touch, in his kisses, in the way he made love to me so intensely.

"Spark. Please, can we just talk about it? Set a date? Something?"

"We've talked about it before, and every single time you bring it up, we fight. I just need more time. How can we have a baby when I'm still doing my shifts at the hospital?"

"I've made enough money to retire. I'll take care of the baby while you finish your residency, and your boards and all," he argued. He was always ready with answers to my every concern.

"It's not that easy. A baby requires time and attention.

Something neither you nor I have at this point in time. We've been through this over and over again!" I did nothing to hide the agitation in my tone.

"I'm sure there's a way we can find a compromise," he answered.

"I've already given in to what you wanted! We're married, aren't we?"

I felt his body stiffen, his arms dropping down to his sides. He slid upwards away from me and pulled himself up out of the water. "So now the truth is out. Our marriage was a compromise." He proceeded to step out of the tub while grabbing a towel and covering himself with it.

"No! Wait!" I leaned forward. "I didn't mean it that way, Tey!"

He turned around to face me, towel wrapped around his waist, head dropped, eyes unblinking. "When are you going to settle down, Anna? What else are you waiting for?"

I held out my arms to him. He responded by clasping my outstretched fingers in his and moving to the edge of the tub. I sat up and wrapped my arms around him. "Okay," I whispered into his neck. I had no fight left in me. Love was all about closing your eyes and jumping in. There was never really a good time for anything; I learned that lesson the hard way five years ago. "Okay. Let's talk about it. Let's plan."

# FOURTEEN
*Jimmy*

"YOU'D BETTER STAND back, I think I'm going to burst right here," I warned, standing in the elevator on the way to the 18th floor.

Dante kept his arm draped around me as the other couples stepped inside. We had just finished a late dinner at one of our favorite spots in Soho and were now on our way to meet Maggie and her boyfriend, Donny. He was now her serious boyfriend, moving to New York to spend all his time with her. His father was the CEO of a popular leather shoe company in Italy and he planned to open outlets in the States.

"You did eat more than you normally do, but it doesn't show one bit," he whispered sensually in my ear while slipping his hand under my dress. "I really love this outfit on you." Dante looked so dashing in a fitted Armani sport coat and slim dark washed jeans. Everything he wore was custom made; his appearance smacked of success. In wanting to match his polished look, I wore a grey leather dress that was fitted and revealing.

"Mmm," I said with a slight moan, staking a claim and defying the envious stares of the women by rubbing myself against him. He attracted them like moths to a flame. "Behave yourself for a few hours, will you?" I teased back, bent on making the night up to him, whatever it took. I wanted to erase the hurt that my words had caused him earlier.

The elevator doors opened and we all filed out in a line. The rooftop bar at the James Hotel was where Dante and I had our first real kiss. We hadn't made a friends-with-benefits kind of commitment, but rather a conscious promise from me to see him in a different light. I had never regretted that decision despite the topsy-turviness of my feelings over the past year. There's so much to be said about closure. I needed it. I knew that if I ever got the chance to have it, I would beg Dante for forgiveness and promise to love only him for the rest of my life.

If only I could. We headed straight to our favorite spot, the blue chairs right by the corner window overlooking the most beautiful view of the city. I hardly had the time to admire the sights before I heard a familiar voice yelling out my name.

"Sparky!" Maggie shouted as she boldly pushed away the strangers who stood in her way. My beautiful friend, with long golden hair and the brightest blue eyes. I was afraid she was going to fall on her face with those five inch heels on the slippery laminate floor. I held my arms out for an embrace. Dante stood up to give her a hug then shook hands with Donny.

"Hi! You're on time for once!" I said.

Donny stood right behind her with a big grin on his face. He was a former soccer player with wide shoulders and ringlets of brown hair scattered all over his head.

"Hi, Donny. So nice to see you again. Come, sit."

Maggie took a seat on the blue stool next to me while Donny sat across from Dante, who motioned for the server to take our order.

"Champagne okay with everyone?"

We all nodded in unison.

He turned his attention to a pretty server in a tight black dress who brought her face close to his in an attempt to hear him speak. "A bottle of Dom Cuvee, please, and four glasses. Wait, hold on." He took my hand and asked, "Baby, is that okay or do you want your Rosé?"

"I'm good with that. Thanks." I squeezed his hand. "Oh, oh, oh, the hotdog thingies. Get the hotdog rolls."

"And the breaded franks, please," he instructed the server.

"And sliders."

"And the sliders," he said, giving me a confused look and shaking his head.

"Maggie's hungry," I said in defense.

She laughed and took my other hand.

"So, how are things?" I asked.

Maggie looked like she was about to blow up. Puffed cheeks, pursed lips, and Donny had a puppy dog look on his face. These two were holding on to a secret that they couldn't keep.

"EEEEK!" she squealed as she held up her left hand to reveal a beautiful diamond solitaire on her ring finger.

I jumped up in glee, almost knocking over the bucket of champagne that sat on the solid wooden table.

"Congratulations! Oh my God! I'm so happy!" I cried.

Dante stood up as we all locked arms in a group hug.

"When? When did this happen?" I asked, holding on to Dante's hand. He had an almost unreadable look on his face. The microprocessor in his brain was running at full speed, and yet he sat there without a change in expression.

"Tonight! Empire State Building! They closed down the Observation Deck for us!" she gushed animatedly.

"She was very surprised. She looked like she was going to hit me!" Donny said.

"When?" asked Dante, trying to hold me down as I bobbed up and down excitedly.

"Next May in Italy! And you will be my matron of honor, Anna. And Dante, Donny wants you as his best man!"

"Me?" asked Dante in surprise.

"Yes, you! He has too many brothers, and choosing one will get him in trouble." The puppy dog nodded his head in agreement.

"Ah. Well, it would be an honor," Dante said with a downward tip of his head. I looked at him lovingly before leaning over to kiss his lips. I knew that this subject would surface later on this evening once we were alone. I was roused from my thoughts when the two men stood up to leave.

"We're going outside for a cigarette," Dante announced. He smoked socially on the occasional night out, especially after having had a few drinks. I never had to worry about him. He was too much of an athlete to allow himself more than a manageable amount.

"Have fun, boys!" Maggie said as she scooted closer to me.

I reached out and popped a roll in my mouth.

"My best friend is getting married!" I exclaimed, squeezing her shoulders.

"I know, right? Oh, Anna, I'm so happy. I can't explain it. He's just the most adorable man I've ever met. And he loves me so much. And can you believe it? We can have babies of the same age!" I didn't have to say anything. She noticed the look on my face. And yet she kept on, trying her best to keep light of the moment. She glanced in the direction of our two men. "Look at them. Our husbands are so hot," she added, pretending to fan herself with her hand.

I laughed nervously. "God, I wish it was that simple." I leaned back against the seat and draped Dante's jacket over my shoulder. "We had—" I stopped cold when I looked up at the line forming for the bathroom. My chest grew tight. The man with his back to me had the same black New York baseball cap over the same black wavy hair, the same compact shoulders with the same strong arms.

"Spark, what's the matter?" Maggie asked worriedly. "What is it?"

He turned around to scan the room. It wasn't him. I let out a sigh of relief. Or disappointment.

"Nothing. Nothing. I just thought—"

"Let's go outside before the men return." She pulled me up and led me outdoors, skillfully maneuvering me through the other exit as we saw Dante and Donny heading back in our direction. We were scrunched to the side, pushed against the barrier surrounding the swimming pool by attractive, scantily clad women and obnoxious, drunk rich men. This was New York, the land of single, eligible, lonely people always on the lookout for potential targets. In no time, we were surrounded by three men around our age, one of whom I recognized as a paramedic who frequented the emergency room to chat with the nurses.

Maggie turned into Maggie as she grabbed my left hand and flashed both our rings up in the air. "Fly away, vultures. We're taken."

The men scuttled away without a word. I laughed through my tears as she handed me a cigarette. I frowned at her as I took it from her fingers, spinning around at the same time to lean against the glass and take in the view. Off in the distance the Empire State Building towered above the others, but it was only one in the multitude of twinkling lights that illuminated the city and brought it colorfully to life.

"Bad influence," I joked.

"Come on, Sparky. That's the beauty of you. You're unorthodox in every single way."

I inhaled deeply, hoping that the smoke would take my woes away as it exited my body.

"Okay. Talk to me," Maggie ordered.

The wind lapped at our dresses and we both held them down with one hand. It was a beautiful October evening, a residual gift of the Indian summer still steadily holding on.

"We had another fight today. He really wants to have a baby. We've only been married for a year, Mags. What's the rush?"

"Listen. No one knows this but me. I see it, Spark. Your refusal to settle down—it's because you don't want to let 'him' go." She enunciated her words with air quotes. "It's your mind playing tricks on you. Give yourself to Dante. He's proven himself to you. And you can't do that if all you have in your head is the guy you think," she paused once again to emphasize the word, "loved you five years ago." She decided to pile it on. "He left you right after you had sex with him, remember? He walked away and never looked back. Why shouldn't you?"

"Whoa. That's harsh." I faced her squarely as the tears dripped down my face.

She stubbed out her cigarette, took out a handkerchief, and dabbed my eyes with its tip. Then she took my face in her hands.

"Sparky, trust me on this. Trust me. He's never coming back. Close that door. You're married. To someone who loves you so much."

"I know, I know." I sniffed. "It's been over for long time. I'm over it."

She shook her head and added an exaggerated rolling of the eyes.

"Most of the time," I laughed.

"There you are!" Dante's approaching voice gave me enough time to wipe the sides of my eyes. I shot Maggie a worried look, but she nodded her head to signal that I looked fine. "We decided to come find you after we were being targeted by some pretty good looking women."

Donny laughed in agreement. "Yes, we started assigning scores to them as they walked past our table."

"You what?" Maggie giggled. "Maybe you should be the one wearing an engagement ring." She hooked her arm in his possessively.

I rushed over to Dante and wrapped mine around his waist.

"Hi," he said, kissing the top of my head. "Let's go order

another bottle of champagne."

# FIFTEEN
## What Can You See?

WE ARRIVED HOME past three in the morning to find the house completely quiet and dark. I slipped off my high heeled shoes and checked around to find that Mikey had cleaned up after himself and even put away the dishes.

"I'm going to my office to send out a quick email," Dante whispered as he laid the keys on the kitchen counter.

"Okay," I said. "I'm going to check on Mike and get ready for bed."

The soft sound of music drifted down the hall as I walked past the study on the way to the bedroom.

The rest of the evening had gone relatively well. Maggie and Donny regaled us with stories about the rush to find a venue for their wedding. We laughed about the slight communication error that occurred when both families met for the first time. It was a happy occasion, and we celebrated their announcement with two bottles of champagne. And although I was lightheaded from the effects of the alcohol, my mind was too wired to call it a night. I took my time in the bathroom, removing the traces of makeup from my face, and taking a quick shower to wash off the smell of smoke and food from my body. I stepped out and slipped on a robe before making my way back to check on Dante.

Silently, I entered the room and locked the door behind me. His gaze was focused on something on the screen of his laptop, and his hands quickly clicked off the page once he saw me sauntering towards him. He wore a pair of reading glasses, something I had never seen him put on before.

"Hi, sexy," he called out from behind his desk.

"Hi." I smiled warmly as I took my place at the edge of the table. "Still working?"

"Nelly stopped with a whole bunch of documents for me to review while you were at Tully." Nelly his ever loyal Executive Assistant/Project Manager. She kept him on task, managed his busy schedule. She was a sexy Latina woman, naturally hot but also very pesky. She got on his nerves way too often for him to feel some sort of attraction towards her. But to her credit, she was the only one who stayed. He was intolerant of incompetence and demanded a commitment to the job that many were not willing to undertake. She had proven her abilities to him and she was highly compensated in return.

He moved the mouse around the pad and typed on the keyboard.

I slid off the opposite side and sat on the table directly in front of him. "I've never seen you wear glasses before. You look hot. Very intellectual."

"It helps me with the headaches, and I can see the screen a bit better." He smiled. "But you're the intellectual in this family."

"I don't like what the stress at work is doing to you," I gently stroked his arm.

He shrugged his shoulders. "I have a feeling that this is my time. I have to just go with the flow, make as much as I can now." Quick, deft circular motions with his hand on the mouse told me that he was eager to shut the computer down.

"Do you want to talk about it?" I asked.

"About what?" he inquired, genuinely clueless about what I was referring to. He slid his chair closer to me and leaned forward.

I held his face in my hands. "Everything. This afternoon, Maggie's engagement. You haven't even made fun of Donny." I teased before kissing him on the forehead.

"Ha!" He laughed. "I'm happy for Maggie, I think she's going to drive the dude nuts with her irritating sweetness, Donny needs to wear his shirt one size larger, his arms are bursting out of their sleeves, and he also needs to gel his hair."

"There he is," I smiled. "The man I know and love." I removed his glasses and placed them on the table directly behind me. And then I kissed his left eye, then his right eye and settled my lips on his right cheek. "I'm sorry about this afternoon," I started to say.

"I know you are," he whispered. "I love you. Maybe it's okay, just being you and me for now."

"No, no," I argued softly. "I meant what I said," I leaned back on my arms and spread my legs seductively. "In fact..." My robe fell open, its right sleeve sliding off my shoulder as if on cue. He licked his lips and settled his hands on my legs. "We are going to try. Right," I tugged at his hands, "now."

"No," he said gently as he pulled me towards him. "I just want you to want our baby in your own time."

"I want our baby. I want you now, tomorrow, next week, next year. You're the only one I want," I whispered, while earnestly trailing my fingers from his chin down to his chest.

"I must be drunk because I'm beginning to believe you," he said.

"Well, believe me." I jumped off the desk and knelt right in front of him.

He watched as I unzipped his pants and held him in my hands before showing him how hungry I was for him. He held my head down and let out a groan. "Don't stop," he whispered.

"I love you, Tey. So much," I said. I wanted to do for him what he was always willing to do for me. To give me love and pleasure and happiness without asking for anything in return. Jude was gone, disappeared into thin air. Gone.

He lifted himself up to make sure that I took all of him in my mouth. "Suck me, baby. Oh God. Fuck me with that dirty, filthy mouth."

I teased, I lingered, I drove him crazy until he lifted my head up roughly, taking me by the shoulders, and settling me on his lap. "I want to be inside you. Put me inside you."

I followed him obediently. I knew that he liked it when we talked during sex. I moved myself on top of him, ground myself into him.

"Tell me, Spark. Tell me how it feels," he said gruffly.

"You're so big, so strong," I said with a whimper. "You fill me up so much. You're all I need. You, just you."

He lifted me up and set me down on the desk. "What do you want, baby?"

"I want you to fuck me hard. Harder, Tey, do it harder."

"Like this? Like this?" He held on to my hips as he drove into me, one of my legs on top of his shoulder, the other spread out across the crook of his arm.

"Yeah," I said with a gasp. "Yeah, just like that." The pleasure never failed to make me forget. And every day, I swore it was getting easier and easier. Teeny tiny triumphs in the one thousand, eight hundred and twenty-five days since he'd been gone.

He leaned over and bit my breast. "This is mine. Your beautiful tits are mine. Squeeze them for me, baby."

I followed his every order, bringing my hands to my breasts and caressing myself. He loomed above me, watching me, invading me forcefully. The force of his thrusts would push my head off the desk; he would pull me back, fill me to the brink before pushing me off the table once again.

"Baby. I'm going to fill you up soon. Tell me you love me."

Whenever I was with him, I lived in these moments. There was no one else. This wasn't a game that I played between two men. I didn't settle for Dante because I couldn't have Jude. I gave up on Jude long before I decided that Dante's love was what I needed in my life. The gentle, unassuming kind of love that lifts you up like the wind and allows you to take flight. It was a liberating kind of love, and except for a few silly bouts of reminiscence and nostalgia, I loved him. I loved Dante.

"I love you. Oh, Oh, I love you!" I shouted. Those words. Of all the words we'd said tonight, those were the ones that made him come. He released himself inside me and collapsed into my arms. The laptop fell on the floor and papers were strewn all over the place.

I tenderly skimmed my fingers along the ridge of his back as he tried to catch his breath. "Did we maybe make a baby? Can we try and try and try?" he asked.

"Are you really going to retire?" I teased back.

"Oh yeah, as soon as you get pregnant, I'll be your house slave," he chuckled. "Baby, you just made me the happiest man on earth."

"Dork." I slapped his butt. "Let's go to bed before Mikey realizes that the noises he just heard weren't in a dream he was having."

"WHAT TIME DO you have to leave today?" Dante asked.

We were whispering under the covers as dawn gloriously settled over Manhattan. The tinted windows that shaded us from the glare of the rising sun were the same ones that opened us up to the beauty of the city. There we were in the aftermath of our lovemaking and proclamations of love and promises of a forever.

"I'll head out at noon so I can drop Mikey off at school on my way there. I'm on the night shift for seven days straight," I answered, as we both focused our attention on the suitcase that laid open on the floor next to the dresser. "I'll try to be home two weeks from today."

"I'll miss you." He lovingly caressed my face as I wrapped my arms around his waist.

"I'll miss you too," I answered, lifting my head up and pinching his nose with my fingers.

"You know, these living arrangements will have to change eventually," he said. "Let me be the one to commute. I can set up an office there. These two weekends a month aren't exactly the best way to start a marriage."

"And what? Leave all this?" I made a sweeping motion with my arm.

He scrunched up his nose and made a face at me. Truth be told, I enjoyed my independence. Those nights away at the hospital were the nights when I allowed myself to miss my mom, to mourn, to cry over what could never have been. Baltimore was far enough from New York to give me the space I needed. He was smart enough to know that. He was also smart enough to drop it for now. "Let's rethink it once you start a new rotation," he concluded.

"Okay," I agreed. "And don't stress out too much about work! If you don't get the deal, you don't get the deal. You'll still be okay. We have enough, Leola."

"Okay, boss!" he said with a chuckle. He flipped me up from under the blanket and tossed my body on top of his.

I let out a giggle as I ran my hands along his sides, trying my best to tickle his ribs.

"You really want to do that?" he warned, before throwing me on my back, locking my arms above my head. He started to rub his chin against my neck.

"No! No! Uncle! I didn't mean to do that! Stop!" I squealed. I kicked and screamed until he released my arms. I grabbed a pillow and threw it at him. Something fell out of it, landed on his head, and fell right on top of my face. The laughing stopped immediately when he lightly brushed my cheek and held up the culprit.

"What's this?" he asked, looking at the object. It was the wooden rosary from a time long ago and a place far away, its tiny beads now old and worn. The knotted rope that held them together, frayed and thinned out by the years. "Is this the same one you got in Thailand?"

"Yup." *Try to remain cool. You are only as guilty as you look.*

"What's it doing in our bed?

"It must have fallen out of the pillow."

"Pillow? Do you sleep with it every night?" His voice was terse with agitation. He sat up and slid inches away from me. His demeanor changed immediately. He held his chin up and regarded me with cold, steely eyes. Ice green and frozen in place.

"I've been praying," I said as I attempted to pull him back towards me. He stiffened his stance and refused to move any closer.

"What are you praying for?" What was I praying for? Many things and nothing at the same time. I held on to the rosary because I wanted to remember. I didn't want to forget. Those feelings that you have, the elation of a first love, they just never happen again. On second thought, that's what I prayed for. I prayed that one day I would forget.

"You, Mikey, my mom and dad. Just life in general. Mostly to give thanks for all our blessings. And peace."

His face relaxed a little, but he swung his legs off the bed and turned the other way.

"Tey, what's the matter?" I asked.

"We have peace. You don't have to pray for it," he said as he quickened his pace towards the bathroom. "Do me a favor and put that away. I'll get you a new one today."

We all waged a war with the memory of a ghost.

# SIXTEEN
## It Ends Where It Begins

THE HALLS OF the hospital were deserted that day. Everyone had left the building, save for a few of us who opted to do the night shift on the eve of Thanksgiving. It had been three weeks since Dante and I had that argument in the bathtub, three weeks since I thought about Jude every single day. Three weeks since I last took the pill, three weeks of making a baby once, twice, thrice a day. Three weeks ago, I decided that I was going to give Dante everything he wanted from me. Three weeks ago, I threw Jude away for good. I resolved to solidify my marriage, I loved Dante enough to trust our future in his hands.

I breezed through the locker room, trying to gather up my stuff, knowing that I had to be somewhere in a few hours. Michael, Dante, and I were going to have a quiet dinner at home, and all I could think about was the fact that the men in my life were waiting there for me. I didn't bother to change out of my scrubs. I checked my phone to find a few missed calls from Dante. He'd been working late for the past few weeks, and I had truly missed him.

I pressed the callback button on my phone and quickened my pace. "Hi," he answered on the first ring. "You heading home soon?"

Home. The holidays with him had been my most cherished blessings over the past few years.

"Yes, sorry. I had to pick up my new badge and security took forever to find it," I said, breathlessly running through the corridor.

"New badge. Hmm. I like it. Tell me what it says." I could picture him smiling on the other end of the line.

I stopped at the door of the locker room. "Anna Dillon-Leola." What a huge turnaround. The first act in committing to start a family.

"Nice, Mrs. Leola. Hurry home so I can thank you for that," he whispered. Mikey was probably in the same room with him.

I hurriedly punched in my code before laying my phone carefully on the wooden bench and placing it on speaker. All I needed to do was change into my shoes and grab my coat.

"I'm rushing to catch the tail end of mass at SPJ by the hospital. You know, the one a few blocks over." I bent down to tie my sneakers. Despite being high-tops, they were very fashionable. I had sworn off Crocs and clogs, the staple of every resident in the entire medical community.

"Why there? Won't it be easier to just stop by St. Pat's on your way home?" He sounded worried, and I knew it was because he wanted me to get home sooner.

"No time, I want to drive straight through." I grabbed my things and headed towards the exit doors with the phone stuck in my ear.

"Spark. Baby. Don't go there. Just go tomorrow," he said.

"No, I want to sleep in with you tomorrow. It's my only day off! Gotta run. See you in a few hours!"

I threw the phone back in my bag and ran down the road towards Charles Street, arriving at the church as the offertory procession was taking place. I was so late that I didn't bother moving through the crowds of people converged in the narthex by the entrance. I stood by the rear doors, intent on moving up through the lines in time for communion, positioned so far away that I couldn't even see the altar. I heard the priest's voice through the central sound system, but my mind was churning with thoughts of my parents. The pain of missing them began on this day and lasted through to the New Year. Sometimes I was convinced that Michael was coping much better than I was. There was so much regret in my heart, and it had changed the things that I wanted out of life.

The phone in my purse rang incessantly. Dante knew I was going to be in church, why was he so insistent on trying to reach me? *The cranberry sauce is in the fridge, I thought to myself, and the potatoes are ready to be placed in the microwave. Don't start too early, they won't be as good if we have to reheat.*

I threw myself back into the moment when the choir started to sing the Communion hymn. Slowly, a line started to form and we painfully inched towards the priest standing at the foot of the large marble crucifix. He was assisted by a few other priests, each stationed along the steps of the four corners of the lectern. I was in no mood to fight through the crowd only to end up in the same place as everybody else, so I remained last in the sluggish, crawling line of people. Step, stop. Step, stop. I looked down at my hands and then at my shoes. Step, stop. Step, stop.

Step.

Stop.

"Body of Christ," said the voice in front of me as he lightly dropped the host in the safety of my hands.

"A—"

*Amen. You're supposed to say Amen.*

I would know those lips anywhere, that nose, those ears, the dark hair that framed the tips of them. I found myself looking into the eyes of the cruelest joke that life had yet to play on me. He jerked his head up and fell two steps back, his face registering fear and shock. Mine quickly turned to embarrassment. What a fool I'd been! There were clues! Theology. Teaching. Planned course of his life.

"Oh my God!" I cried out in a half-sob as I brought my hands to my mouth, the host tumbling to the ground. My shoulders curled over my chest as I bowed down in humiliation. He wasn't dead. He wasn't married, and he definitely didn't have children. He was alive and kicking, and those eyes were everything I had remembered them to be.

All my childhood dreams, my youthful wishes, my dashed hopes, my anger, my loneliness—they all merged together to unleash a fury that I realized had never left me.

We stood in the middle of the church, just him and I, cloaked in an eerie silence as the heat of the parishioners' stares burned through the clothes on my body. My reaction surely gave me away.

I was stripped naked for all the world to see. I wanted to die right then and there. My imaginary reunion killed in the blink of an eye, and taken from me in the place where I thought I would be safe from hurt and harm. I couldn't move my legs, couldn't go anywhere—I was frozen in place and sinking rapidly, drowning in hysteria and unable to save myself. I was too far gone, there was no turning back. Instinctively, my arm jerked upwards freely and slapped him across the cheek. Those beautiful cheeks. Five years did nothing to change that handsome face. I wanted to carve the scars that he left me with on his skin. The same ones that he inflicted upon me when he left me alone right after I lost my mother. He didn't recoil; he stood his ground. The pastor started to walk towards us as the breathless murmurs of the congregation began to get louder.

Screech, went the microphone. It was worse than nails on a chalkboard.

It was as if he hadn't heard it. "Please, please wait for me after mass. I'll be out right away. Please wait."

He must have thought he was whispering, but the microphone on his chest broadcasted every word he said. I glanced around to watch everyone huddle together and cower with unsolicited shame. For a second, I was lost in his wounded eyes. They pleaded, begged, implored for understanding. He extended his hands and tried to stroke my arm, as if to calm me down. When that didn't work, he tried to grab my hand as I took an exaggerated step back. *I don't want those robes touching me. They will melt me and I will disintegrate into a puff of smoke. That's it. That's all I was to him. A puff of smoke.*

"Anna—" No. *I was your Blue. Do you remember?*

"No. Fuck you. Stay away from me! Stay. The Fuck. Away from

me!" I shrieked.

A collective gasp rounded out the sound effects of this very absurd situation. I wasn't sure whether it was the cold air that made me shiver violently but I allowed the hostility in my heart to help me stop the tears. I covered my mouth with my hands and started to giggle. This was crazy. Just demented. There I was, a redheaded girl in a ponytail wearing ugly sea green scrubs and high-tops, going up against a man of God.

I guess I'd never be returning to that church again. I turned on my heel and ran through the long never-ending aisle, across the church lobby, and out the heavy, stained glass doors. I retched and vomited immediately after the doors closed, but no one followed me, no one sought to ease my pain. I was still shaking, still in shock, desperately trying to weave my way around the passing cars, past the hospital, and on to the parking garage to retrieve my car.

Michael was waiting for me, and we had so much to be thankful for. I promised myself I would be strong for him, and so I picked myself up and made my way home.

# SEVENTEEN
## Every Single Day

I SHOVED THE door open and kicked it in with full force, right before charging down the hall and flinging my backpack on the ground. My feet stomped on the wooden floor, calling attention to my presence and declaring my fury to the two people who were waiting patiently for me.

Dante and Mikey sat at the dinner table, staring at the box of pizza that was neatly placed in their midst. I turned my head to find the turkey still in the sink, soaking in the brining bag. I approached my brother and wrapped my arms around his neck.

"Michael, please go to your room for a minute, I need to speak to your sister," Dante commanded as he walked towards me with arms up in the air, ready to take me in.

"Stop!" I yelled. "Don't touch me."

Michael scampered away and up the stairs.

Two steps forward, one outreached arm out. "Spark."

Nothing he said would have made this any easier.

"No! You knew. You knew and you stood by and watched me die for five years. Damn you!" I threw my keys at him, hitting him squarely on the chest.

He slid towards me and grabbed me, pulling me gently towards him while keeping my arms to my sides and holding me down. "Anna, please. Let me explain." He sucked his cheeks in and let out a sigh.

I ignored his attempt to calm me down. "When? When did you know? Let me go!" I bent down and twisted my body around to loosen his hold before breaking free of him.

"He told me after you left Thailand. Said that he was in love with you, but he was committed to entering the priesthood. It wasn't my story to tell." Tears started to form in his eyes. He knew me so well. He knew I was going to leave.

"Yes it was! Yes it was, Tey. It involved me. You based our love on this? On the fact that you knew he would never come back?" I carelessly tore a sheet of paper towel and swiped it across my face.

He raised his voice to get my attention, throwing his arms up in the air and forcing me to listen. "I gave him your phone number! He never called!"

My breath hitched at the pain of his words. So he had a choice. And he didn't choose me.

"And you're telling me this now because?"

The front door swung open. I didn't remember shutting it. The gust of cool air that engulfed us caused me to stop in mid-sentence.

"Anna?"

He didn't look anything like he had that morning. It was the image that I always had of him in my head. Low slung jeans, fitted t-shirt, that damn black baseball cap. Faded somewhat and torn on the edges. Seeing him in the flesh after all this time was too much. I crumpled to the ground in a heap of tears. The shock, the excitement, the tiny hinge of hope… they were all centered on the things that could never be. But then just as quickly, my inner strength took over. I gulped in a deep breath and exhaled out the love that I had for both of these men. I wiped my face with the hem of my top and stood up self-assuredly, ignoring him and turning my head to glare angrily at Dante.

"How does he know where we live?" I asked, my tone steady and even.

"He called after you left the church," Dante answered guiltily as he repeatedly pulled on his shirt collar.

"Ha! You have each other's contact info?" I busted out a low pitched laugh.

"We used my phone in Thailand, Anna. Of course he had my number," Dante answered, his voice thin and weak.

"Great." I moved away and leaned on the back of the couch. "Dante, please tell him to leave. I don't want him here in our home."

Jude shook his head in disbelief before turning in my direction. He placed his hands on his hips and took an admonishing stance. Although we stood just several feet apart from each other, my mind was on an island in the Pacific far, far away. For no matter how much I tried to tune everything out, all I could do was remember.

"Our home?" Jude asked, genuinely confused. It was like a

scene from a comedy. We were all so focused on our individual pain that none of us were listening to each other.

Dante approached him, placed a hand on his shoulder, and began to push him towards the door. "Dude, you'd better go. You can talk to her when she's calmed down."

He waved his hand dismissively. "No. Anna, please! We need to talk!" Despite being furious at him, there it was again, that strange phenomenon that made me want to touch him.

I stood steadfast in my place, arms crossed, feet squarely on the ground. Dante paced back and forth, first towards me, and then towards him.

Jude's look turned from baffled to incensed. He squinted his eyes and shook his head, as if he had just heard the most ludicrous thing in the world. With his chest puffed up like a rooster, his eyebrows drawn together, and his tone marked and derisive, he asked once again, "You two live together?"

"Something your new BFF neglected to tell you?" Interesting. It was my turn to throw the dagger.

"Spark, no," Dante pleaded as he unsuccessfully tried to block Jude from my view.

I deliberately flitted across the room until my face was merely inches from his. He actually thought I was going to kiss him. The way he closed his eyes and tilted his head towards me. The way he sucked in a breath and inhaled deeply. Presumptuous bastard. I needed to rethink this battle strategy, build up a resistance before it was too late. Soon enough, it would happen. He would demolish me and walk away without a second thought.

Dante gasped in fearful anticipation as I formed every single syllable with my lips. "We. Are. Married. And that just means that we fuck. Every. Single. Day. Now get out."

*Dear Fate,*

*Go away. Leave me be. Allow me to live with my loss, the truth, this revelation.*

# EIGHTEEN
## *Departure*

"Annie? Can I come in?"

Mikey knocked softly on my door, seeking permission to enter as I lay in bed wallowing in self-pity. I didn't know where they were, didn't care what happened next. I abandoned them in my outrage while they stood motionless and defenseless.

"Sure," I answered, bundling up the pile of Kleenex on the floor. I propped my pillows against the headboard and straightened up in an attempt to show my little brother some composure.

He tiptoed in quietly and sat next to me on the side of my bed. I pulled him in for an embrace and rested my head on his shoulder for a few seconds before allowing him to lift his head up and take my hands in his.

"I'm sorry for ruining our holiday. I'll make it up to you

tomorrow. Let's go to the mall. Let me get you those basketball shoes you've been wanting," I rambled in apology.

He smiled at me. That sweet, loving face; he didn't deserve to see me like this. He'd been through so much already.

"You don't have to. I have enough shoes," he said. "I just want you to be okay."

"I will be."

"So that's the guy, huh? The one from Thailand?"

"Yeah, that's the guy."

"I'm sorry, Annie. I didn't know that you'd been suffering all this time."

"No, no. I haven't been. That was so long ago. I was just shocked this morning, that's all. I'll get over it. I always do, don't I?" I tried to add some levity to my tone.

"You do." He paused for a second and then his lips began to quiver. "I worry about you, Annie. I don't think you've gotten over losing Mom yet."

"None of us will ever get over that, Mikey. Have you?"

He kept his eyes glued to the view from the window, trying with all his might not to let me see him cry. "I miss her so much. If she were here, I know that you wouldn't be carrying all this on your own. The way that you've been taking care of me. It's not fair that you have to take me on, too."

"Oh! No, baby! No. I love taking care of you! You're the reason why I've been able to get through this! And I will always want to look after you. I love you so much. I'm so lucky that I have you in my life. Don't say that, Mikey. All you need to do is study hard and do well in school. That will be my greatest gift. Your success in life."

He smeared his hand across his face and sniffed. "Thank you for everything, Annie. I love you, too. Dudes aren't worth crying about. You can get anyone you want. Look at the way Dante is crazy about you. He tells me every single day." He crossed his eyes in jest. "It gets kind of annoying to see someone so whipped like that."

I broke out in a peal of laughter. "Whipped, huh?" I pushed him off the bed playfully. "I don't think a guy like Dante can ever love a girl more than he loves himself."

"He said that was before he loved you." The statement warmed my heart.

"Is he here?" I asked as I slid to the opposite side of the bed to stand up. I walked to the bathroom sink and started to rinse off my face.

"Yup. He's watching some Bollywood movie on Netflix. Something about some girl and a Mr. Darcy."

"Ah! Bride and Prejudice. He's watching it without me?" I called out to him while brushing my teeth. "Can you ask him to come in here?" I smoothed my hair in the mirror and wiped my face dry with a towel.

"Sure. Goodnight, Annie. I'll see you in the morning."

"Night, Mike!" I yelled from the bathroom. "Thanks for checking on me!"

"Spark?" Dante entered the room shyly, keeping his downcast eyes towards the floor.

I switched off the bathroom light and settled on the chaise facing the window. The view of Manhattan from this place never ceased to impress me. I spent many nights looking out at the sky from here, wondering, wishing, and constantly convincing myself to enjoy what I had in Dante.

"Hi. I'm okay now. Come sit next to me."

He hurried across the floor and took me in his arms. "I'm so sorry, baby. I didn't want it to go down like this at all."

I leaned into him, accepting the warmth of his body. Whatever his reasons were, I wanted to know about them.

"Tey, what did you think would happen if I found out? For five years, I blamed myself, wondered whether or not I had imagined what happened in Thailand. You watched me go through it and never said a word." Tears started to form in my eyes. It still hurt to talk about the events of the last few years. "All you had to do was tell me."

"I know, and I'm so sorry. When I arrived back from Thailand, your life was unraveling at warp speed. I didn't want to add to your stress and pain. When Grayson told me that he was going to pursue his religious vocation, I saw no point in hurting you even more. And you must know, a large part of it was because I wanted you all for myself. I waited so long, Spark. I waited so long to have you."

"But what you kept from me, Tey. I could've closed the door on him years ago."

"I know," he said, his eyes still glued to his knees. "But through all these years, I've tried to make up for it. Tried to make you forget."

He was right. Our endless trips to every part of the world, his friendship, his loyalty.

I turned to face him, gently resting my elbow on his shoulder. "You will always have me. We've been best friends for ten years. And I'm your wife."

"Married for only a year," he interjected. "You've just

now learned to love me, and he's back to take you away." He tipped his head upwards and stared at the ceiling. Focusing on anything but me.

I laughed at that preposterous suggestion. "Yeah, right. At least not in this life."

"He's not yet a priest," Dante muttered under his breath.

"What do you mean?" I asked, surprised.

"He's a deacon. He said something about it being the last step before taking the vow of priesthood. I knew he was assigned to assist at SPJ, and that's why I told you not to attend mass there."

"Did you guys keep in touch a lot?"

"No, not really a lot. He would text to check in on you once in a while. He knew where you were training and kept tabs on your progress in school through me. But that's it. I would hear from him every few months, tops. I was sure that he'd already been inducted by now."

He watched for my reaction as he explained himself. I could see that he was relieved of this burden. Dante and I never held any secrets from each other, so this must have been really difficult for him. But that didn't change the fact that I was angry at him. That my trust had waned albeit slightly. I needed space to figure things out. Seeing Jude brought back so many feelings, so many emotions. I no longer knew which side was up.

"Tey? I have to tell you something. Mikey goes back to school on Monday. I've decided to stay by the hospital for a while, stay at the apartment close by. I really need to be in my own place and sort things out in my head. This whole thing, it's really shaken me up."

"Are you…" He hesitated. "Are you leaving me?" He turned to

face me, searching for my eyes.

"I could never leave you, Tey. You're the most important person in my life. But I want to love you the way you deserve to be loved. And so I think that being on our own for a while will be good for both of us."

"What about Mikey? Do you need help with his tuition for the semester?"

I reached out my hand to caress this sweet man's face. "No, baby. We'll be fine. I've got a buyer for my mom's car, and I'll use that money for the rent on the apartment. Mikey's school has a monthly plan that takes directly from my paycheck."

"You know, you'll be richer than me once you finish residency, don't you? You'll be supporting me very soon," he said, trying as always not to make me feel inadequate about my current financial situation.

"Haha, right, Mr. Millionaire. Fat chance in hell." I scooted my body so that my knees rested on his lap. He wrapped his arms around me.

"What is it with you and hell lately?" he said with a laugh. "Everything is hell. Hell. Hell. Hell. What about heaven? What about goodness and light?"

"I live that every day. With you," I whispered, planting tiny kisses along the outline of his ear. I closed my eyes and savored the feel of his skin on my lips. He smelled heavenly. He was my blue sky. My sunshine. My light. I pulled his hand to my face and pressed it to my cheek. He leaned over to kiss me, and slowly, sensually, I kissed him back.

"Will you fuck the hell out of me?" I taunted as I slipped my hands underneath his shirt.

"The hell I will!" he snorted. And we both sank to the floor in a fit of giggles.

# NINETEEN
## Figure It Out

I'D BEEN ON my own for two weeks. Dante hadn't allowed me to take all my stuff and move it to my new place. He needed some assurance that I was coming back, so we compromised on leaving a few of my things in the spare room next to his.

I returned to my one bedroom apartment in Pomona, about a thirty minute drive from the hospital. It was more than I could afford at my salary considering Mikey's tuition obligations, but I truly believed that the time away would do us both some good.

There were a handful of co-workers from the hospital who witnessed the incident at the church on Thanksgiving morning. Afihsa asked me about it one day in the middle of a staff meeting. The hushed whispers, the looks of pity that greeted me in the hallway, it all started to make sense after she confronted me about it.

"Was that the guy?" she had asked. "You didn't tell me it was serious."

"It wasn't!" I barked. "It was ten days. It wasn't."

Jude had deserved his shame, but in the end, this was my territory, and I was the one left holding the bag. Small world, great big coincidences.

"Dr. Dillon, please report to the emergency room."

The hospital was abuzz with victims of a school bus accident. There were no casualties, but the five children who sat at the front of the bus were in critical condition. I ran in through the sliding doors just in time to catch a six-year-old boy bleeding from badly mangled legs being rushed in on a stretcher.

"Dr. Stevens is waiting in ER7 to assess his injuries. Please wheel him in there now!" I ordered, clasping his hand and running alongside him. "What's your name, little guy?" I asked calmly.

"Tommy," he cried. "I want my mommy! Where's my mommy?"

"Tommy," I said "I'm going to get your mommy, okay? She's here, waiting for you. But you have to promise me that you're going to show her how brave you are. The doctors are going to make you all better."

"My legs hurt!" he screamed.

"I know, I know, honey. But they'll give you something to make the pain go away, okay? And I'll be right back with your mommy."

He bobbed his head up and down. I released his hand and rushed to the waiting room to find his mother.

"Doctor! My son! Where's my Tommy?"

I took the mother in my arms just as she was about to collapse.

"Please, Mrs...."

She yelped and sobbed, holding on tightly to me. "Monroe."

"Mrs. Monroe, let me take you to your son. He's awake and alert. We're taking a look at his legs right now. We stopped the bleeding, and he's going to be undergoing surgery immediately."

A nurse blocked us from proceeding any further. "Dr. Dillon, she doesn't have any insurance."

The mother started to cry.

"It doesn't matter..." I searched for her name tag. "Melinda. Please let them know that I'll fill out the paperwork later. I'll handle the financial end with Dr. Stevens after the surgery. Let us through."

"This is the second time you've done this in one week." She exhaled loudly as she stepped out of our way. But not before she flashed a smile and waved at someone in the waiting room. I didn't care to see who she had decided to flirt with. I reunited Tommy with his mother. As I left the examination room, I saw that same nurse again and noticed just how pretty she was—a sultrier version of Maggie.

"Your friend is out there again," she said, lips puckered and eyes assessing me from head to toe. She looked like she was in on some mystifying secret, something I was expected to know but didn't. I could hardly hear what she was saying. There were voices coming from all directions and it was hard to discern which was hers.

"What? Who?"

"Your friend Jude. He's been here at least once a month for the past year or so. Looking for you, sitting out there and waiting."

The irony of it all. Waiting for me while I was waiting for him?

I spun around and ran towards the waiting room, shoving my way through the faces of pain and tears and hopelessness to find the one person whose beauty shined a light on them all. And there he was, sitting at the very end of the line of metal chairs, his back against the wall, his face brightening up as soon as I came into view. He jumped up quickly, hands in his pockets, shoulders hollowed, desperate to conceal the slight upturn of his lips.

"Hi. Anna," he greeted me.

"What are you doing here?" I barked. My emotions went from one end of the spectrum to the other. Anger, surprise, worry. "Are you sick? Is everything okay?" I asked.

"Yes, yes. I'm fine. I have the day off so I thought I'd come and see you."

All of a sudden, I felt shy, conscious of the rat's nest on my head, the ugly pink scrubs, and the smell of death on me. I also wanted to punch his face in. He had no right to be there. Not while Dante was out of town. Not while my head was still submerged in the ocean. "I'm working a twelve hour shift today. I've got so much to do."

"Oh," he said, visibly disappointed, the rise and fall of his chest giving it away. Pink little blotches appeared on his naturally tanned face, eyes grazing over the name on my badge. It settled right on top of my heart like a fortress protecting it from invaders.

*It's too late. I'm married now. Go away.*

"It's a crazy day. I have to go and check on my patients."

"Go ahead. I have nothing better to do. I'll wait," he assured me. I ran over to join a group of doctors who were rushing in through the glass doors. "See you in a few hours!" he called after me.

I didn't really know how I felt about seeing him again. It was just too much for me. Too much. Too late.

I DIDN'T GET reunited with my pile of hospital records until 9:30 that night. I spent two hours sitting with Tommy in recovery, and the surgery to reattach his partially severed leg was a success. I rushed through the files, hoping with all my heart that he hadn't given up on his wait. Transcribing the diagnoses for the day took me well over thirty minutes to complete, and by the time I was ready to leave the hospital, it was a few minutes past ten. Things were happening too fast, the opportunity to process it all slipped through the hours, the minutes of that night. I made a conscious effort to stop momentarily to dial Dante's phone number as I stood outside the hospital entrance.

From a distance, I saw Jude sitting quietly on the sidewalk, a cardboard tray filled with food on the ground next to him. I turned around to focus on my phone call.

"Hi." Dante had picked up amidst the low murmur of conversations all around him.

"Hey, just heading out of the hospital. I had a crazy day. School bus collision."

"Oh no. I'm so sorry to hear that. I'm still out with a client. We're having dinner at Gibson." I could tell he had moved to a quieter place as the background noise had died down significantly.

"Jude came to see me today, late this morning. I had to work until an hour ago so I didn't get to speak to him."

"How do you feel about that? Did he tell you want he wanted?" he asked, concerned.

"Not yet," I answered.

"Yet? What does that mean?"

"He's waiting outside for me. I think we're going to go for coffee or something," I professed in all casualness.

"Oh." His tone changed. There was a heaviness in the atmosphere around me. The black clouds of Thailand had followed me home.

"It's nothing. I just want to clear the air with him. I kind of acted like a lunatic that night. We can talk about this sensibly without all the drama that I caused a few weeks ago." The last thing I wanted to do was hurt him. Although I had to admit, I wanted some answers from Jude.

"Should I be worried? I know I agreed to give you some time, but does that involve seeing him?"

"You have nothing to be worried about. I love you," I said lightly, trying my best to cast his concerns away. The lilt in my voice gave away my farce. "If you want I can call you later when I get home and we can... FaceTime?" I whispered suggestively.

He sounded excited. "I can't wait. Call me later, okay?"

"You got it."

WE SPRAWLED ON a park bench outside the hospital, sipping

cappuccinos out of Starbucks cups and munching on sausage croissants. From the corner of my eye, I watched him watch me. This went on until we ran out of things to eat and drink.

"You still look as beautiful as ever, but there's something different about you," he said. "You seem quieter, less enthusiastic than the girl I remember from years ago."

He smiled at me before straightening himself up and tucking his hands under his legs. I walked into this meeting with an escape plan, intent on saying goodbye. There were so many questions to ask him before then.

"It's been five years. We're all older now, more accountable," I answered with a colorless expression on my face. This wasn't a casual coffee date between two friends who were just catching up on life. I needed to get my thoughts out knowing that I was the girl who always ran out of time. "Gray, how long have you been coming to the hospital?" I asked softly.

He sighed deeply and looked away. "How did you know?" he asked, still staring straight into the abyss.

"Pretty nurse Melinda told me. Apparently you two have become fast friends."

He didn't appreciate my humor. He turned towards me, and there was nothing I could do to stop myself from staring at him as he spoke. How many women had he destroyed with that look?

"At first, I couldn't believe the coincidence. Can you imagine? How weird was that? To be assigned to the same hospital you worked at! For a long time, I was content to just see you. To be in the same place as you. To watch you give yourself selflessly to others. What was the point in coming back into your life? You looked happy. Dante would show up to take you home a few times and you looked like everything in your life was settled and in place."

"It was." *Time to revise.* "I mean, it is," I muttered.

"And you married him." He smiled at me as he said this. "Are you happy, Anna?"

"Dante is so good to me. He loves me so much." *Lame answer.* "I love him, yes, and I am happy." *Nice follow up.*

The walkway directly in front of us was filled with people, moving briskly in the chill of the night. The passing of the fall season was evident in the brittle branches of the trees and the lack of life all around us. *You see that branch over there? That's me. I'm about to crack and fall to the ground.*

"That's great," he answered, while bobbing his head up and down.

My emotions began to take over. Memories of the past five years came flooding back, and once again, I felt like I was reliving every minute I spent carrying a torch for him, waiting for him to call me.

He started out once again. "I'm so sorry about what happened at church. I deserved that. What you said to me then, I deserved every word, and the fact that people heard all about it—I wasn't ashamed of what that confrontation insinuated. In fact, I didn't expect anything less from you. I fell in love with that fiery, impassioned, beautiful spirit of yours. And the months that I spent watching you here confirmed nothing but the fact that you're such an amazing woman. What a gifted doctor you are! I once heard a mother and father speaking about how they couldn't have survived their daughter's last days without you."

*Who said anything about love? Love speaks through actions, love grows through interaction. We had none of that in the last five years.*

"Mr. and Mrs. Donovan and their baby, Louise," I mumbled softly. She'd had an enlarged heart and there was nothing we could do but wait painfully until it could no longer survive in her tiny body. I didn't want to talk about my patients, though. I wanted to tell him what I thought so that I could focus my efforts on Dante. Just weeks ago, we were going to seriously plan on having a family together. But tonight, I was no longer sure whether that was what I wanted. I remembered his reaction when he saw us at the apartment and it angered me once again.

"The nerve of you to expect me to wait," I said sadly.

"I never said that." He glanced around uneasily, pressing his lips in a thin line.

"Then why were you so surprised that Dante and I were married?"

"I don't know. I just didn't expect it to be the two of you, I guess. He never told me. All the times we spoke, he never mentioned that you were together for that matter. Let alone married." He paused once again before nervously running his fingers through his hair. His trademark move. When he didn't know what to do with his hands, he took it out on his hair. I could have almost predicted it. Years ago, I spent hours on Google searching for "Signs that He's Into You." Mirroring your movements, combing back his hair is supposed to mean that he's interested. Baloney.

"I'm not a priest," he continued.

"Yet," I countered, reprimanding myself for the upsurge of cautious hope. The push and pull was back. I didn't know what in the world I was looking for in this conversation. So what if he was on the way to becoming a priest? Why did it bother me so much?

"Not until next May," he agreed.

"That's not relevant," I snapped angrily. "You're a deacon. Period. I don't really get why we're here."

"We're here because," he paused to clear his throat, "because I can't keep watching you from a distance anymore. I need to face this, face you. For the last five years I've tried to run away from my confusion. But I never stopped thinking about you, Blue."

"You didn't try to find me," I said, staring at him indignantly. "You're a liar."

My mood had changed drastically. I was embarrassed about the thoughts that ran through my mind earlier that day. There I was, pushing Dante away for an idea in my head that had probably never been there. I sat up straight and began gathering the empty wrappers around me, stuffing them in their original bag with the empty paper cups. This was me, always cleaning up after everyone. Always making sure to leave things the way they should be.

"I want to know," I huffed. "I want to know why you left me that morning."

"I mean, does that make sense to you? To change my entire life's direction based upon a ten-day fling? If I stayed—if I had stayed, I would've been on the plane back to the states with you. And I couldn't let my family down." This guy just kept pulling all the punches. The questions in my head had quickly evaporated. We were in an endless loop of whys and hows and neither of us knew where this was heading.

I lifted myself up, paper bag in hand. "You're right, it doesn't make sense. So I'm going to leave now. Goodbye, Jude. Don't ever show up at my hospital again."

He covered his face with his hands before nodding his head and keeping his eyes on the ground. It was as if he had anticipated my reaction. He swallowed sharply before letting out a deep breath and closing his eyes. I chastised myself for wanting to touch his hair one last time. Or his shoulders. Or his lips. But instead I urged my feet to walk in the opposite direction, as far away as possible from this catastrophic predicament, this calamity, this destruction.

I FOUND ANOTHER batch of missed calls from Dante on my phone, but I didn't call him back until I was home and settled into bed for the night. I didn't cry, couldn't cry. Somehow, the years that passed had tempered my expectations and disappointments, stored them somewhere deep inside. I couldn't seem to find my bearings. Like a flash of lightning or a burst of stars, these tears had manifested themselves in spurts over a steady period of time, and then they were gone. For years I had played the scene of our reunion over and over in my head. And it sure hadn't involved something as unimaginable, as unattainable, as ridiculous as this.

I propped my phone up against the headboard and quickly dialed Dante's number, posing in front of the camera as I waited for him on the other line.

"Look at you, Spark," Dante mused, smiling from ear to ear. You look like an angel sitting among the clouds."

I wanted him to ask me. I knew he was dying inside. I was too.

I wanted to tell him that it would all be okay, but I couldn't. Finally, he broke loose.

"Did you see Jude?"

"I did."

"And?"

"Nothing much really. We just caught up a little bit and he confirmed that he's going to be ordained in May of next year." I scratched the tip of my nose nervously.

"Are you okay?"

"Of course," I said. I made it a point to change the subject. "So, when do you come back to New York?"

"Spark." He rubbed his hands together and leaned forward so that our faces touched on camera.

"You didn't answer me, Tey. When are you coming back?"

"Spark," he said again, this time with a mischievous grin on his face, "it's been two weeks. I'm horny. Show me."

I rolled my eyes. This was such bad timing on his part. "What? No, not tonight. I'm so tired."

"But you promised!" he whined. "Come on, come on, come on," he dared.

I was visibly irritated, flicking my eyes from side to side in coordination with my head. "Seriously? Please! I'm so tired. Let's talk tomorrow, okay? I'm going to bed now."

"Fine," he said, sulking.

"Okay, bye." I hung up the phone feeling horrible. I knew the way that I reacted only served to show him how affected I was by Jude's sudden appearance in our lives. I slid off the bed and stood in front of my bathroom mirror. My hair rested limply against my shoulders, and my eyes looked murky and dark. I leaned against the sink and closed my eyes. What if? What if this was the choice that would lead to my fate? What if I never got this chance ever again?

And suddenly, the clouds disappeared. I saw the sudden burst of beautiful sunshine, the waters of Thailand, the sun, the sea.

It wasn't over. As clear as that one day in the spring, when all I saw was the endless sky stretched out against the blue horizon in his eyes, it wasn't over. I could never stand up against his God. My God, our God. I didn't intend to try to change his mind.

But I would take six months of him. No reservations, no regrets. If I learned anything about losing my mother, it was that time waits for no one. It will shake you off, walk away and leave you in its dust.

I had to call Dante back to tell him how sorry I was for hurting him. I paced around the room, redialed his phone number, and patiently waited for him to answer it. The merry sound of Christmas carols leaked in through the paper thin walls of my apartment; someone was singing along and someone else was laughing hysterically.

"Hello?" he answered testily, the way someone would address a pestering telemarketer.

"Hi. I'm sorry. I can never lie to you. Yes, I'm feeling sucky tonight." I tried to sound as repentant as I could. There were two rosaries on the night table. One made out of wood and another made out of pressed roses. I snatched the prettier one in my fingers and began to twist it around.

"Yeah, okay," he responded in a dry tone.

"You're mad. I get it." *Twist, twist, twist.*

He exhaled loudly. "Look, Anna. I lived in this guy's shadow for the first few years after you lost your mom. I thought you were over him. Apparently you're not."

"Who said that? How do you know that? I—" I started out. No, no. It was time to cut to the chase. "I'm not. And I have to do something about it." I pulled open the drawer, retrieved a golden pouch and slipped the rosary in its case.

"What is it about him, Spark? I'm so fucking angry right now!"

"I don't know."

"Well, find the fuck out and get it out of your system. I love you so much, why can't that be enough for you?"

"But it is! It is enough for me. It's just that I have some unfinished business with Jude that I have to put to rest. I need to do this. I need to find out why he's still here when he shouldn't be. It should be me and you, and yet he lingers, he persists. My feelings seem to feed him, keep him alive in my head. Please, Tey. Let me figure this all out. Give me some time."

"Are we breaking up, Spark?"

"We have to. Separate. I'm done with living two lives. He was always here. In between us, he was always here."

"This is all just bullshit. I can't do this anymore. We'll talk when I get back. In the meantime, good luck with whatever it is you're trying to accomplish."

"Dante, please—"

The line went dead. It didn't go silent, it didn't go blank. It separated him from me for good, it killed us, devastated him, set me free. Our line, our connection, our love, gone. Just like that.

# TWENTY
## Everyone Knew

IT HAD BEEN three days since Dante and I last spoke. There were no call backs, no desperate messages nor admissions of newly discovered doubt or regret. I didn't expect much from him in that sense. In a way, it was a welcome respite from the inevitable decision that I'd made. We were always so good at indulging in the day to day. That's what we were doing. Existing until we would be forced to face the truth. And for his part, Jude had stopped coming to the hospital. Maybe things would work out on their own.

Instead of slowing down for the holidays, the emergency room was bursting with activity. Amidst the Christmas trees and bright lights and gaudy decorations, there were tears of joy and sorrow, some lives saved and some lost. Doctors and nurses tried to keep the upbeat mood by wearing awful reindeer ties and Santa embellished scrubs. I was finally off for two days, intent on catching up on some Christmas shopping before being on call for the rest of the year. My shopping list was short, made up of the only people whom I could really call my family. A PlayStation One for Mikey, bought with my saved up lunch money, a special gift for Dante, some books for my dad, a scarf and hat for Maggie, and something I still hadn't figured out for Donny. For the first time in my life, I didn't get to send out any Christmas cards. The demands of work and home had just spiraled out of control. Never in my wildest dreams did I ever imagine that my life would turn out this way. The reversal of fortune, the task of bringing up a young man full of promise, the loss of my parents and of our home. Through it all, Dante had been by my side. And here I was, casting him aside for someone who had no right to my heart.

That day at the mall, I thought about Jude. I wondered where he was and how he would be spending his Christmas. I imagined what he would look like, all decked out in priestly garb to celebrate the church's most important event. *Is it worth it?* I wanted to ask him. *Is the love of a congregation enough to forsake the love of a woman? Does it keep you warm at night? Does it hold you and support you and steer you through the darkest hours? Does it fill the loneliness in your heart? Does it satisfy your need, fill your soul?*

*I could have loved you,* I wanted to tell him. *I could have given up my entire life for you, followed you anywhere in the world.*

*If only you had chosen me.*

144

THE BRISK WINTRY chill of a snowy night in the city followed me through the front door of my apartment. I arrived home to find Mikey parked in front of the TV, one hand on the game controller and the other around a can of Mountain Dew. The Christmas lights on the tree flickered on just as the timer went off. The place was a far cry from the extravagant living conditions of our former home or of the home that Dante had shared with us, but we had what we needed—a couch, a dining table, a bed, and two nightstands—and it was pointless to fret about furnishing a place that was occupied for only a few days a week. Mikey was only home from school for the holidays, and I was still completing my rotation at the hospital.

"Hi," I greeted him as I unbuttoned my coat, hanging it on the wooden peg in the closet. My gaze settled momentarily on a pair of Chanel ballet flats placed neatly by the corner of the shoe rack. It was the only pair of my mother's shoes that I'd kept, a bit too small, saved as a reminder of our former life and the love that she had for all things fine and beautiful. "What'd you do all day?"

"Nothing much. Just relaxing," he answered, his eyes glued to the screen. "Do you think we can order some dinner?"

"I can make you some mac and cheese," I answered as I walked towards the kitchen counter. "I won't have much cash to spend until payday on Thursday. Sorry."

"Mac and cheese sounds good. Thank you, Annie," he said respectfully.

I headed into the bedroom to change into my pajamas. Minutes later, I laid out some wrapping paper and a pair of scissors on the table before placing a kettle of water on the stove to make myself a cup of tea. I sat on the couch next to him and watched as he packed up his console and turned the TV off.

"So, you know that I'm working on Christmas Eve all the way until the 26th, right?"

"And I'm going to Chicago with Dante."

"Yup. He's going to take you with him to spend the holidays with his family. I'll see you back home on the 27th so that we can drive out to visit Dad." I was plagued with dismay by my very own words. "I'm sorry that I won't be with you."

"No biggie. You know I enjoy being with the Leolas. They're all so good to me."

"They're good people. And they love you." I lovingly reached out to ruffle his hair. It was thick and light and full of curls. He set his eyes shyly on the floor; I missed the days when he was more loving, more demonstrative. As the years went by, I saw the effect that my mother's passing had on the both of us. It was as if showing too much emotion would cause us to break and crumble into little pieces. For as long as we skimmed the surface, the tears could be held in place.

The chime of the doorbell was a welcome intrusion to the wistfulness of the moment, and Mikey stood up to answer it. It was Josh, the college junior who lived on the floor above us, asking Mikey if he wanted to come over. "Annie?" he called out to me. "Is it okay if I go over to Josh's to play video games?"

"What about dinner?" I asked, while walking towards the kitchen. "I can make it right now."

"No need," answered Josh. "My mom made some really good meatloaf. Mikey is welcome to have dinner at my place." Meatloaf? Someone had time to make a meatloaf when I couldn't even find the time to shave my legs?

Mikey pasted a large grin on his face. This kid loved to eat.

"Please, Annie? Can I just have dinner over there?"

"Of course you can, if that's really okay with Josh. But call me every hour just to check in. I want to make sure that Josh isn't having a wild college party up there tonight," I teased them lightly.

Mikey rolled his eyes, though I knew that he always took my instructions seriously. There was no surviving without each other; we protected each other, made sure that we were always safe. He slipped on a pair of running shoes and was out the door in a second.

I breathed a sigh of relief. I needed this time to be alone, to collect my thoughts, to wrap my presents, and write a letter to Dante.

One hour later, as I stood to admire the beautifully wrapped presents placed neatly under the tree, I ran my hands along the pretty little ornaments that Dante and I had collected over the years. We had so much history together—each little figurine on the tree was a reminder of the trips that we had made and the places that we'd seen. The fondness that I felt for him came rushing back; I decided that nothing in my life was more important than to make amends with the man who saved my life. Before doing that, however, I needed to address some unfinished business.

"Hi!" Maggie answered the phone cheerily. "What's new? I tried calling you a few times but you didn't pick up."

I wasn't ready to talk. "You told me that he was never coming back because you knew."

"I did, and I'm sorry I didn't tell you."

"Maggie! How is it that the entire world knew but me?" I asked, annoyed and disappointed at the same time. I couldn't help it, my voice lifted higher by a few notes.

"It killed Dante to keep it from you, Sparky. He really wanted to tell you, but it happened at the same time that you lost your mom, and he didn't want this to add to your pain. And so when we talked about it, I did tell him that I was sure you'd get over it soon. I mean, you knew the guy for ten days! I figured it would take you one year tops to forget about him. I honestly never knew that you would still be thinking of him five years later!"

I took a sip of my tea and sat in silence phone in one hand and fingers picking on the leather piping that ran down the sides of the couch. Outside the gray sky was bursting with snow dust. They floated slowly in the air and melted before they touched the ground.

"Sparky? Are you still there?" she asked with worry. "Do you want me to come over? Donny is out of the country for a few days."

"How long was it before you knew you loved Donny? How long were you in Europe?" I demanded. It helped to throw her cynicism back in her face.

"Spark—"

"How long, Maggie?" I asked, forcing the issue. I clenched both my hands and teeth in distress. The ugly fact was that two of my closest friends had held the truth from me, no matter the intention.

"Three weeks. I was in Italy for two," she conceded weakly.

I had made my point, and there was no need to say anything more. I didn't really want to hurt her; all I wanted to do was to place what she felt for Donny in the context of my ten days with Jude.

"Spark, let me come over," she continued.

"No, no, it's starting to snow outside. And I'm trying to get all my Christmas stuff organized before my shift at the hospital. Thank you for the offer, though."

"What are you going to do?" she asked.

"I don't know. I need to figure things out. But I want to do it in lockstep with Dante. We started this together, and we are either going to continue it, or end it together. We—I mean, I, suggested we take some time off. I can't shake him, Maggie. I can't forget about Jude."

"Hey, listen," she said, pausing to collect her thoughts. "The reason that you and I work so well together is because I'm the ditz and you're the brains."

"Yeah, that volleyball really rattled your brains around," I joked.

She met my witticism with silence. "You've always been the one to use logic in every decision that you've made since I've known you. Take it from the ditz this time. This is extremely illogical, and doing what's right on paper won't work. Do what's right in your heart. Dante is here for the long haul, but he can't wait for you forever. You need to figure out whether you want to put him through some half-hearted relationship when you know that he deserves better."

I heard the creaking sound of the twisting doorknob. "Hey, I think Mikey's home from the neighbor's. I'd better go and spend some time with him before he crashes. I'll call you tomorrow?"

"Yes, call me tomorrow," she replied. "I'd love to see you before your schedule gets crazy again."

"Okay, we'll see what we can do. Talk later. Bye!" I pressed END on the phone just in time to find Dante standing by the door.

# TWENTY-ONE
## *Germany*

I JUMPED TO my feet, anxious but ecstatic at the same time that Dante had driven over to see me. I ran to greet him, throwing my arms around him, and showered him with tiny kisses on his face.

"Hi. I'm so glad you're here. So glad." I proceeded to unwrap the scarf from around his neck, and unbuttoned his coat.

"Hi, Spark. I thought we should talk," Dante explained as he held his arms down to help me slip it off.

"No fighting, no arguing. I don't want to fight with you, please," I begged. He looked weary and dejected, and his empty stare broke my heart. He wore the same unfamiliar pair of glasses; they felt like an intruder in our home. "Your glasses. I thought they were just for reading."

"Apparently I need them to drive now, too," he answered,

lifting me up and carrying me over to the couch at the same time. He took a seat and placed me on his lap. I held on to him, my arms wrapped tightly around his neck. "Maybe I'm just getting old," he said.

"Right. You're not even thirty, Tey. We have a hundred years ahead of us." I pulled off his glasses and gently laid them on the empty seat next to us. We sat for a few minutes, my face buried in his neck, his fingers tracing a path down my sides. I pressed myself against him and rocked back and forth. His body began to relax, the weight of his arms now holding me against him.

"I've missed you. I'm sorry about the other night. I'll make it up to you," I said, blowing gently in his ear before nipping it lightly between my teeth and licking a trail down his neck. He lifted my shirt up over my head, and I willingly removed my bra, exposing myself to him completely. He devoured me hungrily, expertly moving from one side to the other, while his fingers settled themselves between my legs.

"Take me to the bedroom," I murmured breathlessly. I needed him so much, and I wanted to prove to him that nothing would ever change.

"Tell me what you want me to do to you, baby."

He was back, the man who helped me to forget the past five years, the man who loved the broken, messed up parts of me.

"I want you to tear my heart open and fill me up," I whispered huskily. "I need to have you now."

"I WANT YOU to know that I didn't come here to get you in bed with me," he declared as we lay in bed one hour after he'd arrived. We were still undressed, his head and shoulders held up by pillows against the headboard, me facing downward with my head in his lap. I lovingly brushed the hair on his legs with the tips of my fingers.

I lifted my head to look at him slyly, and his face broke out in a wide grin.

"Oh, I want to give you your Christmas present. Wait right here," I said as I slid off the bed and moved towards the robe that hung on the opposite end of the bedpost.

"Spark, you can't walk around like that!" he teased.

"Wait! Hold your horses, buddy. I'll be right back."

I ran back into the room with a square black box in my hand.

"*Et Voilà!* Merry Christmas," I squealed as I handed him my present. He pulled me back onto the bed, and I complied by sitting next to him, facing him with my knees hugged tightly to my chest. "Open it!" I ordered excitedly, while bouncing up and down on the mattress.

He tore through the wrapping paper impatiently, pulling on the ribbon until it snapped in two.

"What is it?" he asked as the box came into view. "Oh my God, Anna You shouldn't have. How much did this cost?" He lifted the watch out of the tissue paper and slipped it on his wrist. Its large round face was etched with gold roman numerals and encased in blurry antiquated glass. The brown leather strap was brand new and so was the golden clasp on its end.

"Wasn't that the one you were looking at? The vintage watch

we found in Palermo?" I asked nervously, afraid that I had purchased the wrong one.

"Where did you find this?" he asked excitedly as he brought the watch closer to his face and scrutinized its bezel. "It still has the original parts."

"Donny had a reseller in Italy who found it for me. I've been paying for it since last year. Sort of an Italian version of a layaway." I laughed. "But wait, turn it over," I instructed, taking hold of his arm and twisting it.

"I need my glasses," he said, looking embarrassed.

I ran to the living room and jumped back on the bed with them in my hand. Gently, I slipped them on his face, careful to lay them on his nose, tucking the stems behind his ears.

He turned the watch around, read the inscription and smiled at me, a brilliant smile that confirmed to me just how much I loved him.

*Dante Leola, Love of my Life. From your Spark, 12-25-2010*

"Tell me, Spark, what does it mean to be the love of your life?" he asked, gently placing his hand on my knee. I reciprocated by laying my cheek against it.

"It means that I love you most in my life. That you are my greatest love. That my love for you is real and true, and it comes from the bottom of my heart."

"And Jude? Who is he to you?" he asked carefully, his words were stilted and unsure.

"He's a ghost from my past." *There are many of these ghosts, you know. They taunt you for what you were, what you had and what could have been. I want to face them, want to jump in and save myself from my own fears.*

"Do you love him?"

"I'm not sure I love Jude. How can I love him based upon the few days that we spent together? He's a force that pulls me towards him, a cliffhanger in a story in need of an ending. I look for him, I want to be with him." I paused as I saw the pain on his face. He shut his eyes tightly and let out a deep breath. "Please," I appealed, "I don't mean to hurt you. I want to be honest with you."

"Go on."

"He's like an unfinished song in the story of my life. The words bombard me every single day, they come to me in my dreams, demanding me to finish them, to complete them. It might not be love, I know it can't be love. But it wouldn't be fair to you to pretend that I don't want to see him, to seek out some answers, to know for sure that I'm over him. You know, I realized in the past few weeks that I met Jude at a time in my life when it was falling apart because of my mom. And then I lost my mom, and I couldn't deal with another loss. So I focused all of my energies on the hope of seeing Jude again because I didn't want to face my problems. If anything, I need to tell him this."

He loosened his hold on me and shifted his body so that his legs stretched out under the blanket. I lay my head in his lap.

"And this is why I'm letting you go, Anna."

I jerked my head back in response, eyes wide with surprise. "You're what?" My wounded pride had overcome my relief.

"I think I made it worse by keeping it from you. You know, the fact that he was a seminarian. If I had told you sooner, I think you would have had your closure. So some of this is my fault, but I really thought that you'd forget him. We meet so many people in this life, look at all the women I'd been with—I thought that he would be the same for you."

"No, this is all me, Tey. And I'm so sorry. I know it sounds crazy, but I do love you. I'm being selfish, I know."

"But you're not in love with me," he argued. "I love you, Anna, more than anything else in this world. But I deserve more than being the backup guy because he wasn't coming back. I'm not going to share you with anyone. And I'm done being your second choice. He's here now. Whether or not you call it fate or a fucked up coincidence. It's up to you to figure things out, to understand what you truly want. Life is short. We can't drag this out. I'd like to have a family with you someday, and when that time comes, it wouldn't be fair to our kids if we didn't have you with us one hundred percent." He lifted his eyes to look at me, and they spoke to me more than his words ever could. "You've changed. You're not the same anymore. You've lost your spunk, your love for life."

"I lost my mother and I've had to raise my brother. Can you cut me some slack?"

"You lost two people on that day. It's like a package deal of some sort."

There were times when he was annoyingly insistent. Today was not one of them. Something was off, but I didn't want to dwell on it, especially because everything he said was true. The tables had turned on me. And in a way, I knew that his feelings were justified. He continued, "You've been through so much, you deserve to find your happiness, your peace. You bring peace to those around you, you take care of people. You need to take care of yourself. Love is like that. I love you and I want what's best for you."

His voice was strong, his words articulate. I realized that he was closing the door on us.

"Oh, Tey." I started to cry. "Please forgive me. I didn't mean to hurt you!"

But I did hurt him. I caused him so much pain, burdened him all these years with my losses and offered him a half empty heart. He leaned his head back against the bed rail and closed his eyes.

"What happens now? Where do we go from here?" I sobbed, my face contorted in pain and apprehension.

With his eyes still closed, he pulled me towards him and rested my head on his shoulder. "We're more or less separated anyway. Take the time to see him, talk to him, figure things out. I'll be in Lake Forest for the holidays, but I'm leaving for Germany the day after I bring Mikey back here from Chicago. They've made me an offer I can't refuse, so I'll be setting up a new office there."

"How long?" I asked, concerned mostly for myself. I would miss him so much while he was gone.

"Three months. I'll be back in three months." He seemed conflicted, as if he was fighting a feud inside of him. "Maybe then you'll have your shit together."

"Why does this seem so easy for you?" I challenged, swiping my hand across my face to dry my tears. I needed to be strong for him. I would make this work—train my heart to love only one, and in three months, he would have me back.

"Easy? Five years isn't easy, Spark. It's been that long. You told me it was going to be a fling, nothing more, and look where we are five years later. You're right. You're in love with a ghost, and you need to exorcise it from your soul."

"You're right," I agreed fully. "And I'm so out to sea at this point. But I'll find my way back. Just you wait."

"Don't promise anything you can't keep. Figure things out and we'll see, okay?" He stroked my hair as I wrapped my arms around his waist. "Get your groove back, Spark. Take it back from him. No one should be able to steal you away from you."

"I know."

"I love you, Anna."

I no longer wanted to take those words for granted. Whenever we ran out of words, this is what he would say to me. And everything would always fall into place.

"And I love you, Dante."

We locked eyes for a time before I settled myself back in the crook of his neck. I no longer resented the sound of Christmas music drifting in through the walls. The cracks on the ceiling, the lint balls tucked tightly in the corner opposite the bed, the wooden rosary and the gilded rosary, I saw them all despite the shadows in the room.

"But you're still angry," he stated.

"Yes. At you, at Maggie. And at Jude."

He brushed my hair with his fingers. "For simply showing up?"

"Yes," I answered. "He had no business coming back."

He nodded his head in agreement.

I continued, "And our lies. You and me. We both lied to each other."

He took a sharp breath and swallowed loudly. The shine in his eyes was replaced by a cloud of tears. "And so this is how we suffer for it. Those irreparable lies."

I ducked my head and hid myself in his arms. For a while, we both strained to listen to the merriment around us. Our tears fell simultaneously, a drop of his, a drop of mine. In the solitude of our tears, we were searching desperately for our peace.

I held his wrist and ran my fingers over his watch. "Do you

157

really like it, Tey? The watch?"

"I will wear this watch every day until I see you again."

I felt his body go limp. He was tired from the long wintry drive, and I assumed that he would fall asleep soon.

"Tey?"

"Hmm."

"Why can't we figure this out together?" I declared in all stubbornness. "Why can't I figure this out with you by my side?"

"What do you think we've been doing for five years?" he answered curtly. "No. This is your deal. It's time to make a choice."

The girl with everything to say was, for once, at a loss for words.

I squeezed him tightly and held him until he fell asleep. Dante had always been a heavy sleeper, so he didn't budge when I unwrapped myself from him to walk back to the living room to make myself another cup of tea. Mikey was fast asleep on the couch, and the timer on the Christmas lights had just turned itself off. The house was dark, and yet it felt like a subtle light was shining on the three of us that night.

It's believed that Christmas is the season of rebirth, of new beginnings, of the casting out of sins, and the dawning of new hope. For the first time in my life, I trusted in this truth, placed all my confidence in it. A feeling of melancholy washed over me as I embraced the stillness of that night. The world didn't end with the integrity of our words; from that day forward, there would be no more secrets, and our lives would be lived in honesty.

It was the simplest of premises, really. Nothing trumps a magnanimous heart.

Dante woke up the next day and found me asleep on the couch.

I stayed there that night, crying tears of loss until the sunlight streaming through the windows threatened to expose me. He climbed in next to me, held me for a few minutes, brushed his lips against mine, and walked out the door.

# PART III:
## A Heart of Flame
## 2010 (Jude)

*"I want a trouble maker*
*For a lover,*
*Blood spiller,*
*Blood drinker,*
*A heart of flame*
*Who quarrels with the sky*
*And fights with fate,*
*Who burns like fire*
*On the rushing sea."*

—Rumi

# TWENTY-TWO
## *Temporary Insanity*

"GRAY, PLEASE REMEMBER."

When she'd uttered those last two words, she cast a spell on me. All I did was "remember," for how on earth could I forget? I relived our days in the sun and under the moon, our dances in the rain. I recalled the touch of the tips of her fingers, the feel of her skin, the sound of her voice.

That kiss at the hut, the last time I ever touched her lips.

I saw my future in that kiss. I wanted to live for it, die for it, to plan my life around it. For years, I allowed it to sustain me. And in keeping me alive, it had killed me. I was a stranger to myself, a man filled with a longing that couldn't be fulfilled. I spent the next few years in a desperate bid to rebuild, to recoup, to convince myself that my truths still existed. And in the end, all that was left was the misery of living a life that I despised. A life without hope. A life without purpose. A life without her.

In the end, I was a coward. I ran away from the endless possibilities offered to me by that one kiss.

The thing is, it all catches up with you in the end. Unless you face your fears, you'll be running away all your life.

The door to the apartment was slightly ajar. From the outside, I could hear laughter and music and lively conversation. With much hesitation, I walked in to find my roommate in the embrace of a woman I didn't recognize. Peter jumped up, embarrassed by the sudden intrusion. Frankly, I was indifferent. I'd been walking around for two hours after she'd left me at the park, and was relieved to see that he had company tonight. There was hope that this would help deflect his attention away from me and steer him from any unnecessary dialogue. I needed to buy time, despite the fact that it was something I didn't have much of these days.

"How'd it go, man?" he asked as his lady friend raided the fridge. She popped open a bottle of beer and leaned against the counter, her eyes following my every move. Peter was fully dressed, although the unbuttoned shirt he wore gave him away. For a moment, we stood rooted in place, assessing the need for more conversation. All around us were unopened moving boxes, some his, some mine, and a week's worth of mail strategically strewn all over the floor.

"Fine." I didn't turn to address him. I continued along until I reached my bedroom door, ready to immerse myself in the familiarity of my only private space. I was hoping that the silence would bring me some answers. Some solace at least from the unraveling of my truth, the unfolding of my lies merely two days ago.

"It's my mistake. I should have seen this coming. Years ago, when you returned from Thailand, you were different." Father Scott paced back and forth in front of me, his voice echoing through the walls of a now very empty church. I sat in the front pew, head in my hands, elbows on my lap. I noticed that the altar boys had forgotten to snuff out the candles by the tabernacle. "You were supposed to be over it, Jude! Over her! You said it was under control, and that you were certain!"

"I'm sorry, Father Scott. I made a mistake."

His voice was forceful, more pensive and direct, not angry. I didn't know how much of his emotions were directed at me for being at this crossroad, or at himself for denying the warning signs. He had been nothing but reassuring to me, a true spiritual guide who encouraged me to think independently. I had lied to him and I was the only one to blame. I lifted my head up to look at him. He stared right back, as if trying to recognize who I was. "You lied to me, Jude. She was right here, right next to your parish. You didn't tell me that. What did you expect to happen? Did you think that one day it would just fix itself? Are you happy about the scene you pulled today?"

"Of course not!" I declared in defiance. I had nothing else to say to that. I knew he just wouldn't be able to understand how, after all the soul searching I had done, I was still as confused five years later as I had been from the first day that I met her. I knew he would never be able to feel the joy and validation that I felt when she looked into my eyes and tears began to form in hers, the pain in her voice, her anger. They all meant something. I still meant something. That momentary high was the only thing that helped me to survive the next blow.

Married.

They were married.

*Everything in that house had been so put together, so well appointed. I wondered whether that was how they lived their life. Everything according to plan.*

*"You have to make a choice!" he shouted. "A choice, Jude!"*

*"It's not a matter of choice! It's a matter of reconciling my heart with my soul. Sometimes, people make choices outside of themselves because that's where their peace resides. And when the time comes, I will know." I surprised myself with my own surety, my own conviction. "I need to step away for a while."*

*He stopped in between the center aisle and the steps descending from the lectern. The vehemence in his voice was gone. "Are you sure you're ready to leave God behind you?"*

*I allowed myself to indulge in a few seconds of silence.*

*"I'm just not sure I'm ready to leave her behind," I said.*

Back to the present with Peter knocking on the wall next to the open door. "Jude? Are you decent, man? Can I come in?" His shirt was buttoned up neatly, his hair now in place.

"Hey. I'm kinda tired right now, can we just catch up tomorrow?"

He ignored what I said, sauntering inside and leaning against the desk. "What'd she say, dude?" His light hair and translucent eyes illuminated that dark corner of the room.

"Nothing. Her husband was out of town, we talked for a few minutes."

"That's good, right? That she's moved on? You just had to see it for yourself."

"Yeah, I guess," I admitted reluctantly. "Pete, how'd you do it? How did you survive in such a different place when you left the seminary?"

"You're not leaving the seminary," he said. "You're on a leave of absence. You don't have to learn any permanent survival skills. In three months, you'll be back where you belong. Because you do belong there, man. Let's just call this your temporary insanity."

"We both left. How does that make us so different?" I challenged.

"Dude. I left for many reasons. My heart wasn't in it, I hated everything about living there, and soon enough I broke every single commitment we were made to uphold. You, on the other hand, remain as pure as you did on the day you signed up."

He took his place on the floor and sat in the middle of the room, but not before grabbing the wooden picture frame that rested on the table next to my bed. "Was this taken in Thailand?" he asked, as he stared into her bright blue eyes. I felt uncomfortable, possessive of her almost. I couldn't bear to have another man admire her in that way.

"I can see why you're smitten. She's a beauty."

I took the frame away from his hands and held it in mine. "She looks even better now. A girl who has turned into an alluring, accomplished young woman. She has the world at her feet, and a bright future ahead of her." I couldn't help but smile as I spoke those words.

"Then stay away. If she doesn't want you, don't waltz into her life knowing that you won't stay. Because you're not staying. You're going back. That's your calling."

I didn't say anything. My thoughts remained focused on her face. I'd stared at this picture so many times before. It was taken on the last happy day we had on the island. She was smiling, peaceful and carefree, with her hands up in the air.

"Look at this!" she'd exclaimed as she twirled around and around the exposed side of the ledge in our little bamboo house. "The most beautiful place in the world. I don't ever want to leave!"

Pete's voice brought me back to earth. "Hey, I forgot to tell you that your sister Katie called."

I let out a groan. My sister could be a major pain at times. She'd also had the biggest crush on Peter when she was growing up. But then again, so did the entire population of girls at our local high school.

"Did she say what she wanted?"

"Nope. She did ask me to join you for dinner at your folks' place three weeks from this Sunday," he said as he finally stood up to leave.

I nodded my head as he headed towards the door. "That's a great idea. You can help me steer through their questions if I survive that long. They're not too happy about what I've done. Leaving the church for a few months to figure myself out—my parents actually thought I had that down years ago."

He turned around to look at me reassuringly. "I'll be there, man. I've got your back. I'll have them focusing all of their attention on me, and they'll forget you're even there."

# TWENTY-THREE
## I Meant Nothing

THREE WEEKS HAD passed since I was with her at the park. It took every ounce of me to avoid stopping by the hospital to see her. What Peter had said the other night resonated with me; if I were to decide to go back, there was no point in seeing her. Besides, she told me to stay away, and these were requests that I had to honor. This situation, what did Peter call it? Temporary insanity?

For the first time in a long time, the holidays had me feeling lost and displaced. This was the first Christmas that wasn't spent celebrating mass at the church, helping out with the choir or leading the youth group in the preparations for their trip to the Vatican. I spent the day at my parents' place, in a house filled with forty of our relatives and friends and nowhere else to go after brunch was over. Every so often, I caught my father glancing at me awkwardly as I stayed glued to the television screen, sprawled out with my legs up on the La-Z-Boy, watching the Cardinals play the Cowboys with a bottle of beer in hand. I proceeded to scandalize my mother by cussing at the terrible plays. It amused me to watch them shake their heads as if they didn't know that the stranger who sat in their midst was the man they had known for thirty-one years, their son, the deacon. That was the beauty of having such loving parents. They stuck with me through my seeming descent into a state of disgrace.

I finally felt like I had overstayed my welcome and stood up to leave about thirty minutes after midnight. It was officially Christmas day. My mother followed me to the front door.

"When do you go back to St. Joe's, *meu anjinho*?" My little angel. She hadn't called me that since I was a child.

"I don't know yet, Mãe. I still have a little more than two months to think about things."

She nodded her head and kissed me on both cheeks. "Come to dinner that weekend, okay? Bring Peter. Mary wants us to meet her boyfriend."

"Mary wants to expose him to our crazy family?"

She shook her head at me and laughed. "Be good, Jude, okay?"

"Okay, Mãe. Love you."

"Love you, too."

THE GRINDING WHIR of the coffeemaker was drowned out by the

loud banging on the front door. *Great, I thought to myself. Could it be another one of Peter's spurned girlfriends?* I deliberately took my time and meandered towards the noise, hoping that whoever it was would change their mind and turn away.

She might as well have kicked it in.

She stomped her way past me and stormed into the living room right after I opened the door. My God she was beautiful. Her hair, her face, her dress. It was short, it was blue, and the flaming red birthmark on the middle of her left thigh was the sexiest thing I had ever seen. She whipped herself around to face me.

"Fuck you. I was happy. I was happy, goddamn it!"

I tried to remain calm by sticking my hands in my pockets, resisting the urge to pounce on her and topple her to the floor.

*She's married. Holy matrimony. Faithfulness. Love. Commitment. She gave it all to someone else. Fuck her.*

She zipped past me and continued on. "Fuck you for messing up my life. What the hell did you want to accomplish by showing up after five years?"

Fuck me?" I yelled back. "Fuck you! You married someone else! So why do you care? If you're so happy and secure with Dante, what the fuck do you care?"

Back and forth she paced, the sound of her high heels clicking on the wooden floor.

"Don't you dare talk about Dante! He left me because of you!"

I was at a loss for words. He left her? She's free? She followed my thoughts with a sarcastic laugh. A low snicker, an evil sounding cackle.

"Ha! You just said fuck," she said.

"I just said fuck. Fuck!"

"Don't you have to go to confession or something? There's a church right down the fucking street. Go cleanse yourself, sinner!" She waved her arms in the air.

Sinner. Despite the blaring veracity of her words, they angered me. It was bad enough to feel like I'd abandoned my faith. I didn't need her, the reason for all this, to judge me.

"Oh, you don't know, lady. You don't know how much cussing I want to do right now!"

"Then do it. Don't be a hypocrite!" she screamed. Clickety clack, clickety clack. She walked around and around in circles.

Leola said that she had changed. That she was more subdued these days. I was going to beat that fucker up. She was still as outspoken as ever. Her rabid eyes lit up like the burning embers on that dark secluded beach and it excited me to no end.

"You're crazy!" I yelled back.

"Not as crazy as you. Stalker."

Once again, she spun around, stomped across the floor and stopped right by the aquarium. Her face grew ashen, drained of all color. She leaned on the arm of the couch to steady herself.

"What's that?" she asked, the prideful attitude still evident in her voice.

"What do you mean what's that? It's a fish tank."

"Are those the…" She pointed to the two blue seahorses wrapped around each other, floating in and out of the bright orange coral.

"Same ones? Not the same ones, no. They don't live that long. These are two years old."

"Oh." She turned to her right and found my open bedroom door. I quickly followed her inside and sat at the edge of my bed, afraid of what she was going to do next. She noticed her picture on the nightstand. It antagonized her so much that she flew across the room and attempted to pull me up with all her might.

"Stand up! Stand up, you coward!" Her nostrils flared as she barreled towards me.

I leapt to my feet and tried in vain to subdue her.

"Face me, you hypocrite! Look at me!" she cried. "You meant everything to me." She struck my shoulders with both hands as I stepped backwards to avoid her. She followed me step by step, smacking me with open palms, hitting me on the chest then slapping me on the face. I caught her hand in mine just as she was about to deliver another blow. Her wedding ring was gone. "But," she said as she used her other hand to pound her fist into my shoulder, "I."

Pound.

"Meant."

Pound.

"Nothing."

That was it. I was pushed to the brink, forced to my limit. "How do you know?" I yelled, my cheek stinging from the force of her hand. "How do you know that I was fine? I was miserable, do you hear me? I was fucking miserable!"

"You lie! You're a goddamn liar!" she yelled, starting to bawl. "I buried you with my mother. You both left me on the same day! Do you know how painful it is to have someone die on you? The hopelessness of never seeing them again? Have you ever felt like you were placed in a box and could never ever crawl out of it?"

The box. That's exactly how I had felt all these years. I was in a coffin, buried by mistake, waiting to die. Not me, I fought hard to say. I was the chosen one, committed to freedom. Why then, had I been locked up in a box, unable to break out of the hold she had on me? I remember being traumatized by a movie on afternoon television about a woman who was buried in a coffin that had been sealed shut. Her hair grew white from fear as she laid there, immobile and trapped, while she watched the maggots feed on her.

I couldn't take it. I couldn't see her this way, couldn't watch this headstrong, spirited woman shamelessly decimated before my very eyes. I started to cry. The sound that I made was unrecognizable. I cried for the years that had passed, the aching, the longing, the wasted time. I was filled with hatred and heartache and lust.

Yes, and lust.

I wanted proof of life. Let her scream and kick and cry beneath me, it would be evidence that she was here in the flesh.

"You killed me," I cried. "The day you married him, you took my future away from me."

I pushed her against the wall and pinned her arms above her head. I brought my face close to hers until her lips drank in my words. "Do you know what it feels like to die every day, to dream of you, to spend every waking hour of the day wanting, needing, craving someone you can never have?" Her face turned to fear. I wanted her to feel my frustration, to match my fear, my anger. "Do you?" I demanded.

She stared at me defiantly.

I banged my fist against the wall. She shut her eyes in a grimace. "I said, do. You. Fucking know?!"

"Yes," she whimpered. "Yes, I do. I do."

And before I knew it, I was savoring the salty sweetness of her tears, kissing them away as I covered her sobs with my lips. She wrapped her legs around my waist and lifted her dress up so she could feel me against her skin. She tasted heavenly, the perfume at the nape of her neck, the pool of sweat between her breasts. Swiftly, she unbuttoned my jeans and pushed them down around my legs.

She threw her head back as I entered her. Slowly, I sat her right on top of me as her back slid up and down the wall. I pushed up and she ground down. Our movements were intense; we didn't hold back. The pain of her teeth as she bit into my shoulder and her nails on my back only served to heighten my pleasure.

I wanted to make sure that she took all of me in, and she yelped as I battered her over and over against the wall.

"Tell me, who do you worship now?" she taunted in between her deep and heavy breaths. The blue in her eyes turned green and her hair felt scorching and hot.

"You, only you," I gasped. "I only worship you."

# TWENTY-FOUR
## Blind Faith

ANNA, MYSELF, AND a beautiful woman with shorn, strawberry blond hair were sitting in the kitchen. Anna had her fingers clasped tightly around mine, both our hands sitting squarely on the table. There were suitcases on the floor, and they looked packed and ready to go.

"Mom," Anna cried. "I want to go with him. I want to go with Jude."

"No, no," said her mom. "It's best that you stay, Anna."

"But we've waited so long, Mom. He needs me. Please, please let me go with him!" she pleaded with the woman who had turned her head to look at me.

"Jude, please leave. Get up and go. She can't go with you. Take your suitcases and leave us be," she ordered.

And then without so much as another word, I stood up and walked out the door.

The door? Was that what I had just heard? Instinctively, I reached my arm out to feel for her, but I found myself alone in the middle of the bed. I jerked up in surprise and looked around the room. There were two dirty wine glasses and an empty bottle of wine on the floor. The covers were hanging off the side of the bed, and the pillows were neatly piled on top of one another occupying the space where she had slept.

"Anna!" I yelled. No. She couldn't have left me. Why did she leave?

Frantically, I sprang out of bed and pulled my jeans on. I didn't care that all I had on was a t-shirt as I ran out the door and flew down the five flights of stairs to the main entrance. My feet felt numb against the freshly fallen snow, but I felt no pain. I had to find her. I ran down the sidewalk until I spotted her walking on the opposite side of the road, head down, shoulders hunched, one hand holding her hat onto her head.

"Anna! Anna, wait!" I shouted at the top of my lungs.

She stopped when she saw that it was me. I ran across the road as fast as my frozen feet would take me. The neighborhood was slowly waking up, people were just about to start their day.

And as we faced each other, I knew that I would live out my days with her. I wanted to touch her but didn't want to scare her off any further. The snow began to fall lightly. *Dance with me*, I wanted to say. *Who cares if the rain has frozen into snow? The music in our hearts will warm it right up.*

"Where are your shoes?" she asked, one hand still on her head, the other in her coat pocket. The morning wind was biting; it stuck to the skin, sharp little pins all over your body.

"It doesn't matter. Why did you leave? Why are you leaving me?" I tried to form the words in my mouth while trying to stop my teeth from chattering.

"Dante will be home to drop Mike off, and I want to see him before he leaves for Germany."

"What about us?" I asked nervously. "I just found you, Anna. What about us?"

"There is no us, Jude."

Tears were about to fall from her tortured, weary eyes. Darkness took me over. I was angry, I was hungry. For her. I grabbed her shoulders, hoping to shake some sense into her.

"No. Fuck no! What happened to last night? What was that? No. We're going to talk about this, figure this all out together. Go back home, get rid of your fucking guilt, and I'll see you later!"

Her head bobbed up and down like a puppet. The feistiness was gone; she didn't want to fight. Slowly she turned around and walked away.

I SAT ON the edge of the tub, soaking my feet in hot water. If I hadn't looked down to find them black and blue, I wouldn't have noticed how painfully numb they had become. I was too distraught, too intent on finding a way to make her come back to the apartment with me. I knew that once we crossed this line, once I got my fix, there was no coming back down from this high. That morning, there wasn't any of the guilt or repentance that one would have expected to feel. After all, I was still under the obligation to remain celibate as a deacon on the way to becoming ordained as a priest. I was no longer considered a lay person; as far as I was concerned I was Judas, the man who had betrayed his master for thirty pieces of silver. Only she was worth far more than that. To me, she was worth the damnation of my soul. A lapse in judgment can be forgiven. That was not my intention. I didn't want forgiveness. I wanted to bury myself deep into this sin.

Despite the pull of my conscience, all I felt, all I wanted, all I was determined to do was to be with her again.

Thirty minutes later, my feet felt better and my head was clearer. As I lifted them out of the water and wrapped them in a towel, there was another knock at my door. He saw the look of surprise on my face as soon as I recognized him.

"Monsignor Ralph!" I uttered respectfully as I kissed his hand. "To what do I owe this honor?"

"I was in the neighborhood and decided to stop by. How are you, Patrick?" he asked as he surveyed the apartment with a peculiar look on his face. He proceeded directly to the kitchen. "Put on your shirt, Patrick, and join me for a cup of coffee."

Quickly I nodded my head, disappearing into my bedroom, and appeared moments later with a collared shirt neatly tucked into my faded jeans.

"Decaf or regular?" I asked, pulling out the coffee filters from the cupboard.

"I'd really rather have a scotch but coffee will do." He smiled warmly at me. "Come, let's sit."

I pulled the chair out across from him, and we sat face to face at the kitchen table. The gurgling sound of the coffeemaker helped to mask the awkward silence between us.

I voiced my thoughts about his visit. "Your neighborhood is forty-five minutes away."

"Ah, I expected no less from you," he said with a laugh. "How are you? I wanted to see how you were doing."

"I'm fine, thank you. Figuring things out."

"When do you go back?" he asked. I knew we were going to get to this eventually, I just thought he would engage in small talk first.

"I have roughly two more months. I'm still on the list for the May ceremony in Rome." I wanted to please him, and this alone should do it, to let him know that I still intended to follow in his footsteps.

"Have you been keeping in touch with Father Scott? He's your spiritual adviser, isn't he?"

"Yes, I call him once every few days."

"Does he know why you asked for this leave of absence?"

"Yes, he does."

"Does he know that it's all about a woman?" He looked straight into my eyes.

I stood up to retrieve the coffeepot and poured some into his cup. He kept his eyes on my face with no intention of letting up. When I didn't answer his question at first, he rephrased it.

"Do your parents know that it's all about a woman?"

"No," I answered quietly. "No, Uncle Ralph, they don't."

My father's brother was my inspiration, my role model, and the man who made we want to serve God. And here he was reminding me of why he was such a special person. He could read minds, could see through to the bottom of a person's soul. He was compassionate and understanding, mindful of the freedom of choice.

He took a sip of his coffee before addressing me. "I remember when you were younger and you told your family that you wanted to enter the priesthood. I went to your father and told him to stop you from pursuing it. I told him that you were too intelligent, too outspoken, too perceptive of the falsehoods of the world, and that you would make a better doctor, or a lawyer, or a father."

Of all the words he had said, I heard only the last one. *God. I could devote my life to having children with Anna.*

"A father?" I encouraged him to explain this to me.

"Not all men are born to be fathers. They say that we're hunters, we're here to provide. But you, the love that you have for your siblings, the way that you are with children, you have that innate gift of being a nurturer." His face broke out in a huge grin. "And the reaction you just had gave away your thoughts. You're thinking of a future with this woman."

"No, no," I said, shaking my head. "I intend to push through with my plan. I'm here to get her out of my system."

He stopped listening only to glance around the kitchen in search of something else. "Scratch the coffee. I'm ready for scotch. And peanuts. Do you have peanuts?"

I nodded my head eagerly and leapt to my feet to get him what he had asked for. A bottle of Johnnie Walker that I'd purchased a few nights ago was going to be my diversion if she hadn't come over the day before. Thankfully, there was one clean glass left in the cupboard. After scooping up some ice and pouring him his drink, I proceeded to peel open the top of a can of roasted peanuts.

"This is more like it." He smiled, satisfied, and then continued to speak. "I remember the first few years, when you had just started out. You were so outspoken, always questioning doctrine as being so outdated. Move with the times, you would say during the family dinners we had at your place. And you never accepted anything on pure faith. Do you remember the time you and I argued about contraception?"

"Yes, I was going to quit right then and there. I just couldn't accept the fact that we would condemn those who used contraception due to financial and medical difficulties."

"What happened to you? Why did you stay around all these years?"

"I decided that a good priest is one who doesn't accept the word on blind faith. A good priest is one who questions, who incessantly strives for answers. Christ became a man for this purpose. He was here to experience firsthand the frailties of being human. He had worries and fears, he felt enmity and anger. A good priest is Christ embodied with a human soul."

I saw the look of pride on his face. "So when do you come back?" he asked, his eyes searching mine, trying hard to assess what my response would be.

"By the end of February, something like that."

"So you're coming back?"

"Of course I am."

What he said next shook me to my core.

"Jude, lying to yourself might be your greatest sin yet. No one will hate you, no one will punish you if you decide that this is not for you. Use these next two months to the fullest extent possible. Have fun. Go out. And if it involves this woman, love her and be with her. This is all being thrown in front of you so that you can make the right decision. Okay, so we thought that your stint in Thailand was precisely for that. But if you have to do it all over again, five years later, no one will hold that against you."

"With freedom of choice comes the freedom to sin," I muttered, my eyes gravely searching for his.

He responded by placing his hands on mine. They felt soft yet steady, strong and protective. "Unfortunately, that is true," he said with a sad smile.

"Uncle Ralph, I thought I was fine. It took me years to forget. And then last year, my mind started to play games with me. I started to get lost in my thoughts about her. They turned from daydreams to sheer obsession."

He let go of my hands and focused his attention on his drink. I remained engrossed in the depth of compassion in his words. "A wise old man, one of the few who had a bigger belly than I do, once said, 'It is a man's own mind, not his enemy or foe, that lures him to evil ways.' Remember that the mind is a powerful thing. You can convince yourself of anything. But at the end of the day, it's your heart that you have to contend with. It doesn't bend as easily as your mind." He tipped the glass over and finished the drink to its last drop. "I have to visit Mrs. Albano now. She's waiting to give me some fern cuttings for my greenhouse," he said as he smoothed down his cassock before he stood up to leave. He pushed the chair back in its place and started shuffling towards the front door. "Jude, do me a favor. Talk to your parents. Your mom is worried sick about you. Tell them the reason, explain it to them. Your mom and dad embody true and lasting love. They will understand."

"Yes, Uncle Ralph," I answered. I walked side by side with him until we reached the door.

He placed his arms around me before letting go and hobbling gingerly towards the elevator bank.

# TWENTY-FIVE
## The Deal

"ANNA?" I CALLED out as I pushed open the front door of her apartment. It was five in the afternoon by the time I'd made it to her place. Even if I had her phone number, I wasn't stupid enough to think she would take my call.

I got it. She was angry, maybe even a bit confused. That made the two us.

I took the chance and stopped over directly after completing my shift at the homeless shelter. The door to her apartment was unlocked, and its slight creaking was the only sound that I heard as I stepped into her place and was met with total darkness. I stretched out my arm, sliding it against the wall until I hit the light switch. She was fast asleep on the couch, bundled up in a blue and white blanket, facing away from me. All I could see were her hair and her feet. I set the paper bag in my hand on the floor and laid my coat on top of it.

"Anna?" I whispered quietly as I tiptoed over to where she rested. I knelt down in the tiny space between the couch and coffee table. A cup of something on the table was surrounded by scattered pieces of Kleenex.

"Go away," she said with her head still buried inside the blanket.

I leaned back and sat on my heels without saying a word. I could stay here forever if it meant having her this close to me all the time.

"Why are you still here? I said, go away," she repeated.

"I'm not going anywhere." I leaned my back on the couch and stretched out my legs on the floor. I figured it was safe to turn around once I felt her move behind me. She sat up reluctantly. Her hair was tied up in a ponytail, her face resplendent with not a single trace of make up on it. Her skin was the pale golden sand and the freckles on her nose were the little tiny shells that lined up along the shore. She reminded me of Grace Kelly, regal with fine features, milky white skin, and beautiful wide eyes.

"He left today," she said sadly. "He said goodbye and left."

"What about your brother?" I asked. "Is he here?"

She shook her head. "No, he went back to the dorm for a couple of days. He'll be back next week," she answered. Her face was sad, despondent, almost.

I looked around and scrutinized the telling little bits of her life sprinkled around the room. Among the mismatched furniture, there were picture frames filled with smiling faces. Her father and brother. A spotted English bulldog. She and Dante in their graduation gowns. Another picture of her and a blond girl her age holding champagne glasses and wearing skimpy black dresses. And then a picture of the woman in my dream. There was a stethoscope on the kitchen table alongside a pile of large, heavy textbooks. Like all other rentals, there was nothing unique about this place. It was a far cry from the digs she shared with Dante.

She remained cloaked in the blanket draped like a shawl over her shoulders. I got up and sat next to her.

"What's wrong?" I asked.

"You know what's wrong," she grumbled under her breath. "He's gone. I still can't believe how easy it was for him to leave!" Her voice broke, and I knew she was on the verge of tears again.

"Blue. It wasn't easy for him. And he'll be back."

"Well, I'm not going to wait for him," she said as she crossed her legs underneath the blanket.

"What does that mean?"

"It means that I'm going to fly to Germany to be with him once I can get time off from work," she said decisively. She settled her legs back on the floor and stood up, still wrapped in the blanket. I could see that she was wearing a red long-sleeved t-shirt and red and black checkered pajama pants. My mind started to wander before going into cruise control. I was getting excited just being in the same room as her.

"Okay," I acceded. I wasn't about to argue with her.

"What do you want, Gray?" She sounded exhausted. She moved along the kitchen lazily, pouring a cup of hot water over a tea bag in a mug.

"I'd like a cup of tea too, please," I answered.

"No! What do you want? Why are you here?" she barked testily. "We just made things a thousand times more complicated."

"You. I want you." I followed her into the kitchen and took my place close behind her. She stepped backwards and bumped right into me before huffing crossly and walking away.

"Ugh. You're driving me crazy right now. Why can't you just leave me alone?" Apparently she found it aggravating to have me lapping around her like a lovesick puppy. "And get your own tea. The tea bags are right there, and there are cups in the cupboard."

An uncomfortable hush fell over us while I made myself a cup of tea and she poked around some logs and lit up the fireplace. She parked herself directly in front of it and I settled myself beside her.

"Not quite Thailand, huh?" I joked.

Her disposition changed as she gave me a half-hearted smile. "I guess not."

"I want to talk about last night. Why you left. What happened between us," I said.

She dipped her head downward and settled her chin on her knees. "Not tonight. I'm not ready. This is all too much for me right now."

"You know, Blue, there's really nothing complicated about all of this," I said, tilting my body towards her. Our elbows touched.

"Oh yeah? Why do you say that?" she asked, her curiosity piqued.

"You love two men and two men love you."

She closed her eyes as if accepting her reality. No quick comeback from her usual self, she didn't deny it. There was a chance that she loved me and I wanted to hear her say it.

"Have you left?" she asked. "The priesthood."

"Not yet. I'm on leave, and on a mission to spend all the time I can with you. All in."

Her eyes lit up with a sudden realization and she turned to face me. "I'm still angry, you know."

"I know."

She returned her aim in the direction of the fire. "How much time do we have?"

"Exactly fifty-eight days." She looked beautiful in the glow of the light. The warmth of the fire brought color to her cheeks.

"And then what?" Still talking to the fire.

"Whatever I decide, I have to go back and let them know."

She sighed. "What is it with you and deadlines, Gray? Ten days, fifty-eight days, I'm always running against the clock, always in a time crunch. With Dante, there are no constraints. He promises me forever."

"I'm sorry."

Silence filled the room. And then finally, she turned to me.

"What did you do, Gray? What did you do for five years? If you felt the same way about us, how did you get through it?"

I paused for a few seconds, fixed upon articulating this to her as best as I could. I wanted her to know the truth that was in my heart.

"I lost myself," I started out. "I lost myself in the laughter of the little children. In the grateful eyes of teenagers who were angry and alone and who contemplated the worse end to their lives. In the cries of the homeless. In the absolution of the dying. At night, I would lose myself to you under the sheets in an endless cycle of guilt and remorse. That's how I survived, Blue. I survived by losing myself."

She inched closer to me and laid her head on my shoulder. My arm shot up to pull her in a little bit too quickly. "I lost myself in

Dante, I lost myself in his unconditional love," she whispered.

She lost herself in him and he would have had her forever. But he wasn't here now, and I was. "Listen to us," I said sadly. "We're both lost. How can we be found? How can we both find purpose?" I buried my nose in her hair and took a whiff. It was our primal instinct at work, using our sense of smell to feel each other out.

"We immerse ourselves in the future," she said. "No looking back. We move on." Her shaking voice was in complete contradiction with the evident portrayal of confidence in her tone.

"No. I want to be found with you. I want to spend the next fifty-eight days finding myself, getting myself back with you."

"And then?"

"And then we go back to what we were before we met. I take my vows and ask to be assigned somewhere far away."

There was no reaction from her end. She knew that it was all a lie. I didn't think she was going to go for it. Not because she wanted me, but because she had become too cynical to even believe that this could happen. The firewood crackled, the flames catching on some old newspaper at the bottom of the rack. They flared up in a rage then slowly petered out. I felt her relax against me.

"This sounds so selfish. We're going to hurt so many people in the process."

"We've hurt ourselves enough," I stressed. "Isn't it time, Anna? Isn't it time we stopped living for everybody else?"

"Why? Why should we do this? Go through the trouble?"

"Because we've both spent years imagining what could have been. What's the harm in playing it out?" I asked.

"I'm married, Jude. I may be separated now, but I'm going to stay married."

"He's given you time to think this through; he deserves better too."

"That's a lot to ask of someone. Putting your life on hold for something that won't amount to anything," she said.

"I know," I answered. "But what's the alternative? How will we know?"

She remained pensive for a while, cocking her head to the side, scrunching her eyebrows and biting the inside of her cheek. She pulled away, lifting herself up, and then dropped back down to the floor a few feet away from me. "Okay," she agreed. "A few conditions."

"Name them." I smiled. *Progress.*

"We make a deal. When you walk away from me this time, you say a proper goodbye. You don't make any promises. Is that too much to ask?"

"No. What else?"

"I get to speak to Dante whenever I want to. You don't interfere in anything that has to do with him. You don't hurt him, you don't tell him anything. We're both clear on the fact that he is my person."

"Okay."

"Wait! There's more!" she added.

"Shoot," I ordered. I knew that no matter what they were, I would wholeheartedly agree to them.

"I make no apologies for loving Dante these past few years. You weren't coming back. I loved him."

This one. This one twisted my gut. I would never get over it. But she had me wrapped around her little finger, and she knew it.

"Awesome," I muttered, with pure sarcasm written all over my face.

"Last one," she interjected. I could see from the look on her face that she was determined to protect him. To protect what she had with him. There was a thin line between selflessness and self-preservation.

"Geez, Blue! You should have been a lawyer!"

"No sex."

"Wait. What?" I asked playfully. I wanted her heart, the rest would follow later. Or not. She stared at me, waiting for an answer, her eyes fixed and unblinking. "Okay, so you're serious."

She rolled her eyes at me.

"Fine, okay. That's fine."

"Good. We have a deal then."

She stood up, dropped the blanket on the couch, and walked towards the kitchen. The pajamas she had on did nothing to curb my desire for her. I looked away for a moment to compose myself. The tension in the room had eased somehow. Slowly, the clouds started to lift and her tone grew light. "I think we should switch to wine now, don't you?"

# TWENTY-SIX
## *Research*

"HI, HAPPY NEW Year!" she greeted me as I stood outside the door. She had light blue scrubs on and her hair was bundled up in a ponytail. Despite the absence of makeup, her lips were red and glossy. I bet they tasted like cherry.

"Happy New Year," I said. "Sorry, you didn't call so I thought I'd stop by." New Year's Eve came and went; she was on duty at the hospital, and I was at the homeless shelter counseling families through two suicides.

"Stalker," she teased.

"Your very own." I answered with pride. During the last week we had seen each other every single day, talking about everything and nothing and getting to know more about the adults we had each become. She was even more amazing than I had imagined, loving and caring, a woman with character and talent. An outstanding doctor and a beautiful human being. She made me feel happy and complete. I was devastated for all the time I lost, for all that could have been mine and wasn't.

"Mikey's home. I wanted to spend some time with him tonight."

"Oh, I'm sorry. I can come back tomorrow," I said, peeking past her to find her brother in front of the television. I really had to see her tonight. Those deaths, the families, the wives whose husbands left for war and disappeared forever. I sought comfort in her presence, to assure myself that there could be a life filled with love and overwhelming joy. That was how I felt that night at my place, and I was desperate to feel that way once again.

"No, it's okay. Come on in." She moved over to allow me to step inside, but I waited for her to lead me through the hallway. "Mike, Jude's here," she called out to her brother. He pushed his headphones to the side.

"Hi," I said as I made my way inside. "I'm Jude, it's nice to meet you." I extended my arm out to him.

"Hey," he said with a wary look on his face.

"What are you playing?" I asked, trying to make conversation. "Is that *Minecraft?*" I was trying to sound cool. It didn't look like Minecraft. There were guys in army gear and blood was splattered across the screen.

"Nope. *Battlefront,*" he said, brushing me off. "*Minecraft* is for little kids." He repositioned the headphones over his ears.

I looked at Anna and shrugged my shoulders.

She responded by doing the same thing. "Don't try too hard," she whispered. "Dante."

I nodded my head in agreement.

I stood there awkwardly while Anna took her place back at the kitchen table. There was something different about her, she seemed jittery and edgy. Her brows were furrowed as if she was trying to suppress something, keep it inside her head. I fished through the pile of books that were scattered on the table.

"What's all this?"

"Research," she answered. "Went to the library to—" She glanced down at the screen of her ringing cellphone. "Speaking of," she said.

"Hi!" she greeted him happily as she stood up and walked towards her bedroom. I could make out his voice but not his words. "Nothing much. What are you doing up in the middle of the night?" She shut the door behind her.

I was filled with a seething jealousy that I couldn't explain. The change in her disposition when she heard that voice on the other end of the phone cut through me like a knife.

I leafed through the pages of the books that lay in front of me: *Fidelity, Remaining Faithful in Today's World, Questions Catholics are Asked, The Holy Orders: A Life of Devotion.*

I didn't hear her come back. "Oh, I see you found my research material," she said, tongue-in-cheek.

"You could have just asked me," I said sternly. I was pissed off at that phone call, although I knew full well that I had no right to be. "How is he?"

"He's good, just working hard. He sounded so close, so clear, as if he were right here. The lines in Germany must be really high tech."

I could tell she was trying to stay away from me; she sat down at the opposite end of the table.

I took a deep breath and pulled my chair next to her. Something was definitely wrong. "When does he come back?"

"He didn't say. Soon, I hope." She smiled as she opened up one of the heavy binders filled with many tabs and pages. "So, anyway, want to hear what I learned today?"

"Hit me," I answered, trying hard to cast away my deep, dark thoughts. I glanced towards the sliding door that led to the balcony. Night was falling, and the dusk was a pretty orange swirl of colors against the clouds. This alone should seal one's belief in a higher power who planned every single detail, including the colors of the sky.

"So you're a deacon, right? It says that you're a transitional deacon, a seminarian in the last phase of training to become a priest. It also says that you will be ordained by a bishop. Deacons assist the priests and bishops in the ministerial aspects of the faith. Deep words there," she said. "It also says that the priesthood is a calling. When did you get yours, Jude?"

I couldn't decide whether or not to condone this conversation. It was personal to me, and I wasn't comfortable discussing the misgivings I had in my mind. I certainly didn't think that this was the right time and place to remind her that if I had my way and if she loved me, I would give it all up.

"Do you really want to get technical about it?" I cautioned.

"Yes."

"There are two levels of calling. One is the calling that you experience when you decide that you want to enter the priesthood. It's the pull you have on a personal level. The phase that I'm in, however, is also called discernment. I am now deciding once and for all whether or not I still have the calling. It's the final decision stage in becoming a priest. If you want to know when I first wanted to become one, it was sometime in the middle of my undergrad when I felt the inexplicable draw towards Christ's teachings and the sacraments of the church."

"Master of Divinity. Sounds so compelling. Is that what you have?"

She was goading me, trying to get me to lose my patience. Ordinarily, I would have thrived in discussions such as these, but not this night. In this instance, I was ashamed of my vocation. I just wanted to be an ordinary man. Because if I was an ordinary man, I would have locked her in my arms and told her exactly what I wanted to do to her right then and there.

"Yes."

"Oh, and here," she said flippantly as she turned more pages. "The most important topic. Celibacy. Hmm," she continued as she skimmed her finger across the words of the book. "This says that deacons are required to lead a celibate life, even before they take their vows." She shut the book and drilled her eyes into my soul. "Uh oh, Gray, you screwed up."

Now we'd arrived at the root of all this. "That's it!" I scowled as I grabbed the book from her hand and threw it on the table. "Do you really want to go there, Blue? Huh? Do you?" I whisked sideways and started towards the door. Mikey had long since left his game and gone to his room with a bag of chips and a Coke.

"Jude!" She ran after me. "Why are you being so defensive? I was just teasing you! Come on, don't be mad!"

I ignored her plea. My hand was on the doorknob, ready to pull it open and get away from the confines of her cruelty. She grabbed my hand and forcibly wrapped my arm around her waist. "Jude!"

"No, Anna. This approach and retreat tactic of yours is killing me! Leave all that to me! It's my decision, my consequence. Don't you ever, don't you ever tell me what I should do, or how I should think." I removed myself from her hold. "I'll see you around."

"Fine!" She stepped back. "Go! Leave! Leave like you did five years ago. Don't come back. Once you step out of this place, don't you dare come back!"

I stopped dead in my tracks "Is this a game to you? Is this all a game to you, Anna?"

"I don't know what to do! I don't know! I'm angry. I'm jealous. I'm envious of God. How sick is that? How can I compete?" She started to cry. "Do you think that I don't count the days in my head? Forty-eight more days. Forty-eight days and then you'll be gone." Her tears flowed, her body went limp, and she dropped to the ground.

The fear of losing her forever was more eminent than the pride in my heart. She had cried enough. I didn't want to be the reason for her pain. I picked her up in my arms and carried her back inside. Afraid to cause a scene, I took her straight to the bedroom and sat at the edge of the bed as I laid her crosswise on my lap with her legs dangling over my thighs. Her arms remained twisted around my neck and her head rested on my chest.

"I want to walk away," she cried. "I want to miss Dante. And I can't do that because you're here."

I scooted us upwards until I was inches away from the nightstand and grabbed a tissue to hand to her.

"That makes two of us, Blue. I'm jealous, too." She looked up at me with understanding in her eyes. "I seem to keep making you cry," I said sadly.

"I know." She laughed through her tears. "I don't know where this is coming from. I'm normally not this much of a sap."

I smiled weakly before taking her face in my hands. "Do you want me to leave you, Anna? I would do that for you. I don't want to be the source of your sappiness."

She snickered as she kept her arms wrapped around my neck. "I don't know what I want."

"That's okay. How about we figure it out together? But from now on, if you have misgivings about my vocation, my future, or even about anything, just come right out and say it. You've got a complicated mind, Blue. You'll drive yourself crazy just keeping it all inside of you. I'm here, okay?" I kissed the top of her head.

"Okay," she said in a weak, childlike voice.

"Blue, we need to talk about that night. Is this what all your anxiety is about?"

Her eyes seemed to change color like the mood rings we played with when we were growing up. They were a different hue every single time. I wanted to spend my life living in her eyes, discovering the colors of the rainbow.

"I feel like Eve in the Garden of Eden. I've ruined you. You've broken your ties with God."

I shook my head in a frenzy. "No."

She looked genuinely surprised at my answer. "Don't you feel guilty about what happened?"

"I used to live in guilt. There was a time a few years ago when I went to confession every single day. Every time I thought of you, I'd cry about the feelings of betrayal that I had for my vocation. But I no longer feel that way. Blue, this is the main reason why I took this leave. I have to decide what I want in my life. And I'm not going to lie to you and tell you that you don't make up a large part of that process. Lord knows how much you mean to me, but nothing in my life will ever make me break my ties with God. The love of God is rooted in our fallibility. He's there more than ever, in the face of confusion."

Her head moved up and down and rubbed itself against my chin. "So you went to the same priest and confessed the same thing over and over again?" she asked, her voice lilted to a slight degree.

I laughed out loud. "Well, I also confessed to cussing a lot. That's one thing that I couldn't stop once I started doing it in Thailand."

There were no more words to say at that point. The stillness in the dark room and the concept of secrecy felt utterly exciting to me. As I held her in my arms, I thought of nothing else but the chance to reacquaint myself with her body once again. And so, instinctively, I lowered myself on the bed until I was lying flat on the mattress and she was facing sideways directly on top of me. Slowly, I rolled her on her back until my face was above hers. She reached out her hand and traced a path down my nose with her finger.

"Blue?"

"Hmm?"

"Can we make out?"

"Define make out."

"Can I kiss you?"

"Yes, you can. Kiss me."

# TWENTY-SEVEN
## *Together*

"YUM," ANNA SAID as she contentedly munched on her sandwich. "You know how I love sausage."

We hid behind one of the large gray columns that marked the emergency entrance of the hospital on a cold January afternoon. Side by side, we sat with our legs stretched out in front of us, our heads bundled up in hats and scarves. For the past two weeks, I'd been dropping by to bring her lunch and spend a few precious minutes with her. She'd been working long shifts, and this was the only way that I could get to see her.

"I got it right this time, I think. No mayo, no tomatoes."

"Yes, it's delish." She took a napkin from the bag and wiped the corners of her mouth. "Thank you."

I leaned over to kiss her. Since that night at her apartment, that seemed to be all that we wanted to do. I couldn't get enough of her lips and kissed her whenever I got the chance. Things changed between us after that night, and we were back to the comfortable banter that we'd always enjoyed when we were together.

"So, how's your week going?" I asked her.

"It's fine. I heard from Dante today; he sounds good. I think he's moved on," she said with a chuckle. "There was noise in the background, and it was obvious that he was out with a group of people. Some woman actually answered his phone. It was kind of awkward, but then we also laughed a lot—he was poking fun about many things."

"Are you okay with that? The fact that he's actually enjoying himself?"

"I am. I just want him to be happy." She unscrewed the cap of her bottled water and took a sip. Those lips, the way she sipped that bottle with her eyes closed.

"Oh, I got in trouble again today. I allowed treatment on another patient without confirming the extent of his insurance."

I shook my head, concerned. "Blue, maybe you shouldn't put yourself out on the line like that."

"It's nothing. They're deducting it from my paycheck." She took another bite of her sandwich.

"But you can hardly afford it with all your expenses," I said.

She shrugged her shoulders nonchalantly. "I'm always going to do the right thing for these patients."

What a perfect opportunity to lean in and nuzzle her neck. "You smell so good," I whispered.

"Hmm," she answered as she gently encouraged me by tenderly skimming her fingers on my face. "I smell like sausage."

"No you don't," I mumbled.

"Deacon Grayson?" I shot up like a bullet in the air. I couldn't believe how fast I got to my feet. "Deacon, is that you?"

It was a young girl from the youth group. What was her name? Georgina. I pretended to look confused, acting like I didn't know her. I was grateful for the cap on my head and the scarf that hid a part of my face.

"Oh, I'm sorry, I thought you were someone else," she apologized. Anna sat silently, observing this exchange.

I waved my hand in the air. "It's okay," I said before dropping back to the ground. There was pure dishonor on my face as I turned to look at Anna. Slowly and deliberately, she brought the sandwich to her mouth and took another bite. "I'm sorry about that," I sputtered out, embarrassed.

Another shrug of her shoulders. "No biggie." And then an afterthought. "Are you ready to be seen with me?"

"What a question. Of course, I am. It's no one's business," I responded with tenacity. I drove the point home by grabbing her hand and holding it close to my face.

"How much," she said in a teasing voice, "how much do you want to bet that you aren't ready? I bet you'll deny me a few more times before all is said and done." I didn't sense any tension in her tone. She was speaking as if it was a known fact, a normal reaction.

"Blue," I said resolutely, "we're together, and I'm proud to be with you."

"WHERE ARE WE meeting her again?" I asked as we weaved through a crowd of shoppers along Fifth Avenue. We had driven the four hours to the city to meet Maggie, who had asked to meet Anna for a day of wedding related errands. She was finally off for the weekend, and I had asked if I could tag along. The countdown was on, and I wanted to spend as much time with her as I could. I held her hand tightly as she stopped every once in a while to admire the window displays as we walked along the street.

"Tiffany's in half an hour," she answered, her thoughts engrossed in something else. I could tell by the way that she walked confidently that she was comfortable in her skin, shopping on Fifth Avenue with the crowd of discriminating shoppers. "Can we stop in for a second?" she asked as she led me through the doors of Saks Fifth Avenue and headed straight to the area that held the designer women's purses.

The rest of that day went by without a hitch. Anna met Maggie at Tiffany's and spent a few hours with her while I roamed Fifth Avenue on my own. I found solitude in one of the pews at Saint Patrick's Cathedral one hour before the evening mass was about to begin.

I strolled aimlessly up and down the aisle of statues and altars and votive candles, lighting as many as I could until I ran out of change. I prayed for many things; I prayed for my family and Anna's family, and I lit a special candle for Leola. In a twisted way, I would never have gotten the chance to spend time with Anna if he hadn't given her up. She would have stayed with him, made it work, and tried her best to forget about me.

In the car on the drive home, I realized that I didn't need to pray for peace. For the first time in five years, I was sure that I had it. I felt it all around me—in the touch of Anna's hand as she rested it on my thigh throughout the long drive back, in her stories as she told me about the day she spent with Maggie, in the sound of her laughter as she teased me about passing gas in the car, and in the look on her face as I watched her with her eyes closed, fast asleep. I found my peace, and I was in a desperate bid to keep it. That's what I should have prayed for. *Let me keep my peace.*

# TWENTY-EIGHT
## *Elephants*

"HI!"

Anna walked into our apartment the next day just as I was putting the away the dishes in the sink. Peter staggered back into his bedroom as I made my way over to greet her. The boxes were gone, the mail had been put away, and the apartment now felt like home, all compliments of Anna. She'd been cleaning up around our place each time she paid me a visit. And it was only because she couldn't sit still for very long. Our movie nights consisted of me camped on the couch while she moved around putting everything neatly back where it belonged.

"Good morning, Peter," she said. "I'm a little early."

"Early is good," I assured her. "We should leave in half an hour."

Our place had now taken on a new look. Two framed street paintings were hung on the wall in the living room and a fluffy grey wool rug occupied the floor directly adjacent to the couch. She took her usual seat whenever she came over, a comfortable easy chair facing the aquarium.

"You look beautiful." I sat on my knees between her legs and kissed her. She wore a short black skirt that showed enough skin, tastefully paired with slim, high-heeled boots. She'd kept her hair down today and it framed her face perfectly. My fingers automatically moved to brush the glaring pink birthmark on her thigh. There we were again, kissing like there was no tomorrow. Kissing and kissing and kissing. That was all we did, and I could have made a lifetime career out of it.

"Are you sure? I know you said casual, but it's been a little nerve wracking, figuring out what to wear to meet your family."

I tilted her face towards mine and kissed her in response.

"Merle looks sick," she interrupted, pointing to the male seahorse who seemed suspended in the water.

"No, I think he's asleep."

"Pearl's just too much for him. Look at her." She laughed as the female seahorse flitted in and out of the coral.

"I know. I get exhausted just watching her. Like a spitfire," I said, looking at her pointedly.

"Uh-huh." She gave me a peck on the cheek. "Go get dressed. I'll be right here waiting."

207

"WHOSE CAR IS this?" she asked as we walked to the parking garage across the street one hour later than planned and got into a silver 2010 Range Rover. Peter had bailed out of this trip, claiming a hangover. "Where's the jeep?"

"It's Pete's," I answered, afraid to look into her eyes. "This drives much better so he offered it to me today."

Minutes later, we were cruising comfortably along I-95, heading north towards Scarsdale, listening to the steady sound of the windshield wipers swishing back and forth as the snow fell quietly all around us. Anna began to interrogate me about my family. You could tell that she was nervous. I, too, was quite apprehensive. So far, I'd managed to speak openly about her only to Father Scott and Uncle Ralph. I had yet to gauge my father's response to meeting her. Today would confirm to the world that she was a part of my life.

"Does your family drive exaggeratedly big bad cars or is this a personal choice of yours?" she asked with a wide smile, running her fingers up and down my arms. "I know for a fact that you're not trying to over compensate." She giggled.

"First of all, a Rover is not big and bad. It's a cool, safe car," I answered. She laughed hysterically at my comment. It was a forced, agitated kind of laugh.

"What do you think they'll ask me first? 'Is it true you're a married woman? Are you trying to send our son to hell?'" She was definitely entering into a state of panic. I placed my hand on her thigh which was shaking up and down. "They know you're going back, right?"

They certainly assumed that. I was the one who was no longer sure.

I steered the car to the side of the road and slowed down to a halt. Parking on a snow filled bank on a two lane road in the middle of a forest preserve wasn't the smartest thing to do in the middle of a snowstorm. But I wanted to hold her, assure that it would all be fine.

"Baby," I whispered, reaching out to touch her face, "if you want to turn back, we can. If you don't feel right about this, we can cancel and just go home."

She leaned her body over the middle console and kissed me on the cheek. "It's okay," she affirmed. "I'll be fine. Let's drive on. Today will be a day of questions and I'm just going to take them as they come." She slipped herself back to her original position and announced without any resentment in her voice, "Now, if you don't mind, I'm going to close my eyes and rest for a few minutes."

"BLUE, WE'RE HERE." I roused her gently as we pulled up to the black gates along a brick paved driveway that led to my parents' home. I watched as she opened her eyes to find the sprawling brick Georgian colonial in front of her. She didn't look surprised at all as she straightened up her clothes and slipped off her seatbelt. I rounded the fountain in the middle of the driveway and parked by the side of the house.

"You have a beautiful home," she said as she stepped out of the car and retrieved the gifts that she had brought for my parents.

"Thank you. We had many happy times growing up here."

"Jude!" My sister Katie came running outside to meet us.

"Hi, I'm Anna Dillon," she said as she extended her hand out to my sister.

Katie looked at me and then at Anna. "Oh, yes! Hi, I'm Katie." She quickly regained her composure and warmly shook Anna's hand.

At this point, I knew Anna realized I had not warned my family that she was coming to dinner with me. She glanced at me but stood unfazed, like a champ.

"Don't say it," I cut Katie short as she was about to open her mouth.

She pulled me to her and said in my ear, "I'm going to. I have to. How? How did you get someone as hot as that?" she whispered.

I gave her a smug look and walked away. "Who's here?" I asked as we headed towards the front door.

"Everyone."

Great.

Anna was relaxed and confident as we entered the house. In fact, she made an effort to stay by Katie and I knew she was trying to give me space.

"Mãe, your favorite is home!" Katie called out jokingly.

My mother and father emerged from the living room, holding hands.

"Hi Mãe, Dad." I greeted them with a kiss. "This is my friend, Dr. Anna Dillon. Anna, these are my parents, Milagros and Pat."

She stepped forward and embraced each of them before handing my mother the bouquet of orchids and my father the bottle of champagne.

"What a pleasure to meet you, Mr. and Mrs. Grayson. You have a beautiful home." Eight-thousand five-hundred square feet of meticulously designed rooms and high-end furniture. My father had migrated from Ireland and successfully broke into the real estate market.

"The pleasure is ours, Dr. Dillon. Please make yourself at home."

"Please call me Anna," she offered graciously.

"Jude! You're back!" I would know that voice anywhere. My baby brother, Max, was the most beautiful creature on this planet. His upward slanting eyes, small facial features, tiny hands and feet—he was the most perfect imperfection ever created. My mother had him after she had been trying for a few years. He was a Down's syndrome baby.

"Maxie boy, get over here!" I yelled. He jumped into my arms, this skinny little boy who was small for his age. "This is my friend, Anna," I said.

She didn't flinch. In fact, she had the warmest, most accepting smile I had ever seen. "Hi, Max. It's so nice to meet you."

"Oh no, Jude, deacons shouldn't be having girlfriends!" he said worriedly.

Anna handled it expertly, and her sweet, reassuring voice filled my ears. "Oh, don't worry, Max. I'm just his friend. You're absolutely right! Deacons shouldn't have girlfriends. Come on, can you show me around? You all have a beautiful house over here." Arm in arm, they walked away.

My brother and my girlfriend. *My girlfriend.*

Dinner was served three hours after we arrived, and Anna's introduction to the family was long and laborious. She affably greeted each and every one of them. Katie's husband, Matthew, and their two children. My sister Mary and her new boyfriend, Sean. My twin brother and sister, Joe and Peg, and seven of their friends from school. My sister Erin and my uncle Ralph.

Yes, Uncle Ralph was there. After the conversation we had in my apartment, I was sure that he would be there to check Anna out.

"So, Anna, how did you meet my brother?" Mary asked, passing the bowl of bread to my mother who sat next to her.

"We actually met in Thailand five years ago. I was on a medical mission, and he was on sabbatical," Anna answered with a smile.

"That explains it," Katie said, turning her head to look directly at me.

I met her stare with one of my own. "Explains what?"

"Never mind. Later. Offline," she responded, directing her words into her glass of water.

My dear mother, oblivious to whatever it was that was going on, began her own side conversation. "Anna, you are working where?"

"Mila, she's a doctor," my dad gently reminded her.

Max and Anna were enamored with each other. After dinner, he took her to the pool house to show her his paintings while I remained at the dinner table with the rest of my family. My mother paced back and forth from the cupboard to the counter, setting aside some food for me to take home.

"Meu, did you want a little of each? The *coxinha* and the *feijoada* too?" My mother had raised us in her Brazilian culture, and she felt right at home with the extended familial ties that my father's Irish family had brought into her life. She loved to entertain, loved life, and loved her children and her husband with all of her heart.

"Yes, Mãe, I'll take anything you can spare. It will save me from having to eat Taco Bell every day."

"She's beautiful, Jude," Katie boldly stepped in and addressed what was on everyone's mind. They nodded their heads in agreement.

"And classy," Erin said.

"Yeah, remember the girls that Jude used to take home when he was in high school? Blech! This one is clearly unimpressed by you for once."

I threw a napkin at Mary. She flung it back at me and missed.

"When are you going back, Jude?" Uncle Ralph asked.

"Thirty-three days," I answered.

"Are you even going back?" Katie asked. She was a traitor. What was she doing?

"What do you mean?" I asked irritably, gesturing at her with my hands.

"Was there ever a plan not to go back? What is going on?" My mother took a seat at the table, turning her head to look at my father, who placed his hand on hers.

"Mãe, that's the girl from Thailand! The one he's been crazy about! This started five years ago!"

"Katie!" I yelled. "What are you doing?"

I looked at Mary and begged her with my eyes to excuse herself. I motioned her with the tip of my head to take Erin as well. I didn't want to embarrass Mary in front of her date. Katie, Uncle Ralph, and my mom and dad were left at the table, and I was shocked that my father had not yet weighed in.

"Katie. Why?" I asked.

"Jude, I've seen the way you've been looking at her all night. You're in love with this girl. I don't want you to be miserable. You don't have to go back."

"I don't know yet," I argued. I felt the heat of their stares on my face. They tried to assess my expressions, tried to read my heart.

My mother looked at me sadly then spoke her words. "Meu, you can serve God in many different ways."

"It's not that easy," I said.

"What, meu, what's not easy? Doesn't she love you? She is here in our home," she said, placing her hand on my arm.

"This is the only life I've known. I couldn't take it if she left me. She's my only connection to a life outside the priesthood."

"Does she love you? Is she committed to staying with you?" Katie again.

"I don't know. We haven't really talked about it," I said sharply. And then I corrected myself. "About the future, I mean."

"She's married," Katie revealed, searching the room for a reaction. My mother bowed her head to avoid my eyes. My father pulled her closer to him. She looked up at him and for a quick second, I saw them communicate with their eyes.

"Separated," I defended. "They're separated."

"Have you thought about an alternate future, son? What would you do if you decided to pursue a life outside of the—"

My dad finally decided to say something and I cut him short.

"Not, really. No. I haven't."

"I would love for you to join the business. Take over for me after I retire, carry on the name we've built for ourselves," he offered warmly. There was a simultaneous nodding of heads around the room. I felt sidelined, filled with apprehension that I would fail at achieving the hopes and dreams he had for me.

"I'm not a businessman, dad."

"Anyone can learn the business. That's what I'm here for," he defended. "Everything you need is set. There's no need to start all over."

How could I make him understand that having Anna in my life didn't mean that I had wavered in my commitment to serving God? My father had always taught me to be honest, to stand up for my conviction. This was the time to make him see that he taught me well. I walked over to my father, knelt down on the floor and held his hands in mine. "Dad, please forgive me for saying this. I still want to serve God in His church as a layman. That plan hasn't changed for me."

He squeezed my hands firmly in affirmation. "Well then, you need to start figuring things out on your own. Although it looks painfully obvious to me. You have one month before you have to go back."

And those were the final words he spoke on the matter.

Suddenly, Max popped up from the corner of the kitchen, Anna standing uncomfortably next to him, visibly shifting her weight from one leg to the other.

# TWENTY-NINE
## Where Was Lola?

"HI, IT'S ME," I said over the speaker on my phone. "Call me, please. I've left so many messages, and I'm worried about you."

Six days had passed since I took Anna home following the dinner at my parents' place. She hadn't said a word as we drove home that night, and she kept her gaze out the window.

"Would you mind if you dropped me off at home?" Those were the only words she said to me that night. I assumed that meeting my family had totally overwhelmed her, so I wanted to give her some space. Six days later, I still hadn't heard back. I knew she was fine because I stopped by the hospital and checked on her through the nurse Melinda. I feared that Dante had returned and that she would soon cut off all ties with me. That, in the end, it would be Anna's departure and not mine that would shred me into pieces.

I answered my phone immediately after it rang without checking the information on the caller ID.

"Hi."

"Hi, Jude. It's Melinda. Just checking in. I thought you'd want to know that Anna is off call now. I saw her heading home."

"Oh. Hi, Melinda." I didn't bother hiding the disappointment in my voice. "Thanks for letting me know."

"She said something about meeting her friend Maggie for dinner and drinks." She had my full attention.

"Did she say where?" I asked excitedly.

"No, not really."

I didn't even know where to start looking. "Huh. Thank you, Melinda. I really appreciate it." I heard her say something just as I removed the phone from my ear.

"Wait! Jude, are you still there?"

"Yes?"

"I was wondering whether you wanted to meet up for a drink tonight. You know, get to know more about each other. I feel like I've known you for a while, seeing you at the ER for all these months."

"Sorry, Melinda, I can't. I'm with Anna." *I'm with Anna. I'm with her. Whether or not she forsakes me. I. Am. With Her.*

That's what had happened. Anna was upset.

A few days before we drove to Scarsdale, she had challenged me about coming out in the open with her. And I had denied her. At the hospital and even with my family.

I had to find her. We only had twenty-seven more days. I decided to call Maggie.

"Hello?"

"Hey, Maggie. It's Jude."

"Jude."

"Are you seeing Anna tonight?"

"Why?"

"I need to speak to her, please. Where will you guys be?"

"Is she avoiding you? If she is, why would I betray her confidence?"

"Because I don't have much time. I have to see her, I have to explain what happened."

"No deal." And then the phone went dead.

FOUR HOURS LATER we were in Manhattan, throwing the keys at the valet as we left the Rover in his dependable hands. Two hours later, we were lined up at a Latin dance club called Copacabana. It was all Peter's idea, all he could do to stop me from sulking around the apartment.

"Do you think we should check out the second floor?" Peter asked as we crisscrossed our way through groups of people. "I think the second floor is the pure Latin floor. That's what the guide said."

"What does pure Latin even mean?" I asked, utterly agitated.

"Latin, man! As in hot Latin chicks!" He blurted excitedly.

We moved quickly through the lobby and up the long flight of stairs. A group of women stopped us as we reached the landing, two of them latching on to Peter while another two tried to lead me to the dance floor.

"Party pooper," Peter said accusingly as we careened through the heavy traffic of dancers, looking left and right. We finally located the bar. I squeezed myself in between two couples and signaled the bartender for a drink.

"Go ahead and have fun," I said. "Leave me here, I'll be okay."

I OPENED MY eyes to a dimly lit hallway in an unfamiliar place, surrounded by unfamiliar people. With distorted vision, I could barely make out the woman who sat in front of me on the floor. But it was Maggie, with her long blond hair and dark blue eyes, examining me closely.

"He's waking up," she said as Anna's face came into view. I couldn't move a muscle; I felt like someone had left a ten ton boulder on my back. She brought her face close to mine.

"Shh. I'm here. It's okay, baby, I'm here."

Baby. I felt like I was in high school, deciphering the meaning behind every word she said. There was a softness to her tone that made me feel a shift in her attitude towards me. Had I died and gone to heaven? Because her love was my heaven, and at that moment, it seemed well within my reach.

"You didn't answer the door," I said in barely a whisper. My lips couldn't form the words correctly. I did remember staggering outside the club and dragging Peter along with me, shoving him into a taxicab that took us to Maggie's place on Park Avenue.

"So you decided to sleep in the hallway?" she smiled.

"Where's Peter?"

"He's here, in the living room." She was all made up, dressed to the nines in a red leather outfit but with no shoes. "Oh Jude, you're a mess. Let's get you inside."

My sides hurt. My head hurt. There was a slicing pain right below my nose. I tried again. "Sorry. I'm sorry."

"Don't be," she said. "I'm the one who should be sorry."

"Why were you upset?" I asked, despite the fact that I wasn't sure whether she could make out the words coming from my swollen lips.

"Long story. Can we talk about it tomorrow? You should rest now. Come inside." She sat on her knees and tried to lift me up by the shoulders. We stood up at the same time and she led me through the house, up the stairs and into a lavishly decorated guest bedroom. Gently, she pushed me down on the bed, laid my head on a pile of pillows and began to tuck the covers around me.

"My father succeeded in real estate. He did well for himself and for our family. Pete owns the Jeep and the Rover is mine."

"I know."

"None of that matters to me. I gave it all up when I decided to live my life in service to others. In fact, my dad asked me to join his business but that's not what I want out of my life."

She smiled at me. There was a look of tenderness in her eyes, of pride, of recognition.

"I know," she repeated.

My eyelids felt heavy. I wasn't going to be able to stay awake much longer. "Why were you upset?" I asked again.

"Tomorrow," she said. "Try to get some sleep."

"Stay. Don't leave. Please don't leave again." I tugged at her arms like a child desperate to hang on to his mother.

"Never. I'm not going anywhere."

I could have died that night with those last words. I could have died and heaven would have been in those words. In twenty-seven days, when this is over, I would take those words with me.

# THIRTY
## *Out of the Fog*

THE ROOM WOULD have been pitch dark if not for a small crack in the curtain. A tiny slice of light seeped through the window, allowing me to see the outline of Anna's hair as she slept soundly next to me. I glanced at the clock by the bedside and wasn't surprised to see that it was already noon. I didn't think we got back to the house until almost four in the morning.

I still felt bruised and battered, but somehow the tingling feeling was gone, and the swelling of my face and lips had somewhat dissipated. I turned to my side to face her, remembering the last time I had the luxury of watching her sleep. I watched as her shoulders rose and fell with every breath she took; I smoothed the strands of hair that fell down her back and lightly twirled them around my fingers. I longed to reach out and touch her, but wanted to give her more time to rest. And so I waited. I shut my eyes and basked in our closeness until I felt the light brush of her fingers on my face.

"Hi," she whispered, her voice thin and weary. She turned her body towards me, one hand tucked under her head and the other against my face.

"Hi," I said, reaching out to feel her lips.

"How are you feeling?"

"Better. But I still have some kind of a headache."

"Let's elevate your head a little bit." She pushed another pillow under my neck with both hands. We remained with our faces only inches away from each other. My eyes fell out of my head when I noticed that she wore a lacy nightgown that peeked out from under the blanket. Her cleavage was deep and inviting.

"Can we talk about why you were upset?" I asked in a hushed tone, mindful of the two people that were sleeping outside the room and the fact that the door to our bedroom was cracked open. She probably did that on purpose.

"Jude."

I trailed my finger along the tip of her nose.

"Aren't you tired of all the questions and the answers and the discussions we've been having? It wasn't supposed to be this taxing."

"Love is worth everything, Anna."

She puffed out a whiff of air. "I was overwhelmed," she answered. "And hurt. And I felt guilty."

"Tell me why."

"Dante hadn't called for three weeks and I missed him. Not because I want him back. I felt so much guilt and blame about having let him down. And then I met your family and fell in love with them. I saw how great an influence they all were in your life. I thought about Mikey and wished he could have met them. And then when you had that conversation in the kitchen…"

I took her hand and rested her palm flat against my cheek. "You heard us?"

Her dancing eyes matched the soft smile on her face. "I love the feel of this." She rubbed the rough stubble below my ears. "Yes, I heard everything. Max wanted to color on the floor next to the kitchen entrance."

"I'm so sorry. I panicked. I was trying to maintain my composure. I didn't want them to think that I was weak and indifferent. I wanted to let them know that my decision wasn't going to be one out of impulse."

"It made your leaving more of a reality to me, and I decided that I wasn't going to play this game anymore. Of all the denials you'd made about us, that one hurt me the most," she admitted with tears in her eyes. "I kept on putting off what I wanted to tell you when you left me at the hut that day, five years ago. And then right when I think I've accepted the fact that you'll be gone in twenty-six days, something happens to fill me with this profound fear of never seeing you again."

"That won't happen."

"We haven't decided that yet," she said with a sniff.

I didn't answer her because she couldn't know yet. It all depended on whether or not she had fallen in love with me. This was decided long ago. It was a matter of aligning my head with my heart.

"I go to bed with the thought of you. I wake up with a deep

longing for you. I'm back to where I was five years ago. I guess the mind has a way of compensating for loss, of moving on."

"Oh, Anna!" I exclaimed as I pulled her towards me and kissed her. "What about Dante?"

"I miss him. He's a huge part of my life and my heart. But he knows that I'm not in love with him."

I noticed something wrapped around her right wrist. I lifted it up and brought it closer to my face. It was the rosary that I had left in the palm of her hand years ago. The beads looked worn, overused.

"I wear it at night when I pray," she said, embarrassed. "Dante got me a new one, but I don't think that one has a direct line to God like this one." She smiled, and then her face turned serious. "Jude, I'm not going to fight Him for you. He found you first, and so it's only fair that He gets to keep you. But when you go, at least you should know that I loved you. When you left me a lifetime ago, I saved these words close to my heart. I thought that if I kept them close to me, I would guard them and keep them until I saw you again. And I don't want to regret not ever saying those words, because everything I had felt, everything I wanted five years ago, is right here in front of me. Again."

"Tell me, Anna. I want to hear them from your lips. I want to feel them from your heart."

"I love you, Jude. I'm in love with you." She was choked up with emotion and her eyes began to moisten; the rain was about to fall once again. All I wanted was to touch her, to feel her. I wanted nothing more than to kiss her and be inside her so badly.

"Say it again."

"I love you." This time the words flowed easily.

I planted tiny kisses along her chin, down to her neck, lower and lower until my head could no longer be seen under the covers.

"Jude—" she gasped, shivering. She pushed the sheets down so she could watch me.

"Let me see you, Anna. Please, let me look at you."

Slowly, she slipped the straps of her gown off from her shoulders and revealed herself to me. Her breasts were the most exquisite works of art, perfectly shaped, perfect for me. This gesture. It meant the world to me.

Her lips, her mouth, her tongue began tenderly showing me the love that she had earlier admitted. I was bursting with emotion. No other feeling in the world would compare to the way your heart soared, your ears rang, your body shook simply from the touch of the only woman you had ever loved in your life.

"Come away with me, Blue," I said, panting in the middle of tender kisses and frantic touches.

"What do you mean?" she asked, puzzled at the sudden proposition.

"Let's just throw caution to the wind and go back to where we started. We only have three weeks left. I need more time with you, Blue. Please. Will you do it for me?"

# THIRTY-ONE
## Paradise

THE PASSENGER CABIN shook vigorously as the plane touched its wheels to the ground. Not even the loud thump of their weight on the asphalt nor the screeching of the brakes could rouse Anna from her sleep. I had spent the last four hours of our eighteen hour flight just watching her as she remained in a deep slumber. I thought about the past thirty-seven days and how my views on life had changed since then. I hadn't lost my faith or my conviction; in fact, I believed more than ever that Anna was a part of God's plan for me. Above all, I felt the power of His love for me, the depth of my certainty only reinforced by the harmony that now existed within the confines of both my heart and my soul.

And so there we were, back in paradise and looking like two honeymooners with a whole lifetime ahead of us. Only we didn't have a lifetime. We had twenty-one days. She opened her eyes to me and I saw the deep blue sea. I saw the sky and the sun and the heavenly clouds even before we stepped foot on the ground.

"Are we here?" She covered a yawn before stretching her arms straight up in the air.

"Yes, sleepyhead. We just lost two days getting here," I said worriedly.

"That's okay. We were together." She paused before laughing. "Even if I slept through it all. Gosh, I'm so sorry, those shifts at the hospital really killed me."

One hour later, we were in a white stretch limo on the way to the resort. She had no idea where we were going, and neither did I for that matter. We drove on a winding highway along the coast to the southernmost tip of Phuket.

"Where are we headed?" she asked sleepily. I was beginning to learn that she snoozed easily on any moving object. The limo was large and spacious, and yet we were scrunched together facing forward near the rear door. She leaned her head on my shoulder and closed her eyes.

"No idea. I think it's a resort called Sri Panwa. Katie made the arrangements for me." I chastised myself for allowing those words to leave my lips. "It's about an hour away still, so more sleeping time for you."

"Katie?" she asked, concerned. "Oh no. Your family is going to freak."

"Katie has my back, don't worry about it. She only wants me to be happy."

She nodded her head casually. "We'll talk about it, right? No matter what happens, you and I, we will find our peace after this trip." Her dainty fingers lovingly outlined the top of my lip. The sharp pain was gone, but the bruising and the numbness persisted. "It's healing very nicely and it's been less than a week."

I tilted her chin up and kissed her. "We're back in business," I announced as she covered her mouth to stifle another yawn. "Go back to sleep, Blue. You're going to need all your energy for tonight."

I was certain that my words were lost on her; she was out like a light in two seconds flat.

"WOW. THIS PLACE." She took a deep breath as she admired the one bedroom villa we had just checked into. The bellman had deposited our bags by the front door and had since left us alone. Check in time was three in the afternoon, but it was almost sunset by the time we arrived in our room. She took my hand excitedly as we toured the place together. "Look!" she exclaimed as she pointed to the splendid view of the Andaman Sea directly below us. We stood in the master bedroom surrounded by glass doors that led directly to an infinity pool overlooking a lush and abundant forest. "Where's the bath—" She spread open two slatted wooden doors to reveal a teak bathroom with two sinks made out of stone and a large Jacuzzi in the center. "Ah, here it is."

"Come look at this," I called out to her.

She followed my path through a side door and out onto a wooden deck connecting the master bedroom to the living area.

"An outdoor shower," she said as she entered the second set of doors and walked over to the L-shaped sofa. "I can just sit and watch the view from here."

"If there's anyone going to be doing any watching, I think it's going to be me."

She moved close to where I sat and settled herself on my lap. I pulled her face to mine and kissed her. We kissed for several minutes, lightly at first, until I was overcome with the need to claim her mouth as mine. Once I took all that I could from her, I moved my lips down towards her neck, intent on repeating the same process of exacting her for my own.

"Gray, wait," she said as she placed the palm of her hand against my chest in an attempt to push me away. "I'm so sorry, something just hit me. I think I'm going to be sick!"

She ran out in a panic then went in the other direction in search of the bathroom. I followed right behind to find her crouched on the floor, her mouth directed at the toilet bowl in front of her.

"Baby, are you okay?" I asked as I poured a bottle of water into a glass and knelt down on the floor beside her. I gently bunched her hair in my hands to hold if off her face. She heaved repeatedly before taking the glass and downing its contents.

"Okay. That's better. I feel better."

"Do you think it's something you ate on the plane?" I asked.

"That or maybe just the turbulence. I think I just need to lie down for a few minutes."

"Here," I stood up off the floor and offered her my hand. "Let's get you to bed. Just relax and don't worry about anything. I'll order us some room service and we can just stay in tonight."

"I'm sorry," she muttered. "Our first night here and I'm

useless."

"No, you're never useless. There's a fight on TV anyway, and the front desk said that I could stream it on pay-per-view. I'll watch the fight and you take a short nap, okay?"

"Okay." She nodded as she stood up and began to busy herself by unpacking her suitcase.

Minutes later, she was washed up and dressed in her pajamas, leaning against the headboard of our king-size bed. Seconds later she was fast asleep.

# THIRTY-TWO
## *The Infinity*

THE COOL AIR of the morning breeze chased after me as I ran along the beach just as the sun was rising over the horizon. From every point within this resort, whether from sea level or from high above our house on the hill, the joy of living was evident. The sun-streaked clouds, the singing birds, the colorful blooms, and the rushing ocean welcomed me as I walked the path that led me back to our villa. Anna slept through the night, only waking up once to smile at me as I climbed into bed next to her. I, on the other hand, had been ready to start my day at five o'clock this morning.

I took a short break and sat on a wooden bench to catch my breath.

*"Uncle Ralph, you there?" I asked nervously as my parents, Katie, and I*

sat around the table on the patio by the pool. I had called my parents the night after I stayed at Maggie's apartment and asked to have breakfast with them in the morning. My mother suggested that I invite Uncle Ralph to attend as well, almost as if she knew what I wanted to speak to them about. Unfortunately, the Monsignor was in California at a seminar, but insisted on calling in via teleconference. It was a rather funny arrangement to me, but I knew that I had to get them all together in one place before I left for Thailand.

"Yes, my son, I'm here. This is good timing, actually. It's seven o'clock here in San Francisco, and we don't start our session until 9:30 today."

"Uncle Ralph," said Katie. "You should see my brother sitting here next to us with a bad case of the Irish flu. His top lip looks bigger than his face."

"I told you, I tripped and fell as I got out of the cab!"

My mother reached out to touch my face in sympathy.

"Good Lord! What in the world happened, Jude? Aren't you too old to be doing that?"

"He got himself hammered over a woman. That same woman, Uncle Ralph," Katie said, tongue-in-cheek, and followed it up with a snicker. "My brother is regressing. He's doing what he should have been doing way back in high school."

I shook my head at her and mouthed, "Enough." My parents agreed by placing a finger over their lips to quiet her. I moved my mouth closer to the speaker phone. It hurt to enunciate my words, and I was too nervous to find anything the least bit amusing about what Katie had just said.

"Well, thanks, Uncle Ralph, for joining us. Mom and Dad and Katie are here too. I wanted to speak to you all about my decision. I'm not going back." I paused to correct myself. "I mean, I'm going back to request for a dispensation."

There was silence from both ends of the phone. Katie placed each of her hands on my parents before turning to me with a smile on her face. "Finally," *she said. "You're being honest with yourself."*

*Uncle Ralph was the first to react vocally. "I respect your decision, son, but let's talk through this a little bit, if you don't mind. Tell us what's in your heart. Why did it take so long for you to decide this?"*

*I took a deep breath and chose my words carefully. "Five years ago, I took a trip to the opposite end of the world to find myself. Instead, I lost myself in the eyes of the most beautiful woman I had ever seen. Her heart was pure, her soul was tortured. From the moment I met her, I knew that I wanted to be a part of her life. At first, I thought that we were meant to meet so that I could fix her. And as the days went by, I convinced myself that it was all we were to each other. When she rushed home to be with her family after the death of her mother, she took with her a part of me that left me with such emptiness that no amount of prayer or good works could even begin to fill. And so for four years, I loved her from afar, keeping in touch with her best friend, Dante Leola, and watching her blossom into her own."*

*My father and mother leaned forward, stealing glances at each other as I continued to speak.*

*"And then one year ago, it no longer became enough for me to live in her shadow. I was filled with such longing for her. What insanity, what a trick of fate that the diocese assigned me to help at the parish that served the hospital where she was completing her residency! I became bolder, more determined to be near her. Sometimes I would blend in with the crowd of people in the emergency room just to be able to watch her at work. There were times when she was close enough for me to touch her. I would inhale the air that she walked in, I would listen in on her conversations. I craved to be a part of her life."*

*"Did Father Scott know of this?" Uncle Ralph asked casually.*

*"I would go to confession and tell him what I had done, resolve never to do it again, and then go back to the hospital the following day to see her again. I sinned so much in the past year that the guilt was torturous, but it was worth*

*every moment that I spent in proximity to her."*

My mother started to cry. She leaned on my father, who gently rubbed her back.

*"Meu, why didn't you tell us? It breaks my heart to think that you went through this alone. Nothing you do will ever make us stop loving you. We are proud of you as Jude, our son, a man, a loving brother. We will always want your happiness first and foremost."*

My father took over with tears in his eyes. *"Jude, there are many things in this life that are incomprehensible. Many people spend wasted hours, years, lifetimes trying to follow a path that isn't set in stone. The decision that you made to enter the seminary years ago was based on who you were then. It may not be who you are now. This choice, here and now, defines who you are and what you stand for. You are a brave and honorable man, and we are so very proud of you."*

I jumped out of my seat and rushed into my father's arms. My mother followed suit, and soon we were mixing our laughter with our tears. Katie held my hand as we sat back down at the table.

*"Jude! Why didn't you tell me you were coming?"* Max ran out of the sliding doors and straight into my lap. *"Is Anna with you? Did you bring Anna?"*

*"Shh. Maxie, we're on a call right now with Uncle Ralph. Let's talk later, okay? Anna is working at the hospital but I'm going to see her tonight."*

*"Oh goodie! I'm going to send her a cupcake in a plastic bag. I made it at school yesterday. Can I, Jude? Can I send her a cupcake?"* he asked excitedly, his hands tightly clasped around my shoulders.

*"Of course you can! Go and wrap it up now, and I'll come in to catch up with you after this call."*

*"Okay!"* he said. *"Now all of you! Stop crying just because Jude came to visit us! He'll be back again soon, right, Jude?"*

*"That's right, Max. Now let us finish this call and I'll be right in," I said gently. He hopped to his feet and ran back inside the house.*

*Uncle Ralph reeled us back into the conversation. "It's not going to be that easy to receive a dispensation. You know that, right? They may ask you to take some more time before making a final decision. You know that's the Archbishop's official seminary, the most prestigious one. You might have to run it up the ladder to Rome."*

*"I know. I'm going to do everything that they ask me to, but my mind is made up. I'm taking Anna on a trip to Thailand tomorrow. We'll be gone for a few days."*

*"I know," my mother teased. "Katie told me."*

*"Katie! Again?" She shrugged her shoulders in response.*

*"Jude. One more thing," Uncle Ralph said emphatically. "It is a privilege to be called by the bishop to the sacrament of holy orders. Never take that for granted in your life. Live a life of gratitude and praise for the honor of being called. Do you remember the book I gave you about saving a thousand souls?"*

*"Yes. It says that everyone has an intrinsic calling to be holy but that each person can choose to serve in a different way."*

*"Yes, whether to the priesthood or religious life, or the single or married life. Which one will you choose?"*

*"Anna and I are going to fill this house with many grandchildren someday. I'm going to marry her if she'll have me. When this is all said and done, I will spend the rest of my life loving her."*

Nothing, not even the reverberating drone of an approaching tuk-tuk that caught me off guard could successfully unglue the smile that was pasted on my lips. She should be awake by now, so I needed to get going. I had big plans for the day, and I couldn't wait to tell her. The thoughts of kissing her again and touching her, and making love to her in the proper way and at the proper time were first and foremost on my mind. I felt free to be a man in love. Despite the occasional pangs of guilt about being in transition, I knew that it was only a matter of weeks before I would announce my decision to my superiors.

I hastily entered our villa, expecting to find her in bed but was filled with momentary trepidation when I realized she wasn't there. I breathed a sigh of relief as I caught her reflection in the window; she was in the pool with her back turned towards me, her gaze fixed in the direction of the sea. Her long red hair, straight and wet from the water, shone brightly from the rays of the sun. Slowly, she turned around in response to the sound of the sliding glass doors.

"Good morning," she greeted me.

"Hi. How are you feeling today?"

I leaned against the glass, content to just watch her, be that close to her. I smelled her, tasted her, felt her against me from that distance without a single touch. Just like the first time we met at the hut five years ago, I couldn't comprehend it then and was still devoid of any answers now.

"Much better. Sorry about yesterday. I think I caught a twenty-four hour bug or something. Do you know that the same thing happened to me when I first arrived five years ago?" She started to swim towards me. "I don't think I do very well on long trips. My shifts at the hospital have just been so hectic, but I'm fine now. How was your run?"

"It was great. It's beautiful down there. I can't wait to do some sightseeing today," I said. "Did you have breakfast?"

"I hope you don't mind. I ordered us some room service. They said it should be here in an hour. What do you want to do today?" she asked.

"I thought we could go to the nearby beach and just hang out. Maybe visit the temple there?" I offered.

"That sounds like a great idea. Hey, do you think we can go back to visit the kids at Takua Pa?" she asked. "If it's too far, that's okay. I just thought it would be nice to go back there again."

"Yes! It's not that far away. I've rented a car to take us there tomorrow." My ability to concentrate was shot—as she hopped in the water and moved closer and closer, the depth of the water proved shallower and shallower, until it completely uncovered her, and she stood in front of me in a skimpy white bikini, her beautiful body glowing and wet from the warm sun and salty sea.

"That's great!" she said, pleased.

And because she knew me, because she was the other half of my soul, and because she wanted it just as much, she began to put my thoughts into action. She reached both hands behind her head, untied her bikini top, and allowed it to fall into the water.

"We have exactly forty-five minutes before breakfast comes," she said.

I didn't need to be told twice. I tore my t-shirt and shorts off, and slipped into the warmth of her embrace. She wrapped her legs around me as I carried her towards the edge of the pool. Our kisses were different this time. They didn't start out slowly; they were deep and hungry, intense and consuming. I enclosed her mouth in mine, intent on tasting her, taking all of her in while she stroked me gently underneath the water.

I stopped in the middle of our passionate kisses and looked at her questioningly. I wanted her to command me, to urge me on.

There were so many things I'd never done before, and I wanted to discover it all with her.

"Do what you want with me," she said. "I won't break." She leaned her head back on the edge of the pool and stretched her arms out to give me complete access to her neck, breasts, and body. She moaned as I slipped two fingers inside of her while devouring her breasts with my teeth and tongue.

"Jude," she moaned. "Jude, I want you, please. Whole, make me whole." The beads of water on her neck dried up in colors under the warmth of the sun.

"I love you, Blue," I whispered, entering her at the same time. She felt warm and wonderful.

Her body was my home, my sustenance. *In heaven, there were many mansions.*

Her lips were my truth; they branded my skin and I belonged to her forever. *There was nothing more liberating than knowing you belong.*

Her touch gave me wings; it inspired me to great heights. *The best and most beautiful things in the world could not be seen or touched.*

Being inside her was my destiny, my reason for living. From that day on, I existed for the sole purpose of filling her, completing her. *There was darkness in intimacy. I craved that darkness with her.*

For a few seconds I refused to move; I wanted time to stand still, wanted to feel her around me for as long as I lived. Every moment with her was something to remember, but the look of satisfaction on her face, her cries, her moans, her rapture—these were flashes of our time together which I knew that I could never again live without. And then as if on cue, she spurred me to move.

"Give it to me, Gray. Give me everything you have." She wound her legs tightly around my waist as I drilled deep, more for myself because I selfishly wanted to take over every single part of her. The places that others had touched, I was going to sink in and wipe out all those before me.

We clawed at each other like animals, took pleasure in inflicting imminent pain. The sounds that we made were guttural—they echoed through the air and bounced up from the trees and into the sky. And when I came, I forgot what it was like to be lonely and confused and alone. She was mine and I was hers, not in the next life, nor in the future life, but here and now. In this life.

# THIRTY-THREE
## Familiar

WHAT HAPPENED IN the pool made me change my plans that day. I wanted to tell her as soon as possible, assure her that I was in this for the long haul. I believed that this would make the rest of our trip more relaxing; it would cast both our worries away and allow us to plan for the future. As far as she was concerned, she thought that we would be over in less than three weeks.

I called for the car while she was in the bathroom getting dressed and I notified the driver that we would be going to Ban Nam Khem instead. They informed me that it was a seventy minute drive to the north. Seventy minutes, seventy days, seventy years—time no longer played a part when it came to her. It was no longer a factor in the equation.

Sleeping Beauty rested in my arms as we drove up the coast

towards the small fishing village where we first found each other five years ago. Not knowing what to expect, I was keen on finding our little hut by the sea and reliving the happy times we shared while we were there. It seemed like eons ago, and life was so much simpler then—she had places to go and things to do, and I had a life plan that required the utmost commitment.

A tinge of guilt coursed through me as a sordid vision of our time in the pool flashed through my mind. But it was quickly dispelled as I felt her heavy breathing against my shoulder. I was hers now and there was no sin in pure and unconditional love.

The sudden braking of the car jolted her from her sleep. A few dogs and cows on the road were preventing us from moving any further.

"It feels so weird that we're in this car when we can really just get out and walk," she said, wiping the sleep from her eyes. "What's wrong with me, Gray? Why have I been sleeping so much?"

"I wore you out earlier," I said with a chuckle. She rolled her eyes. "Seriously, Blue, I really think you're just jetlagged. It will get better in the next day or so."

She reached for the door handle and put one foot on the ground. "Please tell him that we're getting out and walking. Can he park by the bus stop at the market and we can just meet him there in a few hours?"

She didn't wait for me to respond. By the time I gave the driver his instructions, she was walking down the road a few feet ahead of me. I would never tire of looking at her, of constantly describing her beauty. That day her hair was tied up in a ponytail and she was wearing a romper with flat sandals, her legs straight, firm, and endless. It took a great effort to cast those salacious thoughts from my mind. Celibacy had its price, and I was paying for it. Five long years of drought and I was ready to quench my thirst in the stream of her love.

She slowed down to allow me to catch up, and I took her hand as we crossed through the familiar path on the way to the medical clinic. We both stopped when we saw how much it had changed. The tiny structure had doubled in size and was now a bona fide building, complete with a parking lot, a driveway, and air conditioned rooms.

"It feels so different," she said as we walked through the sliding doors.

"Mr. Grayson!" someone called out to me. I could hardly recognize him, but it was Chiayo, now a skinny teenager, pushing a cart full of soft drinks around the waiting area.

"Goodness, is that you, Chiayo? You're all grown up!" I exclaimed as he offered me his hand.

A pretty teenage girl sidled up to me. "Mr. Grayson! It's me, Malee! The girl in your class! Do you remember me?"

"Malee! Wow, what are you all doing here?"

"We help with the drink cart after school," they said in unison.

"You guys remember my girlfriend, Anna?" I saw the look of contentment on her face, and our fingers locked around each other in silent unity.

"Oh yes!" said Malee. "Dr. Dillon!"

Anna happily hugged them both. Her facial expression changed considerably as she recognized her friend from long ago. He was a handsome man, blond with scruffy facial hair and light blue eyes.

"Delmar?" she whispered. She repeated herself, raising her voice this time. "Delmar, is that you?"

The handsome man ran towards her and swept her up in his arms. I felt a pang of jealousy before quickly reminding myself that this had been her past, but I was her future. They'd been housemates five years ago, but she was mine now.

"Annita!" He beamed as he freed her from his embrace. "*Comment ca va?*"

"*Tres bien, merci. Et toi, Delmar? Que fais tu ici?*"

I had no idea what she had said to him. She glanced at me uneasily and decided to switch back to English. "What are you doing here, Delmar?"

"I moved back here two years ago," he answered. "Where is Dante?"

"Two years? You've been here that long?" And then she let out a laugh. "Dante isn't here. He's in Germany on business. But you remember Jude Grayson?"

"Ah, yes, the elusive Mr. Grayson. How are you?" the cheeky Frenchman quipped.

"I'm good, thanks," I said, possessively placing an arm around Anna. This was my punishment. If I had chased her down as soon as I'd arrived back home, I wouldn't be dealing with the ghost of Leola. From the look of it, he'd been a substantial part of her past and I was just going to have to manage through it.

Delmar eyed me with a dubious look then turned his attention to Anna. "Anna, how long will you be here? Milena and the baby are at home; I am sure she would love to see you."

"So you married Milena?" she asked, somewhat surprised.

"*Mais oui.* We have a baby boy named Stephane."

"Congratulations, Delmar! And best wishes to you both. Unfortunately, we are only here for a day."

Our attention was diverted by a loud commotion and then the wheeling in of a man on a stretcher with blood jetting out of his chest.

"Dr. Davignon!" said a Thai nurse. "We need you right away. A boating mishap."

"Anna! Come with me," Delmar said as he ran to attend to the patient. "We could use your help over here."

She beamed at me, her eyes wide and glowing, asking for permission.

"Go, go." I laughed as I watched her dash excitedly towards the operating room.

"THERE YOU ARE." She was out of breath as she found me sitting on the floor of the waiting room two hours later, playing a game of backgammon with Chiayo. "Did you show him how it's done, Chiayo?" she teased.

I lined up the game pieces and handed the board back to him. She offered me her hand and I took it before bringing it to my lips for a kiss. To be able to show your love openly was truly liberating.

"He beat me every single time, Dr. Dillon," the young boy complained.

"Gray! How could you? Picking on a little boy like that!"

"He's a young man and he tried to cheat me twice!" I argued. "Chiayo, you're on the hook for a rematch okay? The next time we come, we can surely play again."

"Okay, Mr. Grayson! It was very nice seeing you."

"You too, Chiayo. Give my regards to your parents, and thank you for keeping me company."

Chiayo stretched his arm out and offered me a fist bump.

"WHERE TO NOW?" she asked as we walked hand in hand down the road leading us back to the village.

"Well, I was thinking that we should visit our little hut to see if it's still there," I suggested. She showed her appreciation for my idea by pulling me in for a kiss. "Or maybe we should go back to the villa," I muttered into her lips.

"Or," she winked at me with a batting of her eyelashes, "maybe we can continue this in our little hut. Just like old times."

"I like that plan," I said. "Let's go."

We moved quickly through the side streets and ran down the path that led us to the beach. We glanced at each other as we noticed the many changes that had taken place in the five years that we'd been gone. The lights that were strung along the leaves of the coconut trees high up in the sky were somewhat too bright and blinding, there were no more bamboo houses, and the beach had been cleared of the wild, growing grass. There was white sand all around us; it felt unnatural and pulverized. The markers that helped us remember where we once fell in love, where we danced and swam and played, were no longer visible. We walked in silence, immersed in our thoughts, afraid to point out the obvious.

*That things had changed and what once had been no longer was.*

Anna was the first to break through the solitude. "It feels so weird, doesn't it? So different." She squeezed my hand to get my attention.

"I know, I've been thinking the same thing."

"I do think that this, right here, is the spot where we first met," she said lightly, trying to deflect us from our saddened disposition.

"You think? The spot where you flung your phone out into the sea?"

"This very spot," she said confidently. "Wait. You saw that?"

"I saw everything. I followed you that night," I finally admitted.

"Oh my gosh! I'm in love with a certified stalker."

"Say that again."

"What? That you're a stalker?"

I yanked her towards me and kissed her. "No, the love part."

"What love part?" she shouted out before running away from me. I let her go for a while and then sprinted right behind her. "I'll race you to our hut!" she yelled, then sped away from me. She was a runner all right, but she forgot just how much taller I was, how much wider my strides were. I caught up with her in no time, lifting her up and slinging her over my shoulders. She struggled in my arms, laughing and giggling, desperately trying to get me to set her back down on the ground. I halted immediately after hitting a myriad of lights in front of me.

What was formerly the place where the little hut once stood was now a resort.

In the place of the pristine yellow sand was a beautifully manicured garden with villas lined up along its perimeter. A large sign connected each of the structures: TLH Resort and Spa.

"Our little hut, it's gone," she said with tears in her eyes. "Somehow I thought it would still be here. But of course not, I should have known that nothing remains forever."

"Blue."

"No, I'm okay. Let's walk back before it gets dark," she said, trying with all her might to contain her emotions.

I decided to take charge. "Come with me," I said, holding both her hands in mine and walking backwards towards the shore. We stopped right as our feet touched the water. The night sky had fallen, but the stars were out in full force. No matter how things changed, how they developed, how masked they became by the trappings of the modern age, the beauty of nature would always shine through.

"I have something for you," I whispered, fishing into my pocket to pull out a teal colored box tied up with a white silk ribbon. My heart was beating out of my chest. I was going to open up my heart and soul to her with the hope that it wasn't too late.

"Oh no! Jude. You didn't have to! What is it?"

"Please open it."

Slowly and with shaking hands, she tugged at the ribbon until it unraveled what was in the box. Tears filled her eyes as she held it up for me to see. It was a golden seahorse, intricately handmade and attached to a long gold hooped chain.

"I found it at Tiffany's while we were there to meet Maggie. The blue stone in its eye is the color of the ocean—I thought it was perfect because that's what I think about when I think of you. You burst into my life like the crashing of the surf and then you pulled me in like the tide, showing me a world of dreams and endless possibilities." I gently held her face in my hands and looked

248

into her eyes. "I will quarrel with the heavens and fight with destiny to be with you."

"How? How did you know about that verse?" She began to cry, tears streaking down her cheeks as I gently latched the necklace around her neck.

"I saw it on your key chain," I admitted. "For a while, I had a tough time reconciling the fact that I've become so wrapped up in this life. With you. When all I ever believed in before you was the life after this one. It took time for me to admit to myself that it's what I want to live for." She stood motionless, willing me to continue. "Anna, I'm found. I'm not lost anymore. I realized that I found myself on the very day that you stormed into my apartment and slapped the heck out of me. I learned that all I had to do was look into your eyes and everything I thought I lost in the past five years was never really gone. You kept my heart for me, nursed it, nurtured it, and delivered it back to me as soon as we saw each other again. I'm never going to stop prioritizing my love for God in my life. I can still love Him most of all, but I can only love Him truly by loving you. Because loving you makes me want to give of myself, loving you inspires me to bravery and courage and truth."

"Oh, Jude."

"Please let me finish." I held my hand up, urging her to keep listening. "I'm not going back. I'll return to the seminary to tie up loose ends and then I'll come back to you. Please, Blue. Please wait for me. I want to live the rest of my life with you, take care of you, love you with all my heart as I do now."

"What about your lifelong dream? The vocation that you were committed to?" she asked.

"I'm not that person anymore. My needs, my hopes, my dreams

for a future are all tied up in you. God is loving and forgiving. There's a reason for all this, why we met, why we fell in love. I know more than anything that this is my fate. To serve God as a man with a wife and a family. To bring up my children in His name and in His love. That's my vocation, Blue. Please say you'll wait for me."

I held on to her arms as I sat on the sand, urging her to take a seat next to me. We watched as the current ebbed and flowed and the rush of the waves teased our toes. She wiped the tears from her eyes and straightened up to compose herself. Tenderly, she held my face in her hands and kissed me. It was a kiss of affirmation, a covenant between me and her with the stars and the moon as our witnesses.

"Jude," she said as she pulled away. "I've been dreaming of this day for years. When I waited for you to come back to me, I held those words close to my heart. I wanted to tell you how much I loved you. I loved you from the first day that I met you. When you sat by my side in the water," she said with a light chuckle, "I loved you then. Because I'd never felt this kind of love before, never wanted to, until you."

We stayed facing each other, our foreheads touching, her body circled in my embrace.

"Do you know how lucky I am to have met you?" I said. "Many people speak endlessly about their love for God. They give huge amounts of money, participate in many other activities, go to church. But that's not what matters. It's what you do that goes unrecognized. What you think when you're alone, your convictions when you know that no one is listening. You are beauty and love and religion all wrapped up in one. You serve God more than anyone I know. You are a blessing. In loving Mikey and Dante, in the nameless patients that you care for, in the fact that you won't go up against God."

I started to cry. I shed my tears because the next few words I was about to say were those that had bound me for five years, kept me a prisoner. And now I was about to set myself free.

"Oh, Anna," I cried. "I am hopelessly, helplessly in love with you."

# THIRTY-FOUR
## It's Time

"YOU HARDLY ATE anything tonight." I covered Anna's hand in mine as we sat side by side in front of the sliding doors leading to our bedroom with our feet immersed in the water. We had just left a hot pot dinner at the resort restaurant minutes ago, and were now relaxing for the evening. The large boiling pot of soup had been surrounded by a vast array of meat, chicken, and fish. There was enough food to feed ten people, and as it turned out, it fed only one.

There were boats parked on the dock a thousand feet below us, and above us the ebony sky was satiny and pristine. She avoided my statement and responded with one of her own.

"Those skittering fish, they look like pearls in the ocean. Did I ever tell you that my mother loved pearls? Well, almost as much as diamonds, I guess they were her second obsession."

"Blue."

She turned to smile at me. "I'm fine. I just wasn't hungry."

"I was jealous of Delmar today," I said without reservation. I was looking for a reaction, a vehement declaration that none of that mattered, that I was the one she'd been waiting for all her life.

She looked away, her gaze directed somewhere far in the distance. "Don't be. There was nothing at all. Those years," she laughed self-consciously, "I thought that casual relationships were the only way to survive the pressures of med school."

I nodded. "Well, did they help? Did they get you through?"

"Every girl at that age needs affirmation, I guess. That's really all they did for me. Casual relationships are just that. Fleeting, transitory, shallow. They never really amount to anything." It was her turn to lapse into wistfulness, and her words did nothing to allay the green-eyed monster that lurked in the dark recess of my imagination. "Jude?"

"Hmm?"

"What was it like living in the seminary all those years? Did you enjoy it like I enjoyed medical school? Did you find fulfillment?"

"My days were filled with prayer and service to others. And a lot of reading—theology, scripture, you name it. I would read for days on end. There was a lot of reflection, but also a lot of interaction with people from all walks of life." I smiled as I remembered those years. Before her, those days were the best days of my life. They were enough to grant me purpose, to lead my direction. In the past three months, I couldn't even remember how I'd survived my life without her.

"Where there women?" she asked.

"Women?"

"Have you looked in the mirror lately? There must have been women chasing you all over the place," she badgered, trying to prove a point.

"Honestly, I never even paid attention. Sure, in college, I did slip up a few times, but the longest relationship I had was probably three months with a girl in my freshman classes who ended up sleeping with Peter." Her mouth hung open in surprise. "Before you say anything, no, she and I were over before he hooked up with her."

"Whew," she said, relieved. "I really like Peter too." The half curve of her lips did nothing to hide her somber frame of mind.

"Tell me what's really wrong, Anna. Talk to me."

"I miss my mom. If she were here, she would be so happy for us. I used to talk to her all the time about these things. She would tease me about being too level-headed for love. I also miss Dante. You know I'm going to have to speak to him when he gets back, don't you? I keep playing the scenarios in my head. I never led him on. I loved him. I've loved him since the day that I decided you were never coming back."

She fidgeted with her hands; I could tell that she was really torn up about it. It irritated me that my profession of love for her would incite this kind of emotion.

"Do you want to be with him?" There was no masking my sullen mood. I stiffened up my posture and crossed my arms in front of my chest.

"No! But I would never hurt him. He's been with me through everything, supported me, defended me, taken care of me," she pleaded with me to understand.

"So don't equate love with gratitude. I get it, Blue. You're thankful to him for everything. But if you love me, then there should be no guilt. No regret. Tell me you don't regret it," I heard myself say loudly. I was angry and I couldn't control myself. I wanted her to take me in her arms and soothe my insecurities about Delmar, about Leola. About all those who came before me. She lifted her legs out of the water, preparing to stand up. I grabbed her right arm and held it down to stop her from leaving. "Where are you going?" I asked.

"To walk. I need to go for a walk. I'm just a little dizzy, and I need to walk it off. It might be the elevation of the resort. It's messing with my equilibrium."

"Let me come with you," I argued. I dried my legs with a towel and slipped my feet into my sneakers.

"No, I just need a few minutes. I'll be right back." She brushed me away as I attempted to follow behind her.

I DIDN'T THINK I had moved since she left. I sat at the edge of our bed and stared at the rose petals scattered all over its cover surrounding two swan shaped towels conjoined at the mouth to form a heart. A flash of lightning in the sky quickly followed by booming thunder and then a deluge of rain interrupted my contemplation. I decided that it was time to search for her, worried that she may have gotten lost. I rushed outside just as I heard her light footsteps on the deck. She arrived as I was shutting the doors that led to the pool, her hair flat on her head, every inch of her showing through her soaked clothes. I missed her so much; I just wanted her to be okay.

"Dancing in the rain without me, are you now?" I teased, controlling the urge to run to her and sweep her in my arms.

"There's nothing to dance about when I'm not with you," she answered as she slowly walked towards me, stopping short as we came face to face.

"Well, I'm here now. And the heavens would be devastated if we didn't accept their invitation to dance," I said as she stepped into my arms. We stood outside in the open air, drenched by the rush of the storm, my arms enveloped around her body, slowly, gently, swaying to the music in our hearts.

"Sing to me the song in your head right now," I whispered in her ear. She stood on her toes and hummed the words of the sweetest song I had ever heard.

*It's a rush*
*I can't explain*
*Like you shot something crazy*
*Into my veins*
*And I'm ten feet*
*Off the ground*
*And I don't want*
*To come down*

And when it was over, she looked at me with so much tenderness that I wanted to cry. I needed to claim her, to be with her. We both knew that it was time to get out of the rain. She took my hand and drew me inside, the droplets of water making light pinging sounds on the wooden floor.

I reached for the towel that hung by the couch and gently wrapped her hair in it. She was shivering from the cold of her wet clothes. Leave it to me to improvise. I ran to the bed and unfolded the two kissing swans before helping her slip out of her shirt.

"Here," I said as I draped a towel over her shoulder. "Let's get you dried up." She slipped out of her shorts and underwear, leaving them in a sodden heap on the floor. But instead of wrapping the former swans around her, she allowed them to drop to the ground, her body still wet and dewy from the rain.

And so there she stood, completely naked before me.

She was Botticelli's Aphrodite, goddess of love and beauty, born of the sea foam with long flowing red hair. She was my strength and my weakness, my courage and my fear, my grace and my sin.

"I'm done running away from you," she said as the tears started to roll down her cheeks.

I didn't wait for her to say another word. I held her in my arms and kissed her. I tried to brush my lips against hers, tried to stay modest and gentle, but she pressed herself against me and took me in her hands. Slowly, she stepped backwards until she was able to sit down on the bed. I towered above her as she urged me to remove my shirt and proceeded to pull down my shorts. Before I knew it, I was laying on my back, rose petals all around me, while she played with me, using her mouth, her hands, her breasts. And then she rose up and lowered herself on me until I filled her to the hilt. I thrust upwards, making sure to keep up with the rhythm that seemed to drive her crazy.

"That night at the hotel after the fight, I was jealous that you were wearing that sexy night gown, that you had planned to wear it without knowing you would be seeing me. Who were you going to wear it for?" I grabbed her by the hips and slammed her down on me.

"Jude!" she screamed.

"Tell me," I groaned. "How do I make you forget him? How do I erase him from your memory?"

"Jude." Her eyes were closed, and my mouth was on her, pulling, biting, nipping.

I took control by raising her up and gently placing her on her back without breaking our connection. I lifted her arms up above her head and held them down.

"Open your eyes, Blue. Watch me give myself to you."

I pushed inside of her; I wanted to see how much of me she could take. And so I pumped in and out, while my lips remained on hers, muffling her words, stifling her sounds.

"Yeah. Is that too much, Blue? Is that too much?"

"No! No! Jude! That was Maggie's! I had ratty pajamas and I wanted to look nice for you! There's no one else. Please! It was always you!"

"Tell me. Tell me you love me," I commanded, the intensity of my thrusts still keeping the same pace.

"I love you! I love you, Jude. I'm so close. I'm so—"

And then the waves took us over, sweeping us both into oblivion. She had drained me of everything I had, and in turn, I gave until I had nothing left.

Everything I had ever owned was hers.

*Rest, my beautiful goddess, our battle has been won. You have slain the* dragon of envy and tonight we sleep in peace.

# THIRTY-FIVE
## It Ends Where It Begins

"THIS IS SO COOL." She smiled as we walked along the beach on the way to visit a temple that was located right by the waterfront. It occupied a large area of land adjacent to the shore, which made it difficult for other developments to infringe on this unspoiled stretch of sand.

"How are you feeling today? Are you sore?" We pledged our love for each other over and over again last night in every single part of the villa.

"No, not really. Just my wrists," she said, laughing. "Leave it to me to pollute a former seminarian."

She was referring to the little bit of role playing that we had done the night before.

"Hey, we're people too. Besides, I'm just a normal man now. A man who loves to be polluted by the woman he's crazy about." I drew her behind the crooked coconut tree and pressed myself against her without regard for the backdrop of holiness. There was no denying what I wanted to do right then.

"Here?" She gasped as I gripped her backside with my greedy hands.

"Here," I growled.

"Shame on you, Grayson. Today is a day for reflection." She rebuked me affectionately by shaking her head and steering us away from the covered grove of trees.

We fell silent as we approached the temple. The sound of chanting and praying flowed out of the open halls. It was tinier than most temples, set in the middle of the beach amidst tall grass and trees. Its strong white columns were decorated with golden leaves, and its multiple-tiered roof was intricately molded and carved. The inner walls of the temple were covered in paintings that depicted the life of Buddha, and there were eight seated monks dressed in orange robes directly facing the cloister. Large yellow candles on golden trays surrounded the four walls of the structure.

Anna and I stood by the doorway, hypnotized by the peaceful vision of the monks in their meditative state. We allowed the time to pass in silence, allowing the stillness to transport us to a place of peace and serenity. We were cloaked in the warmth of the breeze and in the grand design of the universe where man was one with nature and nature was one with a higher power. No matter your faith, I truly believe that there is a plan that's written in the stars and each one of us is merely a part of that constellation.

A few minutes later, I motioned for her to follow me outside. We took our places on a wooden bench facing the dock and sat side by side holding hands.

"In a few days, we'll be back in the States," I said. "I thought we could talk about what's next for us."

"Well, I go back to work." She smiled. "And I guess you'll be going back to Yonkers."

"Yeah, and don't forget that we both return to the dead of winter." I just had to throw it out there. "February 24th is when I go back to speak to my superiors."

"That's in two weeks," she said gloomily. "I'm going to try to reach Dante right when I arrive home. I had a couple of missed calls from him the other day. I tried to call him back but reception at the resort is horrible."

"Thank God for poor reception." I laughed.

She shook her head at me and kept on. "Mikey has a few days off at the end of the month, and I was thinking of taking a trip down to see my dad. They say that he'll be ready to start transitioning out of rehab in March sometime." Her fine, delicate thumbs lovingly skimmed the top of my wrist.

"And until then? Are you still on four day shifts?" I asked, my thoughts sidetracked by a pair of monks slowly approaching us.

"Pretty much," she answered. "I have to make up for this time off. I might take on double shifts until I get caught up." She looked at me with worry in her eyes. I wasn't sure whether they were caused by the monks or something else.

"Are you waiting for me, Blue? Will you wait? I'll submit my resignation as soon as I get back so that we can start our life together."

"Yes," she responded. "Of course I'll wait."

I rested her palm flat on the side of my face and kissed it.

"Mr. Grayson?" an elderly monk addressed me respectfully.

"Yes?"

"We have what you asked for. Please follow us," he instructed.

Anna's eyes searched mine despite allowing me to take her hand. The men brought us to an open area in the middle of the temple grounds. The bright green grass began where the soft yellow sand ended, surrounded on either side by lush, thick flowering bushes filled with butterflies and birds. In the center of the garden were two flattened pieces of rice paper that revealed a bamboo frame when lifted up by one of the monks.

"Oh my," Anna whispered to me. "What are they?" Her eyes grew wide with curiosity; she looked like a child on Christmas day.

The other monk, a younger man close to our age spoke up. "These are sky lanterns. We call them Khom Fai. There is a tradition in our country in which these lanterns are released into the sky during certain festivals. It is considered good luck. It symbolizes the floating away of all your worries and cares." He proceeded to light the candle in the interior of the lantern, causing it to expand like a balloon. Well, a pear-shaped balloon. These lanterns were rather large, about two feet high and one foot in diameter.

Anna laughed nervously, unashamed of the fact that she couldn't wait to hold one in her hands. The older monk asked me to clamp one end of the lanterns down with him, and the younger one motioned for Anna to do the same. The rice paper was fine and slippery. We held them with the pinched tips of our fingers, lightly but firmly, lest they fly away. We stood apart, our arms outstretched, four hands on each one while the wind threatened to tear them out of our grasp.

The older monk began to speak with his eyes closed. "Place all your worries and fears into these lanterns and trust them to the heavens. Cast them away and never look back. Let them go, leave them be. Today, your hearts and souls will be set free."

"Anna," I called out to her, "I'll go first and then you go next." I closed my eyes and announced loud enough for her to hear, "I embrace this love, my new life, my new vocation. I am no longer afraid to stand up for my truth."

The monk lifted his arms up together with mine, and we loosened our fingers until the wind carried the lantern away.

"I will no longer live my life in regret. I embrace this love, this man, and our future." The intensity of the moment filled our eyes with happy tears. The monks bowed their heads in reverence and readied themselves to leave. "Wait!" she shrieked excitedly. "Sir, please, would you take our picture?" She lovingly brushed her fingers on the golden charm that hung from her neck. "This is the happiest day of my life!"

THE REST OF the afternoon couldn't have been more perfect. Anna and I relaxed at Naiharn beach, on a secluded stretch of land that was only known to the locals in the area. I guess Delmar and his insider tips were good for something after all. We arrived back at the villa just as the sun was getting ready to skim its way across the golden sky. Sunset happened right as we got to the front door of our unit.

"Gray! Wait, let's watch the sun from here before we go back in," she said.

"No," I joked. "We have to go in so I can ravish you before dinner."

"Hmm." She stood on her toes and kissed me.

I kissed her back with no intention of easing my hold on her and spun her around so that she was facing the sky. "Here, you look at the sunset while I continue to do this," I whispered as I wrapped myself around her and kissed her like my life depended on it. I pulled her backwards, guiding her with my arms and making sure that I didn't trip her with my big feet, and we slowly stepped into the living room.

"Anna." We pulled apart in an instant to find Maggie sitting demurely on the couch, an overnight bag sitting neatly on the floor next to her feet.

"Mags! Hi! What a nice surprise!" She ran towards her friend with outstretched arms.

Silence. Not a word from Maggie as her eyes avoided Anna's.

Both women stopped short of touching and Anna's look turned to one of horror. She snapped her head towards me then quickly covered her mouth in a distinct gasp. "Oh my God! Oh my God! It's Mikey! What happened to Mikey?"

I started to make my way towards her but she placed both hands up to stop me from moving forward.

"Anna, it's not him. Mikey is fine." Maggie's voice shook, she kept wringing her hands over and over again.

"Is it my dad?" Anna asked, distressed and afraid. "Did he have a relapse?" She dug her heels in and stayed rooted to the very same spot.

Maggie shook her head and reluctantly forced out her words. "It's Dante."

A sigh of relief escaped from her lips. "Dante? He's in Germany on business. Is he here? Did he come back?" She bounced around the living room to see whether Maggie had brought anyone else with her. She couldn't stay still, her shoulders moved up and down repeatedly.

"Anna. Please sit," Maggie begged with tears in her eyes.

"No, I'm okay. Tell me. Is Dante here?" She crossed her arms tightly over her chest. Her hands were shaking; her strong and stable surgeon's hands quivered in perfect accord with the rhythm of her words.

"He was on the way here, to see you."

"Well, he's not here yet." She shot me a look of confusion, her mouth gaping open. "Did you know? Did he tell you he was coming?"

I shook my head vigorously, defensively. "No, I had no i—"

She glared at me, her eyes narrowing, her lips pressed tight. And then she turned to Maggie. "Where is he, Maggie?"

I ran across the room towards her, but she once again held up her hands and ordered me to back away.

"Spark. Please listen to me!" she sobbed. "There was—" She took a deep breath and then spewed the words out so rapidly that they disappeared into thin air. "A plane crash. In the Khao mountains about 200 miles from here. No survivors."

Anna lost her balance and fell on the floor. "No." She swatted her hand in the air. Once, twice, before bringing both hands to her face. "No!"

"Spark," Maggie said, "I'm so sorry."

She let out a laugh. Sinister, hostile almost. "What's Dante doing on a plane? What are you talking about? This isn't funny, Maggie!"

As Maggie attempted to step forward, Anna backed away. Maggie's voice shook, tears began to stream down her face. "Two days ago, he called to tell me that he was coming after you. Said he left you a message, asking you to wait for him."

Anna squeezed her eyes shut and clawed at her cheeks. "What? What the fuck are you talking about?!" she screamed at the top of her lungs. "Will somebody please tell me what in God's fucking name we are talking about?!"

"Blue," I said as I rushed towards her. She tried to fight me off, but I held her down and covered her with my body. She sat on the floor and started to sob uncontrollably before letting out a bloodcurdling wail. It was piercing, penetrating. I would have died for her if only to take away her pain.

She pointed a finger towards the air as if telling us all to give her a minute. "No, wait. Wait, wait. No. This isn't making sense. Just, just. No, wait. I don't want to—"

Maggie quickened her pace and knelt down in front of Anna. "Veronica called me. She told me the news. His family has flown out here, they're staying at a hotel closer to the crash site."

"No!" she insisted through her sobs. "That's impossible! He's been in Germany!"

Her mind had kicked into utmost denial; it simply couldn't fathom this news. The strength of my embrace did nothing to mitigate the violent trembling of her body.

Maggie addressed her quietly. She changed her tone, approaching Anna like a child, and it seemed to work better.

"Sparky, listen to me, okay? Just absorb it all, and if you have questions, I'll try to answer them as best as I can."

Anna nodded her head while her body took in shallow, jagged breaths, her tears continuing to pour down her cheeks.

"It wasn't planned. He decided to come here to talk you into going back with him. He said that he was stupid not to fight for you. That he would make you see how good you were for each other." Maggie had to stop for a brief moment as Anna's howls reached a deafening crescendo. "It was all over the evening news, Spark. When they confirmed that there were no survivors, it became a recovery mission and not a rescue mission. Yes, he was in Germany for almost two months."

And here's where I lost her. Or she lost herself.

She flew up on her feet with a force so strong that she knocked both me and Maggie on our behinds. She stood up, straight and tall, articulating her words through her sobs.

"He's a survivor, Maggie! Why the hell would they give up on finding him? He's alive! I know he is, I know he's somewhere just waiting for them to find him! He's out there somewhere! They need to find him!"

Maggie remained silent.

"What?! Answer me, dammit! What?"

"He's gone!" Maggie began to cry. "Anna, please! Please listen to me. We have to go home and wait for word. I'm here to take you home!"

She hugged herself with her arms and rocked back and forth. "I have to go. I have to go. I have to go," she chanted over and over again. "Let's go, let's go, let's go. Where's my suitcase? Let's go, let's go. Maggie, I'm asking you to help me get ready. Let's go."

She heaved a deep breath and vomited onto the floor. I stood up and ran to the bathroom to retrieve some paper towels, covering the soiled ground and hastening back towards her.

"Here it is again. This is fucking bullshit. Why did I allow myself to fall for this? This is insane! I want to be with Dante! This is fucking insane!"

I held her in my arms and led her towards the bed. "Anna, please, relax. Let me get you something to calm you down. We won't accomplish anything tonight. Your flight is booked for the morning. In the meantime, please relax, you're of no use to him if you're not well. You'll be on your way home in no time." I stroked her head as she wept into my chest. She dug her nails into my back.

*Cling to me, I thought. Cling to me because I will get you through this.*

"Gray, he called me from Germany, right? You saw my phone. He called me from Germany. He was there. In Germany. Germany."

"Yes, baby, yes." I held her tightly. "He did call."

"Let's go. Let's go. Let's go," she continued to chant.

"Yes, my love. We're going tomorrow. We'll take you to Dante."

"Okay. Okay. Okay. I have to. I have to go." She sat on the edge of the bed, swaying from side to side, muttering, whimpering, moaning. "I have to go. Home. Please Lord. I have to be with Dante."

# THIRTY-SIX
## Not In This Life

I LONGED TO give paradise a proper goodbye. The warm breeze, the golden sun, the bright red moon, the bottomless ocean. I wanted to take my time and bid her farewell; after all, it was only fitting to be filled with gratitude for the land that had given her to me. And so in the early hours of the morning, before the rise of the sun and the disappearance of the tide, I tied up my shoelaces for the last time and ran carelessly along the beach. I hadn't slept at all the night before. I held Anna through her tears and stood guard until the medication took over. I was grateful to her friend Afihsa for anticipating her reaction to the news by sending a few sleeping aids through Maggie to help Anna through the night.

The villa was still dark as I noiselessly let myself in, knowing full well that we still had two more hours before leaving for our flight. I was caught by surprise to find Anna sitting in the shadows wearing jeans and a blazer, surrounded by neatly lined up suitcases.

"Blue?" I whispered as I headed over to the lamp to turn the light on.

She raised her hands to shield her eyes. "No. Please don't turn the light on. It's better this way. It's better that I can't see you clearly," she said.

"See me? Why?" I asked as I took a seat on the chair directly across from her. "I can get ready in a few minutes. Let me just jump into the shower real quick."

"No. Maggie is waiting outside. We're taking an earlier flight. I just wanted to say goodbye."

"Goodbye?" My heart fell out of my chest. I knew then what it felt like to be dying. "I'm coming with you."

I saw the outline of her head shaking. "This is wrong. All wrong. I shouldn't have—" She caught her breath. "I need you to do this for me. I need you to stay. I need you to go back to your God. Go and become a priest. Pray for my mother and for Dante. Beseech Him, cut a deal with Him, ask your God to save him, make him come back."

She wasn't making any sense. Bring him back to life? Make him come back?

"Blue, please listen to me. I know you're upset. But I don't even have to go back to St. Joe's when we get home. I can stay with you. We can pray together, get through this together. We can—"

"No! Listen to me! No, we can't! Dante is mine. And I will not share him with you. You bring death with you wherever you go.

When I met you, I lost my mother. Now I'm being punished. God is punishing me for taking you away from Him. He's paying me back for ruining you. He's angry at me for taking His Adam from the Garden. He's shaming me into admitting my sins by taking Dante in your place!"

I tried to find her. I desperately tried to find her through the warmth in her voice, by the way she squinted her eyes when she thought too much, by the slight upturn of her mouth when she was trying to make a point. But she just wasn't there. Her movements were mechanical and robotic. Her hands sat in her lap the whole time, her legs crossed together.

"Please, Blue, no. That's not it at all. We can get through this together. I know that you said no promises. But I'm making you this promise. For now and forever, I will love only you. I love you. I want to spend the rest of my life with you. I can love no one else on heaven and earth the way that I love you. I will die for you, I will kill my soul for you. God has nothing to forgive. What we have, it's nothing to be ashamed of." I leaned over to touch her hands, but she pulled them away from me.

"If you truly love me," she cried, "you will go back to your God and pray for His mercy. Pray for Dante. Ask God to give him back to me."

Dante is gone. Nothing can ever bring him back.

"This is not the way, Anna."

"You. You were never mine. You were always His."

"You don't mean that," I said gently.

"It doesn't matter what I mean. It no longer counts. What matters is that I'm giving you back to your church so you can spend your life praying for us. Your God will listen to you. And when we find him," her voice grew louder, more certain, "and we will find him—when we find Dante, I will promise to stay with him forever."

She scooted herself to the end of the couch and stood up to leave. I threw myself on the floor, dropped down to my knees, and clasped my hands into a praying position. I didn't care that I was crying, I didn't care that I was shamelessly imploring her to stay.

"I worship you and only you. You are my madness, my sanity, my darkness and my light. I will never know one without the other. I don't want to live if it isn't a life with you. Please, Anna, please. I'm begging you, don't leave me."

Slowly she placed the seahorse who saw forever in its eyes in the palm of my hand before leaning over and lightly brushing back the hair on my head.

"A relationship based on death and loss can never survive. Jude. I can never be with you in this life, but I will hope for the next. Live for the next, Jude. Live for the next life."

And then she was gone.

I wish I could tell you that our story ended with the joy of the lanterns or with our whispered promises in the dark of the night. But instead it ended here. In the silence of daybreak surrounded by nothing but suitcases and empty dreams, and memories that would one day fade with time.

This is where it ended. This is where I died.

# PART IV:
## Reborn
## 2011 (Anna)

"Each night, when I go to sleep,
I die.
And the next morning, when I wake up,
I am reborn."

—Mahatma Gandhi

# THIRTY-SEVEN
## Shake, Rattle, & Roll

MAGGIE TOOK ME to the mountain resort where Dante's family had been stationed. Crowds of people jam packed the lobby and spilled into empty conference rooms filled with folding beds and personal belongings. Screams and wails were heard everywhere, people in suits and ties and plastic badges were carefully manning the area, maps and lists were posted on every single wall.

The Leolas refused to acknowledge my presence, blatantly ignoring me as I tried to mix in with the bereaved group of loved ones waiting to hear word from the Thai authorities. It took one day for them to confirm that there were no survivors. Everything happened in a vacuum, and I lived through those days in a blur. The process of identifying the bodies was restricted to immediate family members. I had not one piece of evidence that we were married. Not one form of identity had my married name. In reality,

I wasn't a part of his family, I was no longer his wife. I was an undeserving loved one. I was not even a friend. And so they ostracized me, kept me away, forced me to grieve all alone. I didn't have a right to hope, I didn't even have a right to be there.

And still, I sat and waited. At an adjacent hotel in a solitary room with the curtains drawn, seeking comfort in the despair of the darkness, finding hope in the light of the dawn.

Until Maggie walked in two days later, her eyes swollen from crying, her face puffy yet drawn.

"They found his body," she said as she took a seat next to the edge of the bed.

"Will they let me see him? Will you ask them, Maggie?" I clasped my hands together, brought them to my lips with my eyes closed. The unbearable pain of knowing that I would never see him again had killed me.

"No, Spark. They want you to leave. They want nothing to do with you."

I nodded my head in acquiescence. "I understand. I betrayed their son. I'll wait until they're ready. Let's go home, Maggie."

I ENTERED MY apartment on that wintry night in February, four days after I'd said goodbye to Jude. My phone was filled with messages from him, both texts and voicemails filled with promises and appeals, anger and pain.

*"I will wait for you, Blue. For as long as it takes, I'll wait for you."*

And after I deleted them, there was one message I had yet to retrieve. I would save it for the day that I would need it most. There will come a day when I will hear his voice and it will make me smile. Not that day. Some other time.

I convinced myself to think only of Dante, to channel all my anguish into finding a way to remember the times we had together.

To think that for the past few years, I'd been around death enough to detach myself from it; I had been trained to face it, to humanize it, to socialize it, and to explain it in logical terms. But it kept on brushing up against me, determined to become a part of my life.

Everything around me reminded me of Dante. The cupboard was stocked with his favorite coffee; the refrigerator, his favorite craft beers; the bathroom, his toiletries; and the closet still had his shirts, his jeans, his underwear. I hated him. I hated him for playing this cruel joke on me. Why did he have to leave little bits of himself in a place that was to become my only sanctuary?

"Damn you!" I yelled as I took the bottle of deodorant and threw it against the bathroom mirror. It felt good to watch it break in slow motion—first a crack, then a slight rip, and then the domino effect of its remnants falling one by one. The mirror in the hut in Thailand, my life today, pieces of brokenness spread out across the world. I followed it up by throwing his soap, his toothbrush, his razor. And then I ran into the kitchen and smashed the coffeemaker on the floor. I emptied the bag of coffee beans on the ground; his beer, the bottle opener in the shape of a naked woman, and his favorite coffee cup all came crashing down around my feet.

"Who's going to put me back together when I fall apart? Who's going to love me for who I am now that you're gone?" I cried. "There! Is this what you want? How much more are you going to take from me?" This was fate's final act. Its last revenge. I left Dante to be with Jude and now Dante was returning the favor.

When there was nothing else to toss around, I hurled myself to the ground, holding my knees to my chest, and rolled around and around. It didn't matter that the wood floor was burning my skin or that the shards of glass were dangerously close. I sobbed and wept and thrashed wildly, kicking and screaming ferociously at the top of my lungs. I cursed, I swore. I yelled my shame.

"I wasted five years of my life loving someone else when I should have just loved only you."

And then I begged and pleaded. "Please, please, please. I give you my happiness, I give you my life. I gave him up, dear God. He's yours. Please bring him back. Make this all a terrible mistake. Take away my pain. Bring Dante back to me."

THE CREAKING OF the floor was startling enough to yank me out of my trance. Someone else was in my apartment. I opened my eyes to the bright reflection of the sun against the pure white snow. I was still on the floor in the fetal position, my back stiff from having my knees up by my face, draped in the warmth of a blanket. Someone had come in the night to cover me up.

It was Maggie, broom and dustpan in hand, directing the broken glass away from my body. I continued to lay there watching as she moved quickly around the kitchen table before taking her place next to me. "I can see that you haven't done a thing since you've arrived."

I shook my head, my hands firmly clasping the blanket around my neck to protect me from the sudden chill in the air. It dawned on me that I had turned the heat off before leaving for Thailand with Jude.

"We should get ready for the wake tomorrow. Are you leaving the apartment today?" she asked gently while inattentively scrolling through her phone.

I nodded my head.

"I'm so sorry," she said somberly.

Another nod of my head. I continued to stare into space, aware of the fact that she had reclined herself on the floor facing me. She wrapped one arm around my waist and dabbed the tears in my eyes with the bottom of her sleeve.

"Did you get all those messages from Jude? Are you hungry? Do you want me to make you some coff—oh, never mind," she said, acknowledging the mess she had just cleaned up. "Listen. Donny gets back today. We can both take you to the church tomorrow. Anytime you want."

This time I shook my head.

"No? You're not going?" she asked.

"No, you don't have to take me," I muttered. "Thank you, though. Thank you for being here."

"We'll get through this, Anna. Trust me. We'll get through this. Donny and I will move our wedding date so I can be with you. I'll move in here and we can figure this all out," she assured me. Far in the distance, I noticed two large designer suitcases. She was serious about moving in.

"No," I croaked. "Tey wouldn't want you to do that. He was so happy for you and Donny. You have to go on. At least for him."

"Anna, I know you don't want to talk about this, but we have to address it sometime. Jude. What do you want me to tell him?"

I ignored her question and slowly lifted myself up off the floor.

I couldn't. I couldn't bear to hear the sound of his name. I didn't want to take the easy way out. I deserved to be alone.

*I am a widow. I will mourn for my husband.*

The blood rushed to my head and the room started to spin. I reached my arms out to her to steady myself. "Has anyone told Mikey?"

"Not yet," she said. "I was planning to have Donny pick him up from school if he's done with his classes."

"He needs to come home for the wake. We need to get him," I said. "Can we ask Peter to take my car and get him from school?"

"Okay," she agreed as she looked down to find large droplets of blood at her feet. Her expression immediately shifted to horror. "Oh my God! Anna, your face!"

It was then that I noticed some discomfort. I brought my fingers to my face to find a tiny scrap of glass imbedded in my skin. "Please find me a mirror and a Band-Aid," I told her.

She dashed back with the items I had asked for. "Oh my God! I'm going to die. I'm going to faint right here! There's so much blood! I can't take it! Anna, I'm going to faint!" she said, starting to hyperventilate. I grabbed her by the shoulders to try and calm her down. She was visibly pale and her knees started to buckle.

"No! Listen to me, Maggie! It's a tiny cut. I'm going to fix it right now. Look!" I held the mirror to my face and removed the piece of glass from my skin. It hurt like hell and left me wincing in pain. I affixed the Band-Aid on top of it and forced myself to smile.

"You see? It's all better now," I reassured her, making a mental note to clean the wound out at the hospital.

"Are you sure?" she asked. "It's still bleeding. Oh God."

"I'll be fine," I insisted. "I'm going to take a shower and go. Please wait for me, I'll be ready in a few minutes."

# THIRTY-EIGHT
## My Best Friend

FOUR YEARS AGO, I died alone. In a decrepit old bed, tied up to tubes that did nothing to take my sickness away. I stared into space while my life flashed right by me. Nurses came in and out, asking, "How are you? Do you need more meds? You seem to look fine."

No! I screamed. It's not my body that hurts. Please listen to me. Can't you see? Can't you see my tears through these smiles? Don't you know that I would give this all up—the accolades, the honors, the awards—for my heart? I want my heart back. I don't want to die.

Nobody knew my pain, no one cared. I was trapped in this useless body, pillaged by an overactive mind, slowly deteriorating from a grieving heart. Life was slipping away ever so progressively, and yet no one understood, no one could see my suffering; it was unimaginable how those ten days could have played such a large part in my life.

*Ten days? Oh, that was nothing. There's no way that can be love.*

*You'll forget soon enough. It wasn't long enough, Anna. You'll get over it.*

*He was just a friend. That's all he was. He was a friend you met in Thailand.*

*Take your meds, they will heal you. Drink your wine, it will make you forget.*

*Come party with us, meet other people. Look! That guy thinks you're hot! You'll be fine, Anna. You'll be okay.*

I knew full well how it was to die alone. I could only wish that Dante knew how much he was loved. By me, by everyone else. I hoped he died right away. I hoped that death did nothing to take his dignity away.

I stopped by the hospital to speak to Afihsa, who managed the process of transporting Dante's body back home. I knew she would take part in his autopsy. Aside from that, I wanted to tie up loose ends, take some time off and be there to help Mikey get through our loss. Maggie had dropped me off and was going to try to convince Dante's family to allow me to see him.

I proceeded directly to the public bathroom on my way to Afihsa's office to relieve myself of the bile that kept rising in my throat. During our drive to the hospital, I had kept it in, tried to ignore it, swallowed it repeatedly, and willed it to stay down. But then I decided to purge it completely from my body before walking in and taking charge of my situation. I pulled my hair back and rinsed my face off before brushing my teeth. I needed to ask her for some medication to treat whatever had been bothering my stomach lately. I was sure that it was a simple case of gastroenteritis, a virus I probably picked up on the plane which had caused me to come down with a bad case of the stomach flu.

She didn't look surprised when she saw me sitting in one of the uncomfortable green chairs in the waiting room of her office.

"Anna," she whispered as she pulled me into her arms. I started to cry. "Come, let's go into my office." She shut the door behind her and kept hold of my hand. We sat facing each other on the two seats adjacent to her desk. She pulled a Kleenex from the box on her shelf and handed it to me. "Oh sweetie, I'm so sorry," she whispered.

"Tell me what happened," I said, tears still streaming down my face. They were red and thick, mixed with the blood from my open wound.

*Blood and tears. The miraculous Madonna that cried blood for the sins of the world. All consuming pain transformed into rivulets of sorrow.*

"I will," she responded. "But what happened to your face? It looks like you need stitches. The blood hasn't clotted and your Band-Aid is soaked."

She pulled open the cabinet by the sink and spread out her instruments before motioning for me to move to the exam table. We stayed silent as she worked on me, her hands deft and light like butterfly touches on my skin. She was a skilled surgeon with a steady hand. When she was done, I urged her to continue with our conversation.

"How did he die?" I asked. "Did he suffer any pain?"

"The autopsy hasn't been conducted yet, it's scheduled for tomorrow morning. I'm told there were massive internal injuries."

"But he's here?" I sniffed. "Can I see him?"

"I don't know," she started off, clasping my hands in hers. "You know it's against the rules, and the family... Well, you know, there's still a lot of resentment about the reason he was in Thailand."

"But," I sobbed. "But I never got the chance to say goodbye! Please. I'm begging you. Five minutes, two minutes, anything! I'll die without ever seeing him again. He was my life for so long." I blew my nose and stood up to throw the Kleenex in the trash.

She shook her head and forced out a sigh before arising to retrieve a pile of papers from her desk. "Well, technically, you're still his wife." She sifted through them while tracing the small print with her fingers. "See here," she pointed to a spreadsheet on one of the pages. "They will keep him here until the morning and then send him to the funeral home. I don't imagine his family will be here very late. Why don't you go home and I'll call you when the coast is clear? Go directly to the 7th floor, room 7221."

She ran towards me as I burst into tears.

"Listen, I'll do everything I can for you, you name it. What do you want to do in the meantime?" she asked.

"There's nothing anyone can do," I cried.

"Oh, Anna. You both loved each other very much. Make that fact a comfort to you in this time." She tightened her arms around me.

"I left him for another man," I sobbed breathlessly.

"You left him out of respect. Out of honesty. That was a very courageous thing to do."

I nodded my head, cried a little bit more and then pulled away from her, out of breath but not out of tears.

"There's one more thing you need to know," she added.

My eyes grew wide, I was filled with trepidation.

"His optometrist recommended that he see me. He had an

abnormal growth on the right side of the brain. He told me he would come in for a biopsy after Germany."

*What kind of a God would be so determined to watch you suffer death by a thousand cuts?* I covered my face with my hands. There were no more tears left. And so instead, I wanted to bleed, to hurt, to riddle myself with the pain I deserved.

"Take some time off, Anna, okay? Take a leave of absence."

I nodded my head again.

"I'll take care of bringing it up at tomorrow's board meeting. Will you be able to afford it?"

I had thought about all of this during the long flight home from Thailand. I wouldn't need much. Mikey remained my priority and I had a few months' savings to tide us over. I nodded my head again.

"Anything you need, Anna," she said kindly.

"Thank you." I wiped my tears and checked my face in the mirror before straightening up to leave. My legs were stuck to the floor. My knees refused to unfold, my vision began to fade in and out. There were fire trucks and sirens screeching in my ear and a knife began to dig itself into my heart. My arms became leaden posts anchored to the ground. I couldn't lift them up to save my life.

"Anna?" She looked at me, her eyes crossed in puzzlement as she reached out to stroke my arm. "Are you all right?"

"I-I can't—"

I could no longer hear her voice. In fact, I didn't hear anything. I couldn't see anything, never felt anything.

"OH GOD, NO. What happened now?" I looked around to find myself in Afihsa's examination room.

"You fainted." she said, smiling.

"And?" I asked, annoyed that she seemed to know something that I didn't.

She drew the curtains back and waved a thin white stick in the air. "Are you strong enough to stand up, Anna? I need you to pee on this stick," she said.

"You're crazy," I barked. "I'm not peeing on a stick. I didn't have lunch and my blood sugar probably went crazy."

She turned around and wheeled an ultrasound machine next to my bed. "Then we're just going to have to find out this way," she said calmly.

Afihsa's goofy grin remained pasted on her face. She continued on by lifting up my blouse, inch by inch, careful not to upset me.

"Wait! Stop! I'm not doing this. Stop!" I yelled, holding her hand down tightly against my belly.

"Anna, when was the last time you had your period?"

"I'm not answering you," I said defensively. "I'm fine now. Just have them get me some food. Besides, I used to be on Ortho Novum. I only stopped when Dante and I—" I paused to glare at her. If I had any ounce of energy left in me, I would have smacked that grin right off her face.

"When, Anna?" she asked again.

"November, but... I've been under a lot of stress."

She inched my blouse up again and this time I let her. There was no stopping this foolishness until I proved her wrong. She squirted the warm jelly on my stomach and pressed the round end of the sonar probe on my skin.

"Yup, just as I suspected. Listen!" she ordered while punching some information into the ultrasound machine.

The sound of bubbles, steady gurgling, pulsating beats among a swishing sound of water overpowered the silence of the room.

I was too shocked to say a word. My eyes were fixed on the screen.

"Oh wait. Listen," Afihsa said as she slid the sonar to the opposite end of my belly. "Another one. Two heartbeats!"

She wasn't going to hear a single peep out of me. I was too busy staring at the ceiling, counting the days between Dante and Jude in my head. "And by the looks of this," Afihsa continued, "I would say that you are... let's see," she moved the probe around some more, "you are eight weeks pregnant. This baby—I mean these babies, were conceived around Christmas."

December 26th. That was when I had barged into his apartment and ended up in his bed.

"That's impossible!" I shrieked. "I've been on the pill!"

"Shit happens, Anna," Afihsa said indifferently. "And this is good shit, not bad shit. You're pregnant with twins."

I was caught up in distress over what was right in front of me. Instead of mourning the loss of my love, there we were, graciously celebrating another man's child, another man's victory. Gradually I began to piece together the events of the past few days. Something for something. God was preparing me for a life without Dante. Like a father giving his daughter away on her wedding day.

And then I thought of Jude. I felt the pain of missing him in my bones. What an excellent father he would have been.

"Thank you," was all I could say.

Afihsa quickly changed the subject. "Dr. Malcolm's office is on the second floor. I suggest you still go and see him so you can get formally tested and assessed. He can also give you your exact due date. Congratulations!" She pushed the ultrasound machine back and took a seat on the bed next to me. "This is your reason to fight. Fight to go on, Anna. A new life is waiting. And no matter what happens from this day forward, don't ever, ever lose faith."

# THIRTY-NINE
## Thirty Seconds to Mars

IT WAS LATE into the night by the time I received a text from Afihsa that the coast was clear.

*Come on over,* she had said. *Use your keycard to enter the room. His family left about an hour ago.*

It took me two hours to gather up the courage to drive back to the hospital. Seeing him would put an end to the years we had together, to the time that he stayed in my life. I wasn't ready for the finality of it all. There were pockets in my mind that still fooled me into thinking that this was all a mistake. A dream. That in a few hours, he would saunter back into the apartment, laugh at me and then take me in his arms and assure me that this was all just a big joke. A test.

*I'm back now,* I would tell him. *You never know what you have until*

*you've lost it. I know now, I would say. I don't ever want to be away from you.
Don't do this to me again.*

I held the keycard tightly in my hand as I stepped out of the
elevator and stumbled along the whitewashed corridor, using all
my strength to stay the course, to keep walking towards my
destination. This wasn't the basement, the morgue. I knew that
special arrangements must have been made to keep him in a room
for the day. The Leolas were benefactors of this hospital, and this
was no doubt one of the special favors that were called in for this
circumstance. I was a prisoner on death row walking towards my
fate. Walking in to confirm my fate. For it had been decided for
me less than one week ago.

Seconds later, I stood outside the door of room 7221, awash
with unspeakable fear and unimaginable sadness. How did I want
to remember him? Do I want to linger in my last memory of him?
The day I saw him in his office, before he left for Germany? Didn't
we say goodbye then?

*"Anna, what are you doing here?" he'd asked, his eyes lighting up as he
saw me sitting on the chair opposite his desk. He had rushed in after cutting
short a meeting once his secretary told him I was waiting.*

*Everything in that office was Dante personified. The leather desk with its
matching accessories, couches and end tables and the tall, seamless windows
overlooking the Hudson River. He wore a grey suit with a light blue button
down shirt and a rose colored tie. He looked powerful, invincible, not anything
like the broken man in my bed the night before. Snippets of his successful career
adorned the brick walls that surrounded us. Certificates, awards, life-sized
paintings of New York graffiti art in graphic colors and shapes, golf clubs, an
Artus turntable worth hundreds of thousands of dollars surrounded by vinyl*

*records from every era. He took a seat and leaned back on his chair. We were interrupted by the clicking of high heels and a forced clearing of the throat.*

*"I'm so sorry, Mr. Leola, but your eleven o'clock is waiting in 4 South," Nelly squeaked apologetically. I wondered whether she knew that we had separated. Her skirt seemed shorter, her blouse too fitted.*

*"This won't take long, Nelly," he snapped. "Offer him some coffee, tell him I'm stuck in another conference call."*

*I pushed myself off the chair with my arms. "It's okay," I mumbled. "I can go. I just wanted to see you after—"*

*Nelly had long since then run out of the office. He leaned in. "After what?"*

*After having Jude inside of me. To validate my feelings, say goodbye in the proper way.*

*"Nothing. I just wanted to see you, that's all."*

*"But I was going to stop by anyway, to drop Mikey off, remember?"*

*"Yeah, but…"*

*"Where were you last night, Anna?"*

*"At the hospital. No point in staying home so I took an extra shift." Protecting my secrets with lies. This is what it has come to.*

*"Ah."*

*More awkward silence. Cars zinged to and fro twenty-eight floors below us. Horns tooting, ambulances, fire trucks, loud music from the holiday markets along the riverfront intent on filling us with Christmas cheer. He stood up, circled around the desk and sat down right in front of me. I reached over to lay my hand on his thigh but he flinched and moved away.*

*"I'm so sorry, Tey. I'm beside myself, trying to find ways to tell you how sorry I am. I didn't want this to happen between us. You've been so wonderful to me."*

*"I don't want your gratitude, Anna. I wanted your love."*

*"I loved you." I quickly caught myself. "Love. I love you."*

*"Not enough to want to start a family with me. I understand it now. Your constant reluctance to have babies—you were waiting for him to come back."*

*"No! That's not it! No. I wanted to love you the way you deserve to be loved. I couldn't give you enough of myself with him always lurking in the background. We talked about it! I want to deserve you. I don't deserve you!"*

*"Fuck it!" He grabbed me by the shoulders and shook me before yelling at the top of his lungs. "What the fuck do you think I am? Stupid? Quit dancing around this, will you please? You're scared and confused, but you had to know that one day it would come to a head. This is what you'd been holding out for. Own it, Spark! Tell me what you really mean! Please, have more respect for me than that!" People walking by his office stopped short and peeked inside as they heard him bellow. He pressed the button by the wall to activate the shades. "Tell me the truth!" We watched the blinds roll down in silence until there we were, cocooned in the darkness.*

*I twisted my fingers around my wedding ring until it slipped off, and placed it on the table. "I. I. I want to be with Jude," I whispered.*

*He lost his balance as if taken aback by an unforeseen force. I will never forget the look of pain on his face, the grimacing flutter of his eyes, the sallowness of his cheeks. He clutched his heart before quickly regaining his composure. "So, go. Fucking go."*

*I blocked his path as he moved ahead and stepped into his arms. "Please, Tey. I swear to you! I thought I was over him! If he didn't come back we would've been fine!"*

*He cast a fleeting glance on the diamond that sat atop his desk.*

*"But he did," he whispered as he held me tighter than he'd ever done, stealing whiffs of my hair, nuzzling my neck. I felt cheap, dirty, sullied. This was his way of saying goodbye. "He came back."*

*And with those words, he walked away.*

I let out a loud gasp as the heavy door closed behind me and I caught a glimpse of the large metal bed in the middle of the room. The pain in my chest left me breathless, unable to move my feet towards him. He was draped in a light white sheet that covered him entirely. I stood for a moment before gathering up the strength to move forward. It took ten long steps to get me to his side, one step for each year we had been together. Steps that could never be retraced, never be recovered. Slowly, I pulled back the sheet to reveal his face. He was still as beautiful as ever, sleeping in peace with not a mark on him.

He'd been gone for five days.

This sudden realization knocked me down on my knees, besieged me with convulsions that wracked my body and shook me up with tears. I was sobbing, wailing, banging my fists on the cold cement floor, begging for him to forgive me. I was the prodigal lover who had returned after wandering halfway around the world with another man. How would I explain it? How would I even begin to show him true repentance?

And then when I thought I had no more tears to shed, I sat on the floor, leaned my back against the bed's metal legs and closed my eyes. A distinctive chill took over the room. It was cold in there to begin with, but this time, the air in the room had turned into ice.

"Spark." The unmistakable sound of his voice. I shot my eyes open to find him sitting next to me. Legs folded, arms gathered around his knees.

"Tey!" I shrieked. A feeling of calm washed upon me. I was sitting next to my best friend. I reached over to touch him. His skin felt warm, his eyes were full of life. Bright green and transparent. He wore his favorite plaid shirt and torn up jeans. I was shocked by what was taking place, and yet, the insurmountable surge of love and security that I felt whenever he was around put me at ease. He felt like home; he was my home. I kissed him tenderly on the lips and scooted myself downward so that I could lean my head on his shoulder. His lifted his arm and gently stroked my hair with his fingers.

"Hi," I whispered.

"What happened to your face?" he asked, tilting my chin up to take a look at my cheeks.

"Nothing, another clumsy slip," I answered facetiously.

"My poor baby." He traced his finger right above the jagged line. "Are you mad at me?"

"Yes," I said.

"Like, on a scale of one to ten?"

"Ten."

"Good to know. Will you spank me then?" His tone was light, his voice a bit stronger.

"Tey!" I lifted my head up to see him smile. But the heaviness in my heart gave me away, and I returned his lighthearted comment with unrelenting tears.

He tightened his hold on me while I sobbed uncontrollably. He didn't move or say a word as I released my anger, my sadness, and my fears into his neck. He waited patiently, remained strong and solid, rubbing my back with his hand. I reached for his hand, swiped it across my face, brought it to my lips, and kissed it.

"I'm sorry, Spark."

I sat up and looked into his eyes. "I'm the one who should be sorry. You're gone because of me!"

"I know I never returned your calls. I was trying so hard to forget. I met a woman while I was there and we were together for those short weeks." He glanced at me to gauge my reaction.

"Did she make you happy?" I touched his face with my fingers.

"She did. For the time being, it worked. After all my anger, of course. And then as time went by, she saw how much I missed you. She convinced me to go after you, follow you to Thailand."

"Aha. So this is her fault!" I exclaimed.

He laughed at my doggedness. "Things are falling into place. You were meant to be with Jude." He enunciated every syllable as if he wanted his words to penetrate through my skin.

"Not like this. Not at your expense," I replied. "This is so unfair."

"Okay, I admit it, this is a little extreme." He let out a whoop as he caught the look of humiliation on my face. I dipped my head so that my nose was rubbing itself on his cheek. He reciprocated by holding my head in place. I aligned my lips with his and kissed him. "Seriously," he said as I pulled away, "it would have been you and him no matter what happened. We can't change the master plan, we just have to roll with it. The blueprint was drawn ages ago."

"I'm not letting you go. I'll die if you leave me. It's been proven before, I can survive anything when you're with me. You're part of my program and your love has always been the main act. Jude was the subplot," I said, tears in my eyes.

"I am! I'm a part of your grand plan. But it's me who's the subplot. You see, this is all happening for a reason. Life is short, Spark. We'd been living through this bullshit for five years." I understood what he was trying to do; he was making sure that I would be all right without him. He wanted to hear me say that I was in love with someone else. He waited for me to respond. When I didn't, he continued. "Isn't there something else you need to tell me?"

"I'm pregnant."

"Dang, that guy's good!" My mouth hung open in shock. "Lighten up, Spark! Dead people see everything. I know and it's such great news!"

"I didn't mean for it to happen," I cried. "I fell more in love with him in the fifty-eight days we had together. But it's not that I didn't think of you, Tey. I—"

"Shhh," he whispered. "I know. You don't have to explain anything. The fact that you gave him up for that one tiny glimmer of hope for me. I know."

The dam burst and I became a blubbering mess. I cried because I felt relief. All I ever wanted was to make him understand that I had never stopped loving him. That he was always on my mind and in my heart. "I'm so ashamed. I wanted to do this the right way, you know. When you encouraged me to spend time with Jude, I thought that it would be the only way for me to get over him. To move on. Please believe me, I was going to tell you as soon as we got back from Thailand. I was going to ask for a divorce."

He continued to stroke my hair as I firmly rested my head on his shoulder. We were silent for a few seconds. I was besieged with need for his forgiveness.

"You know now, don't you?" he asked.

"Yes."

"And you know why I didn't tell you." He squeezed my hand as he said this.

"Yes."

Our hearts whispered to one another. But all I wanted to do was to listen to his voice, to hear him speak. And I knew that he had so much to say before we ran out of time. "You would have left him to take care of me. That's just who you are."

I tilted my head back to take a hard look at his face. We locked eyes for an eternity. It was as if he, too, was trying hard to commit my face to memory.

"I just thought… I thought we had all the time in the world," I cried.

He nodded his head and squeezed my hand. "I'm so proud of you. I've never met anyone as steadfast, uncompromising, and principled as you," he continued. "It's been an honor to be in your life. Never change, okay?"

"The honor is mine, Tey. Thank you for loving me the way that you do."

"It's you, Spark. You're the one I should be thanking. You gave yourself to me for one year. I kissed your lips, held your hand, and shared your dreams with you. What a privilege that was for me. I will leave knowing that you loved me back."

*He will leave. He will float around the universe without me.*

"The James." I smiled, remembering the night that started it all for us.

"The best night of my life," he answered. "You truly belonged to me then."

"And now, all I have are those memories. God has punished me, made sure that I suffer for the rest of my life," I said with resentment.

"Suffering is redemptive," he countered. "Didn't he tell you that when he explained the meaning of the breaking of bread at mass?"

"Who told you that?" I snapped irritably. I didn't want to talk about Jude. I wanted to tell him how much each moment we had together meant to me. There was so much to say, and I knew that time wasn't on my side.

"Jude. He said that the breaking of bread is symbolic of brokenness. You have to be broken to be saved. That Christianity is rooted in suffering. Jesus was open about how being a disciple and following in His footsteps will surely castigate you, banish you from the rest of the world. That it was a necessary torment."

"How did—" I started to say. And then I understood. *The dead, they see everything.*

His eyes lit up and the softening of his face told me that this was what he truly believed. There was a lifting of the corners of his mouth. Not so much a smile, but a reassurance.

"Don't cry," he urged. "Please don't cry."

"I can't help it. I'm scared. I'm only crying because I feel sorry for myself. I don't feel sorry for you, you'll be in a better place, I know." I continuously swiped my hand across my face to dry my tears and did it with such a force that for a while, I thought I had bruised myself. I would take any pain but this. Any pain.

"I said some mean things to you when we fought that day you came to my office. I didn't mean them, please know that," he said breathlessly. There were times during this moment that I could hardly discern his words. The volume of his voice drifted in and out like a dream.

"I know. It wasn't you. Those weren't your words," I said. "You are the kindest, most generous, most lovable human being I have ever known. Only the good die young. And I'm terrified that I won't be seeing you for a while."

"Oh, Spark. You're the beauty in this world that life has to offer. You have to know that. You have this great shame about Jude, but you don't see how easy it is to fall in love with you."

I refused to remove my eyes from his face. I wanted to enshrine him forever in my memory—the slightly raised scar above his nose, the tiny mole on his left eyelid, the wrinkle just above his lip, and the lush green forest in his eyes. Everything he said, the way he said them, his voice, his laughter. I wanted to shine a camera on him to record every single detail. How did I do that? How did I keep him with me? How did I keep him when I had to let him go?

"Fine, you win," I gave in. "I'll see you in heaven then?"

"I'll see you." He smiled. "In the meantime, while you're waiting for your turn, know that everything happens for a reason. Don't be angry like you were when your mother passed away, okay? Don't waste your time grieving for me, because I want this. I want you to remember me when I was strong, hot and hunky, funny and oversexed." We both laughed out loud. It was the last time I would hear that sweet, wonderful sound. His laughter. That's what I would miss the most.

"Live life for me. And go to him. Go to Jude. Make lots of beautiful babies." He paused as he strained his eyes to gain focus. "Name one after me. And if you don't behave, I'll be back to set you straight." I settled my cheek next to his and closed my eyes as he continued to speak. The vibration of his voice against my skin, the warm air that blew out of his lips into my hair. I noticed everything, felt every single sensation, bathed myself in his presence and wished that I could absorb it into my veins. "He's a good guy, Spark. He wanted to tell you the truth. I was the one who told him that there was no point in doing so. I was the selfish one."

I couldn't see him through my tears. I blinked several times, afraid that I would lose sight of him.

"That doesn't matter to me now. I love you, Tey. Please, please don't leave me. You promised! You promised you would never leave!" I watched as he struggled to stay with me; the force of death was coercive and deceitful. He nodded his head at something far off on the opposite end of the room.

"You and I, we both need our peace. I want you to have yours. You were not the cause of this—this was simply part of the grand design. You gave me the happiest years of my life, you inspired me to become who I am. You kept me going after my dad died, you taught me about strength of character and conviction. You need to let me go, okay? Let me live out my next life. This life has been fulfilled."

It made sense to me. The reason he was here. "You're here because of this."

"Yes. I couldn't leave without making sure you'd be okay. No shortcuts, Spark. That's never been my style."

Fate had always toyed with me. Given me the opposite of everything I had ever prayed for. I asked him not to leave me, and in a matter of seconds, he would be gone.

"Don't you see? It's all part of God's plan. He won't leave you alone. He gave us Jude to make sure that you won't be alone. Jude is here to take care of you for me. For me, Spark."

I gave in to the flow of my tears. I surrendered to the agony of saying goodbye for the last time. "You can go now, Tey. You deserve your peace. I will always, always love you. And I will always look for you in the stars."

He turned to me and smiled.

It was the most glorious of smiles. A smile from which dreams are made. A smile to heal the most fragmented of hearts. A smile full of love that would last for a lifetime.

I heard his voice for the very last time. "I have the lanterns, Spark. Tell him that I have your lanterns!"

A bright, blinding light shone in through the window and I felt his hold slipping away, but still I gripped and grasped and held on until I found myself clinging to nothing but empty space.

And then like light, gentle rain on a soft bed of grass, a soothing, consoling whisper filled my ears.

*"Remember, Spark. Your name. Fighter. Spitfire. Love. You."*

# FORTY
## *Hole in My Heart*

"SO HOW DO *you like it? Is it good enough for our first date?"* Dante asked as he led me through the door, away from the crowded bar and out into the open air.

"*I love it!*" I exclaimed. "*I think it's nicer than the other rooftop bars in New York. Makes me wonder why there's no one here.*"

He smiled at me impishly but didn't say a word, taking pleasure in the fact that I hated surprises. We took our places on the wooden chairs right by the glass barrier overlooking the city on a windless summer night. The sky was clear, the moon was glowing, and the stars sparkled through the heavens like fireworks on the fourth of July.

Independence. The day I declared myself free to love again.

A group of men appeared out of nowhere and began to play music on their violins. Two waiters appeared with an ice bucket and a bottle of champagne, *and two more waiters with plates upon plates of appetizers followed suit.*

*A beautiful woman with short black hair and a flowing red dress took her place by the microphone, and from her lips came the most beautiful song of love. It was about the night a nightingale sang in a place where two people had just met.*

*"Wait a minute," I said, embarrassed. "You rented the whole place?"*

*"I wanted tonight to be special. There's something I want to say to you," he said as he leaned over to me and took my hands in his. He cleared his throat and began in a shaky voice.*

*"Spark, sometimes I forget how long I've known you. We've been friends for so many years, shared so many experiences, been to so many places together. And yet, after all this time, every day I spend with you is as wonderful and exciting as the first day that I met you. I'm in love with you, Spark. I so desperately want out of this friendship so that I can become your partner in life instead. I want to try to make you happy. I want to love you, to kiss you, to touch you, to make love to you. Please, Spark. Please give me a chance. Please tell me that you'll give us a chance." He looked at me searchingly, waiting for any kind of reaction.*

*"You're saying you want us to date? As in exclusively?" I asked, surprised.*

*He reached for my cheeks and held them tenderly in his hands. Slowly, gently, he pulled my face towards him and kissed me. It was poignant and heartrending, real and authentic. I could feel his love in the fragility of his emotions; I could taste forever in the sweetness of his kiss. For the first time in a long time, I had hope that my heart could live again.*

*"I love you, Anna Dillon," he whispered as the violins played to the melody in my heart.*

*"Guess what?" I teased, skimming my tongue across his lips, believing more than ever that he would be the one to make me forget. I missed being me. I wanted myself back, the strong, silly, outrageously obstinate, happy me.*

"*What?*" *he asked, still holding my face in place and rubbing his nose against mine.*

"*I love you too, Dante Leola.*"


They found me with him the next day. Veronica and Elena Leola, mother and daughter, burst into tears as they walked into the room to find me with their son. I had fallen asleep on the stretcher next to him, my body squeezed tightly against the cold sheet that separated me from his skin. No one asked this question out loud. How I ended up there or how they found us with his hands clasped firmly around mine and his head facing in my direction was never mentioned nor brought up ever again. The two women held me in their arms for a long time before we gently covered him up. I planted one last kiss on his lips before they led me out the door. And into the Psych Ward.

On a rainy day in the middle of March, just two weeks shy of turning thirty and surrounded by friends and family, Dante Leola was offered up to the heavens. I wished I could say that I jumped up in fear when I woke up that morning, but I didn't. For one hour after they found me, I longed to remain hidden inside his arms, refusing to step out of the confines of his embrace. I'd never known a world without him in it, never imagined I would have to learn to live in one. I was fraught with the need to absorb his peace, for I knew that once I emerged from his protection, I would be left destitute and alone in this world. But in my heart, I knew that he wanted his rest and had finally achieved it.

I allowed the stars in the sky and the God of the universe to lead the way without any question, and I willingly gave up all my diffidence.

But nothing changed the fact that there was a hole in my heart and I didn't know how to fill it.

Fate leads to choice leads to fate. I gave Jude up so he could pray for us, but I should have known that no amount of prayer could deviate your life's plan.

On the day of his funeral, the world compressed itself into a single space where all the people that mattered to him gathered around in a testimony to the exuberance that he had brought into our lives. Donny, Kingston, Peter, Delmar, and Mikey stood proud and tall as pallbearers and as friends. His parents, his cousins, his aunts and uncles reminisced about the naughty little boy who had been so full of energy, so full of life. Maggie was my compass; she guided me forward, helping me place one foot in front of the other. Milena was slightly showing with her second baby on the way.

But Paulina, she was the one who truly stole my heart. She was me five years ago, the young girl who had waited for the man who promised he would call. I cried for her because she had never gotten the chance to truly know Dante. At least I could say that I had fifty-eight days with Jude.

When I stood up to deliver the eulogy, I had a change of heart. Instead of speaking about the man himself and the millions of ways that he had graced our lives, I spoke about the people that he loved. In life, Dante was never as vocal, as demonstrative about his feelings. But I, of all people, knew just how much he loved them. I narrated what he used to say to me about them, the stories he would tell, the experiences that meant the world to him. I wanted to open up his heart to the people who loved him. I wanted them to know with utmost certainty that Dante was thankful to have had them in his life.

Jude was there, at the funeral, standing in a dark blue suit and tie under the great big oak tree that had witnessed the tears of the grieving for hundreds and hundreds of years. I saw him rush towards me when my knees gave way as they lowered my best friend into the ground and I begged him not to leave me. No one knew that my tears weren't for Dante; they were for Jude. They were for him and the children he would never see.

I don't know what I would have done if he had ended up standing next to me. I guess it didn't matter now. He was gone shortly after that. He had paid his respects and returned to his church to pray for our souls.

Two days after I last saw him, Jude left a voicemail message on my phone.

"Anna. The thing about…" He paused to collect himself, and I could tell that he was crying. "The thing about the clouds is that they never stay in one place for very long. The winds will come and carry them far away from you and me. And when that happens, the sun will come out and the sky will become blue once again. And our lanterns, you will see them, Anna. Dante is holding on to them just for us."

FOUR WEEKS AFTER the funeral, life was slowly becoming more tolerable. Mikey went back to school, and I spent most of my hours at the hospital, stopping by the apartment only when it was absolutely necessary. His things remained untouched—his towels, his pillows, his clothes - they were tucked away in a place I could never revisit. All I remembered were the good times, the happiness and love that we both once shared all but a few months ago. And I prayed. Lord, did I pray. I begged God to make me dream of him, but the angels had taken him away to their side, and he was just too good to mingle among mortals. He was one of them now.

And I was just one of me.

I finally found the strength to listen to his last voicemail. The one he left on the way to Phuket. The one he recorded as he walked down the jetway to board the plane. I could hear his footsteps as they pounded lightly on the metal floor, I heard the flight attendant welcome him and I heard the click of the safety belt as he settled himself into his seat.

"Spark, I just boarded the plane for Phuket. I should be there in fourteen hours. I found out from Peter who found out from Jude's sister who—oh, never mind. Listen, Spark. The most important thing is that I want you to know how much I regret giving you up so easily. I mean, we had a few good years together, right? They were happy, weren't they? They count for something, don't they?" There was a slight pause as he addressed the flight attendant who was probably telling him to power his phone down. "Okay, I have to go. But I'm coming for you. I don't know what's waiting for me on that end, but I know that I want to fight for you. I'm going to fight for you. I don't want a divorce, Anna. I'll be there soon. Wait for me. I love you. I love you so much."

Maggie remained in town, always catering to my needs despite the fact that she was deeply embedded in her own hectic preparations for the wedding.

One Saturday afternoon, we took a break and ventured out into

Antique Row to look for little plates and furnishings to fill Maggie and Donny's new condo. The line to the register was endless; it seemed that everyone and their mother were out looking for antiques on that breezy spring morning.

"I love the golden glaze on these antique plates," I said as Maggie carried a basket full of them and we lined up at the counter.

"Geez, remind me next time never to come here on a weekend," she said exhaustedly. "Spark, are you okay? I don't want you to stand too long. Why don't you find a place to sit while I pay for these?" Everyone still called me Spark in honor of his memory.

"Yeah, if that's okay, I'm going to sit for a few."

I walked away, eager to find a chair to rest my legs for a few minutes. Lately, I'd been feeling a little heavier. I hadn't gained any weight yet, but the morning sickness that had ravaged my body during the first trimester had really worn me out. I found a newly upholstered chair in the middle of the aisle on the opposite end of the store. I sat down and fixed my eyes on my bulky, swollen feet.

"Annie?" A man's voice stirred me away from my musings. I looked up to see him standing next to a young woman pushing a stroller with two baby boys sleeping soundly side by side. He looked older, still handsome but with visible lines around a ragged looking face. "Is that you?"

"Jack," I said, alarmed by the serenity of my reaction. I held no anger for my mother's former lover, had no urge to run away.

"Are you—"

"Yes." I laughed nervously. "Quite big for four months, I know." I placed my purse on my lap and nervously twisted its strap over and over again until I feared it would come apart.

He turned to the woman who had the clearest, most innocent

311

eyes I had ever seen. "Honey, do you mind if I speak to Annie for a few minutes?" She pushed the stroller away from us and headed in the opposite direction. "That's my wife, Nadia. And those two little boys are Ethan and Cameron."

Nadia. Arabian for the beginning. The end of my mother was the beginning for Jack and his new family.

"They're beautiful."

"Listen, I want to apologize for not trying to contact you. It's just that it's taken me a long time to come to terms with everything." He pulled a flimsy looking stepstool from underneath a shelf and set it down next to me.

"I understand," I said.

"How is your family? And your husband Dante?"

"Dad gets out of rehab this week. Mikey is doing well in school. And Dante…" I paused for a moment to collect myself. "There was an accident. He passed away a few weeks ago."

"Oh! I am so sorry," he mumbled. "How are you holding up? Are you okay? Is he the—"

"Father? Yes, yes, he is. Was," I said, trying to shut it down. I didn't want to share any more than that. I knew that the uncomfortable silence that followed was because he was waiting for the right time to tell me something. He made an attempt to take my hand, but I shied away, pretending to brush my hair to keep it busy.

"I loved her so much, you know," he said sadly. I believed him now. Only true love could have made her that happy. The look on her face that night—she was luminescent. "We were going to be married after she filed for an annulment. You know your mom, she was a very religious woman. She wanted to do things the right way.

Despite the fact that we had an affair, she wanted to make it right. In the end, she just ran out of time."

Maggie came running down the hall with three large bags that clinked and clanked in cadence with her steps. "There you are! I found more things to buy." She laughed, ready to hear me make some snide comment about her shopping habits.

Jack stood up abruptly as soon as he saw me attempt to get out of the chair.

"Mags, this is Jack Laurent. Jack, this is my best friend, Maggie."

Maggie eyed him cautiously but reached out her hand to him just the same.

"We have to go, Jack. It was very nice seeing you. I'm glad that things have worked out for you. Congratulations on your new baby boys and I wish you all the best," I said as I started to pull Maggie in the direction of the door.

"Bye, Annie. You take care, too, and I'm very sorry for your loss."

# FORTY-ONE
## Letter from Outer Space

ON THE NIGHT of my day off, one week after seeing Jack at the antique store, I arrived home to find a letter from him waiting for me. I wished I hadn't run into him, wished I didn't have to remember. I was so engrossed in my grief over Dante that I set aside the loss that I had suffered six years ago. I was filled with guilt to think that my mother meant any less to me than my best friend. They were different and yet identical in so many ways.

I began to detect a pattern, a predestined flow in the events of my life. Dante was there for me when my mother passed away. He helped me through my remorse, my regret, and the times when I missed her so much that I wanted to crawl under the bed covers and die. He constantly reminded me that she was happy before she passed, and he relentlessly snapped me out of my depression by taking me on trips and showing me new places.

Before he left, Dante wanted Jude to do the same for me. Replace him, take his place. Now Jack was back, and he too played a part in the second act of my life. Bound by loss and united in despair, he formed a part of my cluster of stars and together we cruised the midnight sky.

I sat on the floor in the middle of my apartment and tore open the white linen envelope that revealed two completely different sheets of stationery.

The first one was neatly typed on business letterhead. It was a letter from Jack.

*Dear Anna,*

*Once again, I sincerely apologize for taking so long to send this to you. For years, I struggled to hold on to anything and everything she owned, touched, and loved. You see, I had no home with her, no children, no memories, no tangible items to keep with me as a remembrance of our time together. When she wrote you this note on the night of her surgery, I was furious at you for refusing to come home from Thailand. I didn't think you deserved this letter. And as I watched you break down at her funeral, my reason for holding this letter changed into one of sympathy for the remorse that you felt over not seeing her before she passed away.*

*Your mother loved her children more than anything else in her life. If you had asked her to leave me, she would have done so in a heartbeat. To her, your happiness always came first and foremost. As a future mother, you should be proud of the example that she set for you.*

*With warm regards,*

*Jack*

He was a good man. And he loved her. I wished she could be with me now, I wished she could see what was in my heart. We were molded together, fused by the similar experiences in our lives. We took what we could, little scraps of time. But the love that we had for the men in our lives—whether it be months or years or fifty-eight days—there were millions in this world who had never had the privilege of finding a love that was this deep and real and true.

The second letter was from my mother, written on college ruled paper. I smiled to myself when I remembered the trusty notebook that she kept in her purse everywhere she went. Mikey and I bought it for her after I caught her writing her ideas on a square sheet of toilet paper from a public women's restroom.

*To my dearest, darling daughter,*

*Sometimes, there comes a time in one's life when there's an unshakable feeling, an inkling that something big is about to happen. Don't call me paranoid, but I truly believe that I won't be making it out of surgery this time.*

*I'm so sorry for hurting you so much. I was selfish and unthinking about the consequence that my actions would have upon our relationship.*

*I met Jack on the night that I stayed at the hotel across the street from your school when I came to visit you a year ago. He was there on a business trip, having dinner at the restaurant by himself just like I was. Your father and I had been over for so many years, but I didn't realize it until I met Jack. He is kind and gentle, and he brings out the best in me. From the minute I met him, I knew that my life was going to change.*

*I love you, Anna Banana, more than you will ever know. Please forgive me for the way that I selfishly destroyed our home, for the hurt that I inflicted on your father. I am so proud of the woman you have turned out to be. You are strong and smart and independent. But what matters most is that you have a heart as big as the universe.*

*I love you with all my heart.*

*Mom*

*P.S. How is Dante managing himself with all those beautiful Thai women?*

Dante had gotten his peace, and at that moment, I was certain I had mine. For the first time in months, I could relive my memories without gasping for air. For the first time since I said goodbye, it no longer hurt to breathe.

# FORTY-TWO
## *There is a Plan*

MAY 27TH, 2011. The eve of Maggie's wedding. Six years after my mother had died, three months after Dante's passing and I walked away from Jude, and five months after he had planted the seed of life inside of me.

The executive floor of the Waldorf Astoria in Rome had finally quieted down. It was a few hours past midnight, and the room was tranquil and still. As my body changed, as the babies grew inside of me, the hole in my heart expanded with every waking day. The emptiness that I harbored—it was consuming, constricting, crippling. I was desperate to fill it, but I didn't know how; desperate to fill the void that all three of them had left behind. Here I was, a single mother of twins, whose life had spilled out into emptiness.

There were times when I hated having his life inside of me, and there were times when I was so grateful to have a part of him that could never be taken away.

Hours before, it had been a madhouse. Hotel guests walked up and down the halls, knocked on people's doors, laughter and music filled the air. The rehearsal dinner at La Pergola was an experience in itself. We feasted on a nine course menu which included tartare, scallops, veal, tortellini, and a host of wine and cheeses. I consumed everything placed in front of me, except for the wine, of course. Despite the intimidating imperial furniture, the opulent setting and the unparalleled views of the city, the night was warm and cordial and intimate. The love between the happy couple emanated through their actions, their words, and their inner excitement about the commitment that they were about to make together. It was the perfect time to celebrate life and love and the future. Kingston, Delmar, Paulina, and Milena—they were all in attendance, sharing the happy occasion with us all. Peter had also become an essential part of my life in the last few months; he played a huge role in the weeks after I lost Dante. We whooped out loud, we joked, we reminisced about our days in Thailand. We spoke about the past and pondered about what was to come. And although my heart still hurt to hear their names, I welcomed the mention of Dante and Jude; after all, they had been a part of our history, a part of our past. As the priest gave the blessing over the food, he cited Dante's name and offered a moment of silence in his memory.

I heard the news that very night.

As we sat at the table after a hefty serving of dessert and

admired the panoramic windows that opened us up to the most impressive picture of the city of Rome, Peter was reminded of something.

"Hey, look out there. That's the dome of St. Peter's, correct?" Milena pointed towards the fully illuminated structure not too far in the distance. Its lights were so bright that you could actually see the statues lined up along its base.

"Oh yeah," Peter answered as he leaned in to whisper something in Milena's ear. She shot me a look then turned her head towards Maggie.

"What?" asked Maggie with a devilish grin. "Spill, Peter."

"Nothing," he said as he looked down and stared at his empty plate.

Milena spoke up. She reached out to take my hand in hers. "Peter, I think you should take Anna outside so you can speak to her."

He nodded his head morosely and tilted it upward to catch my gaze. I offered him my hand across the table. "It's okay, Peter. Whatever it is, it's okay."

He pushed his chair back, stepped over to where I sat, and waited for me to join him. We walked back towards the entrance of the restaurant and stood near a row of couches by the podium.

"Anna, let's sit," he suggested.

"No, it's okay. I can stand," I answered nervously. I felt a slight inward tug on my belly button. I think the babies were anxious to hear from him as well.

He took my hand in his. "I would never do anything to hurt you, you know that, right?"

I shook my head recklessly in response.

"Jude's rite of ordination takes place tomorrow at St. Peter's Basilica."

Wham. A kick in the gut. I wasn't sure whether it was imagined or real. But it didn't matter. This was it. The finality. Another death. Another mourning. Another catastrophic event in the life of Anna Dillon. It wasn't that I was hoping for anything more from him. It was knowing that I would be here in the same place and at the same time that he would be making his vocation a reality. The vocation that we once thought was going to include me.

"Anna?" He tried to assess my facial expression. I remained standing there, surprised by my own personal fortitude.

"What time?"

"One o'clock." He moved his hands up so that they were grasping the tops of my arms. "We don't have to go back inside. Let's find a place to sit and talk."

"No, I need to be alone for now. Would you please apologize to the bride and groom for me? Let Maggie know that I'll be there to help her get dressed in the morning. Mikey has a key to the room so he can just let himself in."

"Anna, please. I'm sorry, I didn't see the point. I kept my promise to you, I never told him about the babies."

"And thank you for that. I'll be okay, Peter. Really, I will. I'm walking back to the room now." I ran into the elevator without looking back.

I DIDN'T KNOW how much time had passed before I opened my eyes to find myself alone in bed, completely fenced in by darkness. I must have fallen asleep before Mikey let himself into the room. For the first time in so long, I didn't feel apprehensive; the palpitations of my heart from previous nights were gone, and I felt calm and collected. I smiled to myself as the tears rolled down my cheeks. I felt their presence, I was sure of it. The gentle breeze from the open window and the endlessly vast mosaic in the sky, studded with stars, sprinkled with planets and streaked by the passing of comets assured me of that truth. The movements of the universe, its near misses, its combinations and its collisions are all planned, harmonized to a fault. We are all a part of that. We must keep moving unless we want to get left behind.

I thought I saw both of them, sitting side by side on the gray cushioned chairs right next to the balcony overlooking the fascinating city. The warm beige scalloped window treatments hung high above them, and a beautiful orchid floral arrangement sat on the marble table between them. I surveyed the room just to make sure that I was still in the same place. Gold inlaid fabric lined the couches and chairs, solid, wooden hand-carved dividers between the bed and the living area. Mikey was on the sofa bed across from me, wheezing soundly in his sleep.

My mother looked gorgeous, just as she had when I was a young girl, with her smooth white skin and her long, long legs. And Dante, it was the same outfit that he wore during our date night at the James. He had the same handsome face, the same magnificent body. They weren't really there, of course. They were in my mind, in my heart, and their eyes spoke a multitude of words to me. Words of love, words of encouragement.

*"There is a plan, Anna. A great plan for you. Let it take you over, revel in it, embrace it, and stay the course. Live in the present, not in your memories."*

For weeks I had wallowed in sorrow, bereft at losing the two people who were closest to me forever. I desperately tried to recall their touch, their faces, their voices. There were times when things came back to me so vividly and clearly that I watched as my life played out on a big screen before me. There were also times when no matter how hard I tried, I couldn't, for the life of me, recollect a single thing about them. I was left with some memories, but they were all jumbled up in my brain. The everyday stories, the ordinary events. Did he do this? Did she say that? When did that happen?

The dream that had just occurred. They were real, they were here, and they were just as I remembered. Whether through a dream or in reality, God had sent them back to me with a message of hope. I believed that at the right time and in the right place, I would see them again. That all I had to do was hold on to my love for them, just like I held on to my love for Jude. I wasn't ashamed to declare with confidence that it was possible to love two people at the same time. They were ensconced in two very different compartments of my heart—the smiles they elicited, the feelings they caused—they were distinctive to each one and divergent to both. The warmth that I felt when I thought of Dante and the pain that I constantly had of missing him was unequaled by the craving that I had, the longing that existed in my heart for Jude. He was my soulmate and I was in love with him. And although I had chosen to love Dante, I would always be tied to Jude. And my mother? Well, she will always be my inspiration. I could only hope to be half the mother, the woman that she was.

Just like every book with a beginning and an end, I decided to proclaim that night as the genesis of my life's story. I guess that was the wonderful thing about starting over. Although you never forgot the past, it's what happened from that day forward that truly mattered. It became clear to me that instead of harping on the fact that God didn't grant me my one big miracle, I should be relishing in the little ones I received from Him every single day.

Tomorrow, I thought to myself, as I yawned sleepily into my pillow—tomorrow I would begin to live again. I wouldn't disappoint them and I would honor my promise to Dante.

# FORTY-THREE
## *Our Lanterns*

"YOU LOOK SO stunning, Mags," I said as she stood in front of the majestic mirror in the lavishly decorated dressing room of the hotel. I slipped a clip in her hair to keep her veil from falling off. "Donny is a very lucky man."

"Thank you, my dear friend. If only you could see yourself as others see you. You're glowing, Spark."

"Ugh. Growing, you mean." I laughed. "I feel like a kangaroo despite being in this beautiful Peter Langner dress. But I love the way its length covers up my swollen legs."

"Pregnant or not pregnant, you're beautiful, Anna." She wrapped her arms around me at the risk of getting my makeup all over her dress. "Are you okay? Will you be okay? You left the dinner early, and I know you needed some time alone."

"Things changed after last night, Mags. I had a dream about Dante and my mother," I said.

"And?" she asked curiously. Her eyes brightened up as she smiled at me.

"And they're okay. They really are okay. I can stop worrying about them now."

"I'm glad," she said. "I love you, Anna. And I regret with all my heart that I didn't tell you about Jude five years ago. I was wrong to belittle what you had with him. I am so sorry, and I can never take back your tears. But things will get better, I promise."

I didn't want to see the droplets of rain in her eyes. Today was a day for sunshine. "Please don't cry. This is your special day. I love you too, Maggie. I know you were just trying to protect me. It just wasn't meant to be. It's time to go. I'll see you at the other end of the church. Here's to new beginnings!"

I WATCHED HER walk down the aisle with tears in my eyes. She was a sight to see—a vision of loveliness gliding through the clouds to join herself with the man of her dreams. As the bridal chorus began to play, a collage of images started running through my mind. The beauty of the moment, the love in the air, the friendships, the sorrow, and the continuation of life for the living. It all started to make sense. Everything is part of a plan. I was meant to learn about Jude's ordination because I needed to give him his peace. Step by step, as she got closer and closer, each moment in time was suspended in the air, and I was soaring along with it. I glanced at my watch to see that the wedding had started forty-five minutes late. I had fifteen minutes to get to him.

I wasn't going to stop him from giving himself to God. What I needed was closure. I wanted to tell him how proud I was of him; I wanted to share his special moment, be there for him, be strong for him and assure him that things would all work out. That he would go on to live a remarkable life filled with service and grace. That everything did happen for a reason, and that he had restored my faith in God.

I stood impatiently as I waited for Maggie to reach me, shifting my balance from one foot to the other, straightening my dress, swinging my hands back and forth. Did she have to take so damn long? Poor Donny had been waiting for a year to do this. Hurry up!

Finally she was here, her father in tears as he handed his baby girl over to Donny.

"Psst. Maggie!" I hissed, just as the priest walked down the steps of the makeshift altar to begin his blessing.

She turned her head towards me in surprise. I motioned for her to come closer. She did, and so did the rest of her ten foot train. She left her place beside Donny and stood right off to the side of the room.

"What's wrong, Spark? Is it the babies?"

"Maggie! I have to go! Your wedding is so damn late! I have to go and see Jude!"

"Why? Why are you going?"

"God helps those who help themselves. I have to let him know that things will be all right."

She let out a squeak that rocked the entire room before pushing me away in the opposite direction.

"Go! Go! Just go! I'll see you when you get back!" She turned to the confused audience and screamed at the top of her lungs. "Peter! Peter! Where are you? Go with her!" But before he could even react, I was gone.

I'D MADE A lot of stupid decisions in my life, and this one would go down in the books as the ultimate one. I hopped on the shuttle bus, still wearing my bridesmaid's dress, and sat restlessly as it made its way through the traffic in the city. They said that Saint Peter's Square was all but two miles away from the hotel, but it took an eternity to get there. All throughout the grueling ride, I got up a few times in an attempt to get off the bus and walk. But each time I tried, the high heels on my feet reminded me that riding the bus was a better option than waddling down the cobbled streets of Rome. It was almost two o'clock by the time I hobbled up the steps to the church, ran past the tall colonnade that flanked every corner, and wove my way around the sea of people that were here to witness the same thing that I had come for. The grandiosity of the basilica, with its painted ceilings and endless aisles, overwhelmed me. The prayer alcoves, the saints and statues, they looked at me with pity in their eyes.

*"You fool," they said to me. "You had the chance to take one of ours, and you gave him up. You should have known that we don't make trades. Life's*

*too precious to engage in barter. Fate has no negotiation."*

I tried to find him, tried to see through the crowds, but the men at the altar looked like tiny ants from where I stood. The church was quiet, filled with somber silence as I arrived in time to watch ten men dressed in white robes lie face down on the floor as an aria of song filled the air. There were so many men with dark hair, and I was sure he was one of them, so I focused my attention on the man at the end of the line and imagined that it was him, promising a life of service and honor to God.

"Remembering that you have been chosen among men and constituted in their behalf to attend to the things of God… with the sole intention of pleasing God and not yourselves," an elderly voice rang out clearly through the speakers surrounding the pulpit.

I had seen enough. This validated the end of the line for me; in my heart, I had endorsed his decision and I prayed that he would find his happiness and peace. I couldn't bear to live in grief any longer. I had to leave him be. The upsurge of self-reproach consumed me; I felt suffocated by my own actions, so viciously hauled back into the reality of this day. A vow is forever. From here on out, nothing in the world could erase the choice he had made.

He had his absolution, now who would give me mine?

I sank to my knees and dissolved into tears as I reached the end of the steps that would lead me back to the Square. I was determined to empty my heart out, leave my love for him in this sacred place, but instead here I was, filled with distress at the thought of a life without him. I covered my face in my hands and sobbed, aware of the fact that I must have looked liked a jilted bride on the morning of her wedding. People came and went, the sound of their footsteps, their conversations, their silent wonderings floating all around me.

"Anna?" said a voice directly in front of me. I peeked out through my fingers, embarrassed at having been recognized. "Anna?" he said again as he settled down in front of me and gently pulled my hands away from my face. There he was, looking so composed, his voice soothing, his touch healing.

We faced each other as we knelt on stone, as if in prayer, in worship, in atonement.

"Jude?" I had to blink once. Twice. Three times. It was him, or maybe not? He wasn't dressed in priestly robes; he wasn't even dressed in black. He looked like a normal human being, with the trademark New York Yankees baseball cap, a white t-shirt and jeans, and a backpack slung across his shoulders. *Another trick of fate,* I thought. *What else? What else could it be?*

"How did you find me?" I marveled at the power of happenstance. I began to realize that there was really no such thing as coincidence.

"I will always find you." He beamed despite the clouded look in his eyes. "I'm so sorry, Anna. I'm so sorry for your loss. I prayed so hard. I wanted God to take me in his place. I just wanted you to be happy. I know how much you loved him."

His teardrops began to fall softly like the rain.

*I should dance in them,* I thought. *I could dance in his tears and wash all my wounds away.*

It was then or never. I had to tell him everything, tell him how much I loved him before he walked away forever. I lowered myself to the ground in supplication until my head was at his feet.

"Please forgive me. I have loved you all these years. I pushed you away, I let my bitterness and pride get in the way. You're the price that I paid and I will always regret it!" I cried.

"Oh, Anna. No, no." He pulled my face up and held my chin close, our tears intermingled, our words obscured in sorrow. "Listen to me. You'd said that our love was born out of death and loss. That's not true. Our love is a gift from God himself, born out of courage and adversity. No love is more real than this."

The draining emotion and the weight of my stomach caused me to tip back and sit on my feet. My arms fell to my sides as I placed them on the floor to keep my balance. His eyes quickly settled upon my midsection. It was hard to miss; I was wearing a maternity dress after all.

"Is that... are you... Did Dante know?" He stayed in place, afraid to touch something that wasn't his.

"I'm five months along," I said as I wiped my eyes dry. "Dante knew. It made him so happy."

"Five months?" He paused for a few seconds. "December?" He closed his eyes and allowed a few tears to fall. And then he broke out in a jubilant smile. "That was morning sickness. In Thailand."

I nodded my head slowly. "Twins." I began to cry again. These children were conceived out of love. Too bad that same love could never ever be.

"Is it over? Are you a priest?" I asked, fully expecting him to say yes.

"What?" He shook his head in bewilderment. "No, no! I was here to get a dispensation, and I received it yesterday. I went to the hotel to try to see you this morning, but you were busy taking care of Maggie. And then Peter called me to tell me that you were on your way here."

"You left the church. For me?"

"It wasn't a choice. It was always you."

He chose me? He chose me. I couldn't begin to describe the feeling in my chest, the sudden rush of air into my lungs, the lightness of this moment; bit by bit, the remnants of my heart began to form like puzzle pieces coming together. It's funny how things could change in an instant. One minute you're broken, your world exploded around you, and the next minute you're whole, your soul rescued, your torment erased.

I smacked his arm as he lightly brushed my tears away. "Why didn't you tell me?" I asked.

"Tell me that you wouldn't have argued against it."

"I would have." I smiled through the thickness of my tears.

"Exactly," he said with a chuckle. "I never went back, Blue. I told you I'd wait. I promised you that I would. From the day that I saw you again at the church, I knew I wasn't going back." He brought his lips to mine and kissed me. It was the kiss on that one dark night six years ago, the kiss in the hut over the ocean, the kiss in the rain. It was the kiss that paled all the others, the kiss of beginnings, not endings.

"Why here, Blue? Why did you come here to watch me leave you?"

"I wanted to tell you that I understand everything now. You were right all along, why this all happened. And that I was sorry I didn't believe you," I said, my hands held tightly together in repentance.

"Here," he said as he reached into his pocket to pull out the familiar teal colored pouch that had meant so much to me. "I believe this belongs to you." I turned sideways to give him access to the back of my neck. The seahorse of forever was back where it belonged.

With me.

"Tell me what this means. Tell me where we go from here," I pleaded.

There is sacredness in tears, someone once said. What I learned that day was that without pain there could be no deliverance; without sin, no salvation. That in this life, it is only through sadness that one could truly experience joy. And although you are shaped by experience, you are ultimately defined by your destiny. Jude was my gift from God. If we paid enough attention, we'd find tiny little gifts imbedded in every single drop of misfortune.

"It means that when I wake up tomorrow, I'll find you right next to me," he said confidently and without a care in the world.

"It means that our children will know a great love between their parents," I added.

"It means that Mikey will have a family again, and the rain will bring us song after song," he went on.

"And it means that you are mine in this life." I smiled triumphantly.

He wrapped his arms around me from behind, pulling me tight into his embrace and leaning his chin on my shoulder.

"I love you, Anna Dillon. Always have and always will. A love like this could never be wrong."

"I love you too, Jude. No more running, I promise."

We gazed up at the sky to find the sun peeking through the clouds and the spectrum of colors reflected by a rainbow.

"Huh. Twins," he said. "Max will flip out! He loves babies, he practically lives with Katie because of that."

Gradually, he leaned himself back and leapt to his feet before pulling me up with both hands. It was as if he knew that I'd been having balance issues as of late.

"Let's go home, Anna," he whispered in my ear as he held me close, one arm around my waist and the other with the palm of his hand flat against my stomach.

"Yes, let's," I said.

And as we blended in with all the others, with the thousands of believers who were here to affirm their faith in the land of the great empire and in the city where past and present converged in harmony, I had a thought. A thought that filled me with certainty that the path that God planned for me had just been set in motion.

"He has our lanterns!" I squeaked happily as we walked hand in hand, rushing back to make it to Maggie's reception.

"Who? Who has our lanterns?" He leaned over to kiss me on the cheek.

"Dante! He told me!"

For a fleeting moment, I believed that I saw Dante's eyes reflected in his. "I have no doubt that he has them. No doubt at all."

We were but two tiny stars in the galaxy, Jude and I.

That was all we were.

Two stars among many, in the infinite constellation of the universe.

# EPILOGUE
*March 2015*
*Today*

"MOMMY, CAN I sit outside with you while you talk to Uncle Dante?" Her golden hair blows freely in the wind as I fire up the pit on the fourth anniversary of his leaving. I can't wait to meet him under the moon again tonight.

"Of course you can, Danielle, but I don't really talk to him much. I just visit with him while he's up in the stars watching over us," I say as she makes herself comfortable with her head on my lap.

"I'm sleepy, Mommy, but I want to stay while you visit with him too." She stretches her little mouth into a big, loud yawn.

"Okay. Close your eyes so that you can see him in your dreams," I say, leaning down to give her a kiss before spreading the blanket on top of her. A heavy raindrop plunks itself down on her head, rolls down her forehead and settles in her eye. She lets out a grunt and squeezes her eye shut.

"I hate the rain, Mommy. It's cold and icky."

I laugh as I run a finger across her cheek. "Oh, honey. Some of life's best moments happen in the rain. Besides, don't you remember what happens after every rain?"

"Rainbows!" she squeals with delight, clapping her hands together.

*Rainbows.*

I sit in silence for a few minutes and watch the pieces of wood begin to catch fire. The view from our deck reminds me of the days of our youth, the dances in front of the bonfires and the warm nights on the beaches of Thailand. It isn't difficult to imagine, since our home in the Outer Banks brings us the best of the sand and the sea. We live in a three-story house overlooking the ocean in a seaside resort town filled with visitors and tourists and overcrowded roads. Our days are filled with the laughter of two little girls, busy schedules, hospital shifts, and fried oysters from Spanky's. Our nights are filled with stories and songs, love and pleasure, happiness and peace. My private practice allows me the flexibility to be with the girls more often, and Jude's work as a youth counselor and permanent deacon at our parish church allows him the luxury of being home in time for dinner with his girls. We live a simple life. After all, working three days a week as a part-time physician doesn't really equate to a successful career in the medical profession. I didn't discover a cure for cancer and Jude didn't change the world. But what we found was so much more. We found ourselves, and together we are writing the love story of a lifetime.

The glow of the fire calls me to begin this year's letter. I have everything that I need next to me. His glasses, his watch, and his blanket were the only things that I saved when we cleaned out his apartment before moving away.

*Hi, Tey. Happy Anniversary!*

*I miss you. I know you've always said that I was a little bit unusual. Do you suppose that's why everything seems to have the opposite effect on me? Instead of missing you less, I miss you more each year. Can you see Dani on my lap? Look how much she's grown! She seems to be the one more like me. Teah not only looks more and more like Jude, she's also got his personality; while Dani is loud and giggly, Teah is quiet and introspective.*

*Anyway, here's my annual report for you. So much has happened this year—Jude was finally installed as a permanent deacon. Everyone in the parish loves him. We receive at least five pies a week from the little old ladies in the bridge club. And don't get me started on the women from the divorce support group. They never miss a meeting when it's Jude who facilitates the sessions. Once Father Dan steps in, the room clears out and there's no one there!*

*Dad's doing well. He's working as a consultant for his old company. We drove up to Seattle last January to meet his new girlfriend.*

*And the mission. Oh wow. So, we finally got all the paperwork settled for the foundation under your name. Delmar is managing it from Thailand. Okay, don't get mad. I know you left it all to me, but I thought that the memory of your generosity would live longer in the hearts and minds of the kids over there. I did as you asked, and the money that you left for the girls' college education is locked up in a 529 plan. I know you said Harvard, but can we wait to see what they want to be when they grow up? After all, they're only four, Tey.*

*Guess who were the very first recipients of the Dante Leola scholarship? Malee and Chiayo! We saw them last June, and oh, my gosh. Malee is beautiful! Chiayo has grown to become such a responsible young man. The two of them have blossomed into such brave individuals—so outspoken and confident, so sure of themselves. You would be so proud of them.*

*Peter is finally getting married in August, and Jude is his best man! And Maggie—her little king is flying all over the world with her and Donny as he sets up his new chain of stores in Asia. Delmar, Milena, and Paulina came to visit last November. I think Paulina has met someone from Germany. Her email said that she's slowly falling in love with him. Isn't that great?*

*Your mom and stepdad stayed with us for two weeks last year. Jude's parents invited them to New York for Thanksgiving, so we'll be seeing them in a few months.*

*Mikey. I have happy news! He got a job! Guess where? Goldman Sachs! Not quite Blackstone, but number two! We raised him well, you and I.*

*Merle and Pearl are still going strong. They've surpassed their average life spans, but those two seahorses are still spending their days tangled around each other in the middle of our living room. They're a family of six now, and Jude is constantly on me about following in their footsteps soon.*

*And me? I'm really trying, Tey. I know you can see that I still have my moments. Sometimes the pain becomes so unbearable and I don't know how on earth I will ever find a way to move on. The other day, while cleaning out the girls' closets, I called your cell phone. I had this ridiculous urge to hear your voice and hoped that your voicemail message was still there. It wasn't, of course, but it made me feel connected to you in some weird way. I think about you every day. I see you in every happy place. I see you so clearly every time there's goodness and laughter, and my heart, though still broken, is held intact and kept whole because of your very selfless gift. We will be celebrating our fourth wedding anniversary in two months—can you imagine Maggie and me sharing the same wedding day? After all, you did ask me when I was going to start my life and I took you up on it. And I can breathe now, Tey. Even when I cry, the overwhelming heaviness is gone and the air that fills me gives me solace. Thank you for bringing him back to me. Thank you for Jude.*

*Well, now I'm going to shut up and listen to you, okay? I don't know how the reception will be from here this evening. Last year was pretty clear; I saw you in the stars right before the storm came.*

*Tonight, will you be here? I can see some stars right now.*

*Which one are you, Tey? Which one is Mom?*


Jude walks outside right when my tears begin to fall, and my heart still reacts the same way whenever he's near. He's holding two green balloons with one hand, the same colors for every year that I don't get to see Dante's verdant green eyes. In his other arm is Teah with ebony dark hair, wide awake and ready to jump into my arms. Jude places her on his lap as he takes a seat next to me.

"There you are, Mrs. Grayson." He looks at me with so much love. My husband. My lover. My fate. My air. My everything.

He kisses me before wiping the tears from my eyes.

"Are we ready?" he asks cheerfully, trying to rouse me out of my reverie. "Teah, wake up your sister so we can send the balloons up to Uncle Dante."

"I'm not sleeping!" exclaims Danielle. "I heard everything, Mommy! You said I was giggly."

Jude and I laugh as we hand the balloons over to the girls.

"Ready?" says Jude.

"Set?" I say.

"Go!" yell the girls as they release the bright green balloons into the dark blue sky.

Jude goes quiet and whispers something up in the air. The girls don't hear him, but I do.

"Thank you, dude. Thank you for my Blue."

"WE LOVE YOU, UNCLE DANTE!"

We all scream out loud, and the winds carry our voices across the sky and into the sea.

"SEE YOU NEXT YEAR!"

WHAT HAPPENS TO the living when the performance is over and the final curtain call has ended? The characters in your life story, they come and they go.

But every so often, there are those who are cast, whose roles despite fleeting and brief, become the essence of your story. They live on forever in the words that are spoken, in the songs that are sung, in the scenery of the stage, in the days and nights when the audience is nowhere to be found.

The living must go on. And Dante will always be a part of our living. He may not be here, in this life, but his presence will shine through everything that fate has planned until the day that I see him again.

This isn't a story about death or the dying or the sadness or indescribable emptiness that comes with losing someone that you love. This is a story about the infinite bounds of true love and commitment, and the redeeming gift of hope.

It is a story of a girl who loved two men in her life. It wasn't a love triangle; she wasn't confused nor was she apologetic. She set out to prove to the world that there are different kinds of love that can only be experienced once in a lifetime. She became living proof that sometimes, you have to lose faith in order to truly believe. That you may never find a Jude or a Dante, but through adversity and tears, you will always end up finding *you*.

And boy, does this girl believe.

She places her faith in the stars and the skies and the alignment of the universe. And then she places her trust in the One who forgives, who loves unconditionally, who only gives what one can take. She places her trust in the hands of God.

It may not be the same for everyone else, but to her, it's the only way.

# ACKNOWLEDGEMENTS

The stars dropped out of the sky two years ago and shook my world like you wouldn't believe. During that time, I prayed for clarity, for purpose, for an end to my confusion. I was filled with anger and disappointment when my prayers weren't answered. Why didn't God want me to be happy if He loved me so much? This book is a testament to that time, that darkness and the hope that was never realized. It is a lesson learned – that fate is fate, and what's meant to be will be. No amount of prayers will change what God has planned for you, and with that acceptance comes peace.

This book would not have been possible without the help of the following people:

**Nelly Martinez de Iraheta** - her encouragement, her friendship and her collaboration in writing this book. Some of these words are hers. **Trisha Rai**, who stuck with me through hundreds of versions of this story. **Leylah Attar**, who has become such an important part of my life. **Jim Thomas**, best editor in the world and **Italia Gandolfo**, my agent, who believed in me even when I didn't believe in myself. What an honor to work with the two of you.

**Rick Miles** just knows too much about me and I am thankful for his friendship. **Erin Dauer Roth** read this book as former editor and always friend, and it means the world to me. **Angela McLaurin** has never let me down, always just a text message away.

**Luisa Hansen** who read this book at the last minute and found the time to help me make it better. **Becca Manuel** for shining a light on my book with your trailer. My friend **Lindsay Sparkes**, for another beautiful cover creation.

I've learned so much in the past two years, I don't even know how to thank everyone who has taken this journey with me. Thank you to my **Butterflies**, loyal friends, who loved me through my whirlwind of a year, who have stayed even when there has not been a book to talk about – you guys keep me going - **Vasso V., Daiana S., Maricar A., Anna G., Christine A., Karolin D., Donna D'A., Lisa R., Melissa J., Suzanne W., Alisha J., Laura W., Barb M., Emma F., Kissy M., Manuela F., Robin S. (times 2)** – to name just a few. YOU are my inspiration and I am so lucky that you are all a part of my daily life.

Thank you, CB Philippines, **JM**, **Jem** and the rest of the Sinclairs – **Dianne, Majul, Sayyeda, Zarce, Anne, Rafael, Luigi, Jane, Rose, Mabie, Danna, Amanda, Hannah and KC**, and all of you who welcomed me even when you didn't know who the heck I was. I love you so much. You made my dream come true.

To the staff at National Bookstore for your genuine support and interest in this book, **Xandra Ramos, Chad Dee, Lola Tumaneng.**

All the bloggers who have supported me through all four books – **Vilma Gonzalez, Angie McKeon, Brandee Veltri, Tammy Zautner, Denise Tung, Lisa Kane** – you are special to me because you read my book without putting me through the always humiliating act of asking to be read; **Cris Soriaga Hadarly**, who has never left my side.

**Tarryn Fisher,** for teaching me how to embrace my life. And for never wavering. Thank you for protecting me and for showing me that it's okay to be a mess sometimes. I bet you don't realize just how much you do for me. The world looks so much better (and funnier) when I see it through your eyes.

**You,** for teaching me all about unconditional love. This is your shout out, Agent Orange.

And as always, to my family especially **my husband**, whose love and encouragement allows me to blossom and grow. I owe you everything. And this book is for you.

CB

# ALSO BY CHRISTINE BRAE

*The Light in the Wound*
*His Wounded Light*
*Insipid*